GRIFFIN'S WAY

"A blessed companion is a book"—JERROLD

GRIFFIN'S
WAY

★

FRANK YERBY

THE COMPANION BOOK CLUB
LONDON

CONTENTS

*Made and printed in Great Britain
for The Companion Book Club (Odhams Books Ltd.)
by Odhams (Watford) Limited
Watford, Herts*

S.1064.UA.

BOOK ONE

CANDACE TREVOR

★ I ★

"ANYBODY ever tell you you're a mighty pretty woman—I mean lady, Mrs Trevor?" Hector Griffin said.

Candace looked at him, quickly. She saw at once that he wasn't getting out of line, that he was merely making conversation, falling back a little helplessly on the Southerner's belief that the only way to talk to a woman was to pay her compliments. Her gaze flickered over him, seeing his knuckles white where he was gripping the reins too hard, the beads of perspiration among the red-gold hairs on the back of his hands, and even on his forehead under his wide-brimmed planter's hat. Which didn't make sense. It was only the second day of April (April 2 1870, she thought with genuine surprise, only seven years, not the seven centuries I'd have sworn it's been) and it wasn't hot enough, even here in Mississippi, to make a man sweat like that.

"Why are you so nervous, Mr Griffin?" she said.

"Lord, but you're a smart one, ma'am!" he chuckled. "Yep, reckon I am kind of nervous. You—you're so different, and——"

Candace Trevor smiled. She had a good smile: a sudden flash of even white out of dogwood pink; and saying that she was mighty pretty wasn't far off the mark after all, Hector decided.

"You mean," she said, "that I'm a dadblamed Yankee and you're worried about what kind of reception I'm going to get at Griffin's Way. That's it, isn't it, Mr Griffin?"

"Well—no'm," Hector said. "What I reckon I do mean is that you're a lady—a real lady—and us Griffins—Lord, Mrs Trevor, what I'm trying to say is that I hope you won't pay attention to everything you'll hear about us. Some of it just isn't so. . . ."

She caught the emphasis, slight as it was, that he placed on the word some. But a goodly part of it will be, she thought. You've got the look—Aloud, she said:

"Don't worry, Mr Griffin, I don't pry. The only questions I'll ask will be about my patient, and only those that I think may help. . . ."

Hector's eyebrows rose towards the brim of his hat.

"Help?" he said. "Thought I told you that Paris is beyond help, ma'am. . . ."

"I know," Candace said: "but I'm a Vermont Yankee—stubbornest breed there is. You say that your brother's young——"

"Yes'm. He hasn't turned thirty yet. . . ."

"And handsome——"

"Heck, ma'am, Paris is almost too goodlooking. That's why Pa named him that. Pa was one fine scholar. Could quote the Iliad and the Odyssey in the original Greek. And Latin—he'd spout Virgil by the hour. . . ."

"Paris," Candace said, "King Priam's youngest son. The abductor of Helen. The coward who killed Achilles with a poisoned arrow to the heel——"

"Well," Hector grinned, "it all fits except that poison arrow business. Paris never was a sneak. Good man in a fight. Only now—"

"He's mad, you say. A lunatic who needs a nurse to take care of him. But nothing you've told me sounds like lunacy. He doesn't rave, or laugh at nothing, or talk to himself, or think he's Caesar or Napoleon. He's just quiet——"

"Too quiet, Mrs Trevor. He's hardly addressed a mumbling word to anybody since he came back from the fighting. Not even to—to his wife. . . ."

Candace stared at Hector. There was a sudden tightening of her mouth.

6

"His wife?" she said. "You didn't tell me he had a wife. Why didn't you, Mr Griffin?"

"Well——" Hector hesitated.

"The truth, Mr Griffin!" Candace said.

"All right," Hector said quietly, "the truth. I thought you wouldn't come. I thought you'd ask why won't *she* take care of him."

"You were so right. You saw the state that my husband's in——"

"I promised you that you could bring Mr Trevor to Griffin's Way as soon as you got the feel of things," Hector said desperately. "That way you could take care of them both. Oh Lord, Mrs Trevor, ma'am, don't go back on me now!"

Candace looked away from him out over the sweep of fields. There were clouds in the sky, huge piled-up masses of blue, grey and white. But from behind them sunlight spilled, lancing earthward in broad shafts, ruler-straight, pale golden. On the far edge of the world there was a fragment of a rainbow—like a welcome, she thought suddenly, or a benediction. She turned back to Hector Griffin.

"I won't go back on you," she said gently. "I can't. I need the money. But don't you think I ought to know *why* Mrs Griffin doesn't take care of her husband?"

"Yes'm," Hector said slowly; "You ought to. And I'd tell you if I knew myself. Only I don't rightly know. Not all of it, leasewise. Say that Laurie's spoiled. Selfish. Too damn beautiful, and knows it. Not the kind of a filly who'd go out of her way to look after a fellow for five minutes after that fellow was no good to her any more——"

He saw the warm tide of blood climbing her cheeks.

"I'm sorry," he said; "I thought, seeing as how you're a married woman, yourself——"

"And one whose husband is no good to her any more, too —You're right. I'm being excessively prudish. You've seen Henry. He's been like that—paralysed from the waist down —for seven years now. Only, it seems to me I faintly recall some words: 'For better, for worse, for richer, for poorer, in

7

sickness and in health'—it does say that, doesn't it, Mr Griffin?''

" 'Until death do us part.' Yes'm. And you live up to it. Only, ma'am, there're an awful lot of people—who don't. Who can't. Who haven't the kind of strength it takes to— Please, ma'am—if you can, don't go making judgments ahead of time. Laurie's a sweet kid. I like her. You're asking too much—all those looks, and character, too! "

She smiled at him.

"I hope you won't misunderstand me, Mr Griffin. What I'm going to say is an observation, nothing more. You, it seems to me—have all those looks, and character, too. Plenty of both.''

"Why, thank you, ma'am!" Hector said. "Only I reckon you'd better go slow about judging again—'til you find out more about me. As for my looks, you just wait 'til you see Paris. And, as far as my character is concerned—heaven never was my destination, ma'am. What I am, you're going to run right smack dab up against—and I'm sorry. I wish it could be avoided. I'd like you to go on thinking well of me.''

"I think I shall," Candace said, "no matter what. Because I'm sure of one thing, Mr Griffin——"

"And what's that, ma'am?"

"That though you may be guilty of many things, there are others I feel sure you're incapable of: treating people badly—any kind of people, lack of pity for your fellow man, inability to—to love. Am I right?''

Hector sat there, thinking, a long slow time.

"Yes'm," he said at last, "reckon you are. I don't hate anybody. I don't care what colour a body is. And I got too much pity in me, maybe, and a damn sight too much love. . . . But down here, all those things are considered wrong. The wrongest things there are, some of 'em——"

"I know," Candace said; "that's precisely what I don't like about down here. Oh—is *that* Griffin's Way?"

Hector looked at the white-columned house, far off and small at the end of the alley of trees. His eyes were bleak, suddenly.

8

"Yes'm, it is—the big house, leasewise. Well, reckon we'd better be moving along. . . ."

Hector pulled the horses up before the house, and the Negroes swarmed out to take the reins. Hector got down at once, ignoring the chattering blacks, and put up his hands to help Candace down. But she didn't move. She sat there looking at the house; and the conviction that you couldn't do anything really well with slave labour came back to her with renewed force. At a distance, the manor house of Griffin's Way was lovely. Seen from a few yards, it was a mess, like nearly all the neo-Grecian monstrosities scattered over the South. Her father's tart comment that it always took three slaves to come anywhere close to the productive capacity of one Ohio farmhand had its counterpart in this, too. You could whip a man to work; but the very element of force precluded the most necessary attributes of any art or craft: love—and pride.

"Like it?" Hector said.

The Vermont ginger in her veins wouldn't let Candace be polite.

"Frankly, no," she said. "My uncles on my mother's side were shipbuilders, Mr Griffin. Carpentry like this would have made them weep, and New Englanders aren't given to easy tears——"

Hector turned and stared at the house, seeing it, she was sure, for the first time with really critical eyes.

"I'll be gosh darned if you aren't right!" he said wonderingly. "Hardly a joist with speaking acquaintance with its corresponding beam. You've got a good eye, ma'am—"

"And a loose tongue," Candace said gently. "I apologize, Mr Griffin."

"For what?" Hector said. "Heck, ma'am——"

Candace smiled at his watered-down profanity, the gosh darn's, and heck's that Southerners customarily used around women with whom they felt at ease, but nevertheless continued to respect. She had come a long way in the course of the ride from Vicksburg; she had performed the difficult

9

feat of making Hector Griffin her friend. She had lived in Mississippi ever since the Spring of '58, so she knew how hard that was to do. Southerners, she had often remarked to her husband, are only at ease with coloured women, and with the fallen sisterhood of their own race. The ladies of the South had their husbands' homage, respect, even, curiously, a love akin to worship; but their companionship, never. "I'd rather be married to a Yankee millhand," she'd said impishly to Henry once, "who'd occasionally pinch me where I sit—than to one of these hand-kissing bowers and scrapers. . . ." And, remembering her husband's expression of shock when she'd said that, she suddenly laughed aloud.

Hector turned his gaze downwards, away from the veranda, and the slim figure of the girl who had appeared upon it, attracted, doubtless, by the sound of their voices, and his eyes were troubled, suddenly.

"Oh, I am sorry!" Candace said. "I wasn't laughing at you, Mr Candace. I was remembering my husband, and thinking how much you Rebels are all alike. But I shouldn't have said that about your house. It was something like telling a woman that her petticoat's showing, and that it's dirty, to boot. . . ."

"It *is* showing," Hector said; "But I don't reckon it's dirty. Laurie's mighty finicky about being clean. Hope you won't pay her too much mind, ma'am. Laurie comes from the up-state part of Louisiana. Pine-barren folks, though she doesn't look it. Talks all right, too. But, sometimes, I'm afraid she acts like it for fair. . . ."

"Oh!" Candace said, looking at the girl at the head of the stairs. "I hadn't even seen her!"

"Well, take a good look, ma'am," Hector chuckled; "'Cause it's generally held hereabouts that Laurie's a treat for the eyes. . . ."

Candace stared at the girl. Early twenties, she guessed. And perfect. Wears that tight bodice because she knows what she's got to show off. Sullen-looking mouth. Broom-straw between her teeth like—like white trash. Which is what Hector probably means by pine-barren folks. But, heavens above! A waist like that! I don't believe it's stays; I can see her breathe; precious little under that bodice. Shameless. A bit of a hussy. Black Irish ancestry. Black hair and blue eyes are Celtic, Father always used to say. . . .

She saw then that the girl was coming down the stairs. Her way of walking was a sight to see: lazy, slumberous, like a willow sapling, wind-driven; with a tiny hip sway calculated to bring out every drop of the feline in any other woman who witnessed it. Before she was half-way down, Candace was absolutely sure that she was going to hate this woman with all her heart.

"Help me down, Mr Griffin," she said. By the time her feet touched the ground, Paris Griffin's wife was there. Draped languidly over the balustrade. Staring at her with that ice-blue gaze that made even a casual glance an effrontery and an insult. Candace stared back, just as coldly, seeing with a curious kind of joy that the antipathy was mutual; that Mrs Griffin was paying her the supreme feminine compliment of instant dislike.

"Laurie—" Hector's tone was noticeably uneasy, "this is Mrs Trevor. . . ."

"How-do-you-do, Mrs Griffin?" Candace said, and put out her hand.

Laurel Griffin stared at Candace's hand, but made no move to take it. She shifted the broomstraw to the corner of her mouth with a lazy motion of her tongue.

"Howdy, Nurse Trevor," she said.

"Laurie!" Hector said.

Laurel put out a slim hand; touched Candace's fingers; let them drop.

"'Scuse me," she drawled; "Hec should have told you I haven't any manners. Us clay-eaters don't have much home training. . . ."

"Laurie," Hector groaned, "can't you behave yourself, just this once?"

"Yep," Laurel said, "for your sake, brother, dear. . . ." She flickered that pale gaze of hers over Candace's face.

"Hec wrote me that you're married," she said. "Your husband didn't come with you?"

"He—he'll be along later," Hector said nervously. "He's crippled, Laurie. We kind of have to arrange things to accommodate——"

"Crippled?" Laurel said. "You mean he got hit during the fuss?"

"Yes," Candace said crisply, "he did."

"Poor fellow," Laurel said; "Reckon he was mighty brave. . . ."

Candace stared at her. What was there about this black-haired snip of a girl that made everything she said offensive?

"No," she said quietly, "Henry wasn't brave. In fact, he wasn't even a soldier."

"But you said——" Laurel began.

"That he was hit during the War. He was. Like a great many other civilians in Vicksburg during the siege: even women and children. A Yankee gunboat lobbed a shell through the roof of our house. Henry took a shell splinter through the lower part of his spine. Left him paralysed from the waist down."

Laurel grinned.

Don't say it! Candace thought. Don't say it, or by heaven and hell, I'll slap you winding!

But Laurel didn't say that. When she finally spoke, all she said was:

"And you?"

"I—I wasn't at home," Candace said lamely.

Laurel's grin widened.

"Us modern women!" she said.

"Laurie," Hector said solemnly, "I ever tell you that folks most in generally don't appreciate your sense of humour?"

"Yep," Laurel said, "frequently, Hector, darlin'. Anyhow, all I meant was 'twould be better for Mr Trevor to come—look better, anyhow, since Mrs Trevor is going to have to dang near live with Paris. And, even if her old man's crippled, living there in the same house, folks wouldn't be so quick to think——"

12

"Laurie!" Hector said again.

"But," Candace said quietly, "don't *you* live with your husband, Mrs Griffin?"

"No'm," Laurel drawled; "he gets on my nerves. I purely can't stand loonies. 'Course Paris isn't much trouble. He's nice and quiet. Fair drives a body out of her mind, that way he's got of not even hearing what's said to him most of the time. And when he does answer, what he says most in generally makes no sense. . . ."

But what *you* say, does? Candace thought acidly. She said:

"May I see my patient now, please?"

"Why sure," Laurel said. "Duke!"

"Yes'm?" the Negro who was holding Hector's horses said.

"You let some of the young ones hold those nags," Laurel said; "and you go saddle Prince for me—and"—she swept a critical gaze over Candace—"and old Bess for this lady. Get going now!"

"Yes'm," Duke said.

Laurel turned back to Candace.

"You *can* ride, can't you, Mrs Trevor?" she said.

"Yes," Candace said; "but why do we need to? Doesn't Mr Griffin—I mean your husband——"

"Live here? No'm. He lives in Pa Griffin's hunting lodge. Besides, he wanders. We'll probably have to hunt him all over hell's half acre. . . ."

"Oh," Candace said.

"'Scuse me, Mrs Trevor," Hector said; "reckon I'd better be getting along home, myself. I—I'll see you tomorrow——"

Candace stared at him.

"Then you don't live here, either?" she said.

"Nobody lives here but poor little me," Laurel drawled. "And I'm getting the feeling you ask a sight too many questions, Nurse Trevor. 'Sides, you sound like a Yankee when you talk, anyhow."

"I *am* a Yankee," Candace said, repressing the impulse to add, 'Thank God!' "My husband brought me to Vicksburg three years before the War."

13

"Why?" Laurel said.

"Because it was his home town," Candace said. "But speaking of asking questions, don't you think you ask a few too many, yourself, Mrs Griffin?"

"Reckon I do. But seeing as how I'm hiring you——"

"One minute, Mrs Griffin. I was under the impression that it was your brother-in-law who was hiring me. It so happens that I'm free, white and over twenty-one. And, among the things that freedom implies is the right to choose the people for whom I'm willing to work, not to mention the kind of treatment I'm prepared to accept." She turned to Hector.

"I'm sorry, Mr Griffin, but I'm afraid I can't——" she began.

"Now, just you wait a minute, Mrs Trevor," Hector said; "I'm hiring you. Laurie's got nothing to do with it, beyond the fact that she's against the whole thing, and is doing her damnedest to run you off the place by yapping and showing her teeth like a fyce terrier. I had the idea that you Yankees don't scare easy—or we'd have won that fuss. You won't have dealings with Laurie—only with my poor brother. I'm asking you, out of humanity, not to quit before you at least see him, see what can be done, maybe——"

"Then she won't quit," Laurel grinned. "Loony or not, Paris is mighty pretty. . . ."

"Laurie, for God's sake!" Hector began.

"It's all right," Candace said quietly; "I've lived down here a long time now——"

"And you don't like it," Laurel supplied.

"And I don't like it," Candace said; "but then I don't like ignorance, bad manners and plain, downright injustice, wherever they occur. . . ."

"So you're a nigger lover?" Laurel drawled. "That's what Yankees most in generally mean when they start talking about injustice. Hec, what d'you say we give her Samson to help her with Paris? That way she'll have the strongest black buck in Mississippi to—to take care of her. . . ."

"Just what do you mean by 'take care of' me, Mrs Griffin?" Candace snapped.

"You figure it out," Laurel said. "You look mighty smart to me. . . ."

"Laurie," Hector said, "'fore God, if you don't quit talking like that, I'm going to take my buggy whip to you!"

"Please don't Hec!" Laurel laughed; "Doan you go 'n whup dis heah po chile! Can't you see how I'se a tremblin'? Plumb shakin' all over, I is!'"

"Oh, hell!" Hector said disgustedly.

"Don't worry about it, Mr Griffin," Candace said; "I can take care of myself. And I'll tell you one thing: I'm not going to quit, if for no better reason than that she so obviously wants me to. It will be most interesting to find out—why."

Laurel stopped smiling.

"Poking your nose in things that don't concern you can be mighty unhealthy down here, Nurse Trevor," she said. "But here's Duke with the horses. So let's call a truce—for now. After you've seen my dearly beloved husband, you can decide how noble you feel like being—or acting. Same thing, likely. C'mon, now. Hec, you drop her baggage off at the lodge. We'll be there as soon as we find Paris. . . ."

"All right," Hector groaned. "Mrs Trevor, ma'am, I'm sorry——"

"You needn't be," Candace smiled. "We lost quite a few battles during the late unpleasantness. But we always win the one that counts: the last one. Don't worry, I'll teach her to spell Appomattox, yet!"

"A—pee, Ap," Laurel began mockingly, "Pee—oh, po, m—ay—tee, mat, tee—oh—ex, tox. Appomattox!"

"Why, go to the head of the class, Mrs Griffin," Candace Trevor said.

"There he is," Laurel said, pointing with her crop, "right where I thought we'd find him—in the family burying-ground. Talking to his pa and ma and his baby brother, Ulysses. Only folks he'll condescend to talk to, now: the dead. Well, goodbye. Sorry I acted like that; but it just comes over me, sometimes. . . ."

"Aren't you going with me?" Candace said, a little breathlessly. "To introduce us, I mean?"

"'Twouldn't do any good," Laurel said, and Candace was surprised by the genuine note of sadness in her voice. "He listens to other folks, sometimes: Hector, and Roberta. 'Specially Roberta. But me, never. I—I don't think he likes me very much. . . ."

"Why?" Candace said. "Have you done anything to hurt him?"

"If I have," Laurel said in that same toneless voice of sorrow, "he sure Lord doesn't know anything about it. Leasewise, I don't think he does. Mrs Trevor, ma'am, you reckon lunatics can read folks' minds?"

"No," Candace said. "Now, what do I do? Just march up there and present myself?"

"That would be best," Laurel said gravely. "I'll send you Samson, like I said. Now, don't you take on. You'll need him for the chores. I'm not trying to rile you any more. . . ."

"But where are you going?" Candace said, "in case I need to get in touch with you—to ask you something. I mean. Are you going home?"

"Nope," Laurel said, "not home. . . ."

"Then where?" Candace persisted.

"Told you once you asked too many questions," Laurel said. Then she yanked her black gelding's head around savagely, and got out of there, leaning forward on her horse's neck, heading for the dark woods near the river, riding at a gallop, going on.

Candace stood there looking at Paris Griffin. Paris, she thought; it fits. Out of the Achaean legends—this face of a slumbering god. Apollo's face, set upon the body of young Hercules; because you have none of that almost feminine softness that the sculptors gave to Apollo, do you? No wonder she sounded sad! If you were mine, I'd——

She stopped short, appalled at the direction and surging

16

sweep of her thought. 'For better or for worse,' she told herself mockingly. That's what I said to Hector, throwing it up as a reproach to your—your wife, before I'd seen her—or you. Oh God, isn't all virtue cloistered virtue in the end? And untested strength, no strength at all?

She stood there before him, staring at him. But, she realized at once, she might as well have not been there at all. He gazed through her, his blue eyes fixed upon far distances, while his strong well-shaped hands went on stirring in an ant-hill with a stick. He struck down, killing dozens of the insects with every stroke; but with, Candace saw, complete impersonality and without malice. Then he changed his tactics. He held the stick still against the mound, so that the ants, driven by terror (Did ants feel terror, pain?) raced up it. Laughing, he lifted the stick, flicked it like a whip, and the little crawling things (Smaller than the other crawling things he had seen at Donelson, Island Number Ten, Shiloh, Corinth, Vicksburg? Unable to scream, at least at a pitch his ears could capture . . . ?) were flung outwards through the air to come to earth yards away. He did it again and again, kept up his idiotic cruel game until Candace took a step forward, and her shadow fell across him.

He looked up. For the first time he seemed to have recognized that she was both a stranger and alone, because he whirled and stared at the diminishing figure of Laurel and her horse, racing towards the woods.

"She didn't want to come," Candace said, fighting furiously against the sudden quaver in her voice. "It—it upsets her too much to see you the way you are now. . . ."

Paris didn't answer her. He went on holding his stick so that the ants could crawl up it, then snapping them out in an arc that brought them down—where? Beyond their world's rim? Candace asked herself. Beyond the edges of recognition or even hope? Comparable, perhaps, to that formless, shifting wasteland into which he, himself, had been flung?

"Paris," Candace said gently; "why do you do that?"

17

He looked at her, his blue eyes clear and serene.

"God," he said; "I'm playing God, ma'am. . . ."

Candace took a backward step. What came to her mind was a quotation: 'Though this be madness, yet there is method in it!' Men—and ants. Smash them, and they don't know why they're being smashed. Fling them out of the familiar, the loved, deprive them of recognition, take away their feeling of belonging, and——

"But why, Paris?" she said again. "Tell me why?"

Paris looked at her solemnly.

"Does *He* ever tell us why?" he said.

"No," she whispered, "He doesn't, does He?"

Paris was staring at her curiously.

"You—you're pretty, ma'am," Paris said.

"Thank you, Paris," Candace said, and put her hand out to him. "Come on," she said; "get up from there. I have to take you home, now. . . ."

"What's your name, ma'am?" Paris said.

"Candace," she told him, "Candace Trevor——"

He stood up then, towering above her like a young oak.

"Pleased to make your acquaintance, ma'am," he said, and took her hand. His grip was strong, but gentle. Candace pulled her hand away from his, and caught him by the arm.

"Come on; we'd better get there before dark," she said.

2

"Paris," Candace said; "what did you do before the War?"

"War?" Paris said.

Candace bowed her head. Stared at the toes of her shoes peeping out from under her skirt until the edges of the world were hard and clear again. Until the hot tangle in her throat subsided. Until her voice could be trusted not to shake.

"The fighting," she said. "People shooting at each other. Cannon roaring. Like this: C a a a r r a h h—boom!"

"Boom!" Paris said, and smiled at her.

Candace turned her face away from him. Sat there staring out into the night.

Get a grip on yourself, 'Dace Trevor, she thought. You're a nurse, remember. You've worked in hospitals where the stench of gangrene would floor a buzzard. You've heard men scream until their voices were gone and after that go on screaming with their eyes until they died. So why should this get to you? What is there so much more horrible about this magnificent male body housing this broken mind?

She turned back to Paris.

It is though, she thought; and it does get to me—it does, it does, it does!

"Why," Paris said wonderingly, "you're—you're crying, Candy!"

"I know," Candace sniffed; "that's because I'm over-tired. Come on, let's go inside. Samson's getting your bath ready. . . ."

"All right, Candy," Paris said.

Inside the lodge, Candace sank wearily into the big chair. Paris sat down on a stool by the fireplace. He didn't say anything. Was there, Candace thought bitterly, anything to be said?

I'll write Ingra Holm, she told herself (knowing what

19

she was doing, perfectly aware that she was arming the thresholds of consciousness against the insupportable, the unendurable; smashing the mirrors of recognition so that she could no longer see the image of herself as she had become now; using the bright-edged slivers remaining from that destruction to top the walls against truth's unspeakable ugliness, so that it couldn't reach her, so that it must rip itself to shreds trying to pass). Dear Ingra. She promised to look in every day on her way home from school to see how that lazy black slattern is taking care of Henry. Ingra's too pretty to be a school teacher. The perfect Scandinavian beauty—and teaching Negro children, at that. Which I approve of. Of course I do. I haven't become that Southern, yet. Still—they're so—unwashed. So—physical—and so dreadfully black! Lord, what's happening to me? I'm so tired. So very, very tired——

"Miz Candy," Samson said from the doorway, his voice a bass rumble that made the windows rattle even when, as now, he was trying to talk quietly, "the water's all hot, ma'am. . . ."

Slowly, Candace stood up. She was truly tired; and she would have much rather stayed where she was. She thought about telling Samson that, as a nurse, she had bathed hundreds of wounded soldiers, both Confederates and Union prisoners, with her own two hands during the War, so the fact that he was going to scrub Paris Griffin in the big wooden tub before the fireside—as she'd told him to do— was a matter of indifference to her. But she didn't tell Samson that. She knew he wouldn't understand her professional disinterest before male nakedness, that he would drop her, in his mind, out of the ranks of the "Quality". And, considering how much she had to depend upon the big Negro, that wouldn't do. That wouldn't do at all.

"Be gentle with him, Samson," she said. "Sometimes I think you don't know your own strength."

"I'm mighty strong, all right," Samson said complacently; "but I'll be careful, ma'am. 'Sides, Mr Paris is mighty

20

strong hisself. 'Taint like he was a wounded soldier. . . ."

"Oh yes he is," Candace said sadly; "perhaps worse wounded than any man I've ever seen. . . ."

She went outside again. It was a white night, moon-washed, star-blazed. She leaned against an oak, feeling the tiredness inside her like a weight. And yet she knew she was hours away from sleep, that, even if she were to go to bed this instant, her mind would go on, until almost morning, grinding out the unending thoughts: Why? Not a mark on him, and what those Army doctors say about concussion is nonsense. I saw too many cases of concussion in Vicksburg, during the siege. I may have suffered from it a couple of times myself. But, if being knocked unconscious by a shell-burst affects the mind, wouldn't it always affect it, or nearly always? And it doesn't. Very, very rarely. If at all. Let me see: Those Union gunboats pounded Vicksburg from June 1 until Independence Day—all of thirty-three days; and I saw concussion cases daily, more of them than real wounds. Bad ones, too. People bleeding from the mouth, nose, ears, and sometimes even from the corners of the eyes, and far gone in shock. Yet, when they came back, they were all right. I was blown across the ward twice, was out both times; and I'm not mad. Have I ever seen a case like Paris's? No, never. In spite of all the sterling opportunities I've had. Wait a minute! That Baker girl—Sally Baker. But she was feeble-minded *before* the war. She did go insane during the siege, though. So maybe concussion can make a mental case worse. An already existing tendency—only Hector says that Paris was perfectly all right, before. But—was he? Hector's not a doctor. And even doctors know precious little about the mind. Maybe the explosion they all insist upon attributing Paris's condition to—more comforting that way, isn't it? Removes all suspicion of a hereditary factor, a taint in the Griffin's blood—was the last straw that broke the camel's back. Being married to her probably had him teetering on the edge of insanity anyhow, and——

Just one moment, 'Dace Trevor! she brought herself up short. Now you're not being scientific. You have absolutely no reason to believe that she didn't make him happy as a lark, and vice versa. Because, at the moment, slapping her teeth out seems to you one of life's most dearly anticipated pleasures doesn't mean that Paris responded to her the same way—or that any other man would have, for that matter. In fact, I'll bet that around men—except her brother-in-law, who doesn't really count, being out of the sweepstakes—she purrs like a kitten and is just as soft and cuddly! Women! If men knew what we're really like, they'd all take the vow of chastity and let the race die out. . . .

She heard, suddenly, old Bess's whinnying snort. She drew herself upright, standing away from the tree she had been leaning against, going a little rigid at the sound. It was a lovely night. A moonlit ride would maybe weary her tingling flesh to match the deadly tiredness of her nerves, her mind. Then, perhaps, she could sleep. If some corn-fed Macbeth had not murdered it, she thought.

"Samson!" she called out.

"Not yet, ma'am!" Samson said. "I ain't nowheres nigh done with him. . . ."

"I know. Could you get him to bed without me? I think I'll ride up to the big house and have a chat with Mrs Griffin. . . ."

This last was a lie, an invented excuse. But then she thought: Why not? Perhaps I can squeeze a little information out of her without her realizing it. . . .

"Why sure, ma'am; you go right ahead," Samson said.

She hadn't got five hundred yards away from the hunting lodge when she saw the horsemen. She pulled old Bess up and sat there, trembling, though whether from fear or rage or disgust, she didn't know. They went by in Indian file, led by a big blond man on a magnificent grey gelding, making no sound at all, no hoofbeat, nor stirrup jangle. And then she saw that their horses' hooves were padded with rolls of cloth, so that the animals seemed to be wearing turbans on their feet. The riders hadn't covered their heads with the tall conical hoods yet, so, as they rode through that wash of moonlight, Candace could see their faces clearly. From where she sat on old Bess in the utter blackness under the trees, she had time to study those fifty-odd faces one by one. Even after the white-robed Klansmen had all gone by, she sat there still, wondering what it was that made those faces so terrible.

Because they hadn't looked any different from any fifty men, picked at random from any section of the land. They had varied in age from forty downwards to less than twenty. Some had been thin, some fat, some rather handsome, as faces go. They hadn't seemed fiends incarnate out of hell— just a group of average, rather ordinary men, riding quietly through the night.

Their robes? Ridiculous coverings of sewn-up bed-sheets. The hoods they carried? The whips coiled around the saddle horns? Or even the fact of knowing who they were, what their mission probably was? No, she decided; it was none of these.

Then, startlingly, it came to her what the terrible thing in those faces was. It was the identical attribute her father, the Reverend Llewelyn Matthews, had tried all his life to instill in her without ever quite succeeding: simple, unquestioning faith. And she knew then that there was nothing worse, not anything in this world.

These Klansmen now, sustained by their faith that the pigmentation of their skins, or rather the lack of it, was a God-given badge of superiority, could commit acts of obscene barbarity without the faintest tinge of remorse. Their cause was holy. God was on their side. God and all the angels stood smiling their approval while these masked fanatics whipped a Negro to death, burned a schoolhouse, made war even upon children. And all through history it had been this way, Candace realized: the crimes of the wicked paled into insignificance before the hecatombs piled up by the righteous, the self-appointed just.

Oh God, she prayed, grant me always the humility of a little decent doubt! Then she pushed Bess into motion, rode on towards Griffin's Way.

She came almost to the alley of oaks leading to the house. But, as she had cut across country, riding through the woods, she had missed it by a few hundred yards. And, as she sat there, trying to get her bearings, a screech owl cried out, ripping the very fabric of the night apart. The sound tore through her, left her shaking. Why, she breathed, it—it's only an owl. Why am I so nervous? A regular fraidy cat. I never was like this before. Used to think I hadn't any nerves. Effect of the way I've had to live these last seven years, very likely. Now, there's a modest thought, 'Dace Trevor! Modest or not, there it is. As big as truth, and just as ugly. Henry was —sweet, before. But now he's a wreck; and he isn't even nice, because being crippled certainly doesn't help the disposition. While I—I want—I need—I hurt from loneliness. Oh God, I——

She kicked old Bess into a walk, her penny-brown eyes widening, feeling the waves of heat rising in her cheeks.

Lord! It really doesn't take a mortar shell, does it? Griffin's Way is quite enough. Father forgive me, for I *do* know what I do. Only stop me—stop me, Father, please!

And it was then, with an almost conscious feeling of relief, that she heard the hoofbeats. They cut through old Bess's placid clipclopping like rising thunder pounds through a splatter of rain. It was very dark under the trees so that Candace could see neither horse nor rider; but that they were coming towards her, she was sure. Half out of fear of being ridden down, and half out of a leaping, instinctive sense that those hoofbeats fitted into the pattern she was trying to discover, Candace pulled the fat old grey aside.

The horse and rider swept by her, passed into a gap between the trees where the moonlight flooded through. For a long moment, Candace sat there, hugging herself with unholy joy, before she pushed old Bess into motion. Because, just before the woodland darkness swallowed horse and rider once again, the blaze of moonlight had illuminated the pale oval of Laurel Griffin's face.

Then her feeling of exultation died. She wasn't going to be able to follow Laurel—not riding old Bess, and with

Laurel mounted on Prince. I'll ask Hector for another mount, Candace thought angrily. "C'mon, slowpoke! At least walk, won't you, please?"

But old Bess plodded on, no faster than before. Then, suddenly, the silence rode in upon Candace. There was no hoofbeat thunder up ahead. And Laurel hadn't had time, even at that beautiful swinging canter at which she rode, to have got beyond earshot. Far from it. Which meant——

That she had stopped. That she was waiting for Candace to catch up with her. Had seen old Bess as she passed; had even recognized—No. That, no. Because she hadn't so much as glanced in that direction. But, she *had* stopped. There wasn't any sound. There! Again. Louder now. An even slow trot instead of a fast canter. But was it the same horse? There was something about that gait. . . .

Candace eased old Bess forward. Came to the edge of that clearing, daybright in the wash of moon. Saw the two horses, the sleek roan and that magnificent grey, side by side; the two riders become one figure in the closeness of that embrace.

Why you little—Candace thought. Then she stopped. Because she didn't know the word. Not the right word, any-how: the one that fitted Laurel. Wasn't it, maybe: brave? The valour needed to break your world between your hands and reshape it nearer to your heart's desire? What was the difference between doing a thing and merely thinking it—except, maybe, the reckless courage it took to go ahead? Was a woman supposed to live all her life upon the memory of what used to be, but no longer was? How far did duty extend? Dear Lord, how far?

She felt the bitter tears sting her eyelids.

Why, bless you, Laurie, darling, she thought with sad self-mockery. Have fun for me, too, dear—for this pillar of nega-tive virtue, whose only grace consists in this: the recognition that these so white hands weren't made for throwing stones. . . .

She tugged at the left bridle to draw Bess's head around;

but then she saw that Laurel had jerked away from the man, and was gesticulating angrily.

You know what, dear? Candace thought; I'll tell you a secret: I'm not going to leave. Not now. In fact, wild horses couldn't tear me away!

Then she dismounted. Tiptoed through the woods. Made a semicircle that brought her out behind a screen of brush, close enough for their voices to reach her. From where she was, she could see them clearly. Then, abruptly, almost before her mind had recorded the corroborating details: that splendid grey gelding, the whip around the saddle horn, the white robe rolled into a bundle behind the saddle, the flutter of muddied rags that before had covered the horse's feet, she knew she had seen this man before; and where. With the nightriders. No, not merely with, but leading them.

"No, Di!" Laurel was saying. "That's why I came to meet you. You can't come to the house any more—not with this Yankee nurse around. She's smart. Too smart. She'd catch on so blamed fast——"

"Aw," the man called Di said; "Why should she care? What's it to her? Long as the old witch gets paid, I don't see——"

"You never see, boy—Baby," Laurel said; "but then, there never was a Cadwallader in human history who ever had a blamed thing 'twixt his ears; 'cept, maybe, Barry——"

"Now listen to the Queen of the Red River Valley!" the man grinned. "Well, Laurie, all I've got to say is that us Cadwalladers may not be the smartest folks on earth, but at least ain't none of us ever been scared loony by a little gunfire. . . ."

Then Laurel slapped him. Hard.

"Laurie, for God's sake——" the man began.

"Shut up! Told you I wouldn't have you talking that way about Paris! You watch your filthy tongue, Dion Cadwallader!"

Why, thank you, Laurel, dear! Candace thought; thank you very kindly. Name: Dion Cadwallader. Age—about

26

thirty. Big. Strong as an ox. Not quite as stupid, but almost. Hasn't learned the first thing about women; doesn't even know that contradiction, inconsistency, changeableness are our middle names. She loves Paris, you oaf! And she's only using you to still a certain annoying little itch—here I go again; me with my aseptic, clinical little mind—because Paris is *hors de combat*. And the minute I cure Paris— because I will cure him, I will! —she'll drop you so fast. . . . Then where will I be? Answer: right where I am now. With poor, dear Henry. Living upon the hard crusts of resignation. Cheerful thought, isn't it, 'Dace Trevor? Like all my thoughts. Like—my life. . . .

"Laurie, damned if I can figure you out," Dion Cadwallader said; "Sometimes you talk like——"

"I'm fond of Paris? I am. He was always good to me, never did me any harm. I wish I wasn't such a bitch. You see? I talk 'most as dirty as you do. Only I'm going to quit it. I'm going to learn to talk like *she* does, so prim and proper, using the right words in the right places, so that everything she says sounds like it comes right out of a grammer book. . . ."

"Lord!" Dion Cadwallader said. "She's really got you up a tree, hasn't she? I'd better have a look at this old witch."

"No, you don't Di! I know you. The minute you see her, you'll be off like a snakebit coon hound baying the moon. . . ."

"You mean she's cute? That this here Yankee fluff ain't half bad?"

"I mean she's pretty. Doggoned pretty. Prettier than I am, maybe, if only because she doesn't look stupid the way I do. And she may be a little older than I am, but not much. And she's already got Paris——"

"Then she's got herself a mighty heap of nothing!" Dion chuckled.

"You didn't think so once," Laurel said tartly; "and you won't again, if she brings him back to his senses, which it appears to me she's going to——"

27

"And if she does," Dion said; "just what do you aim to do, Laurie?"

"Go right back to him so blamed fast it'll make your head swim," Laurel said. "I'm his wife, ain't I?"

"Look, Laurie," Dion said, his voice heavy, menacing; "'Pears to me you're forgetting a couple of points. One, you were mine before you married him. Two, it was me, not him, that that freakish fool, Hiliary, ought to of gone gunning for. Three, when I came home on leave that time and he was still off at the fighting, you didn't know then whether he was loony or not, now did you?"

"No," Laurel said.

"Yet you climbed into the hay with me mighty willingly —long time before you had the excuse of his craziness——"

"So I'm no damn' good. I already admitted that," Laurel said. "What's that got to do with my loving him and going back to him? Long as he's with me and sound of mind, you don't even tempt me, Dion Cadwallader! You nor nobody else——"

"Still, you ain't a-going back to him. Not never. So get that through your pretty, stupid little head, Laurie."

"Why not?" Laurel said.

"Because I still got those letters you wrote me. And the day you start taking up with him again, I'll see that he reads 'em. Every living one of 'em. Then he'll have to meet me and——"

"You'll kill him. Or he'll kill you. And, either way, I'm sunk. 'Cause, even if he outgunned you, he wouldn't even so much as spit on me afterwards. And if you won, I'd have puking fits everytime you tried to touch me with hands covered with his blood. 'Cause it wouldn't wash off, Di—not never——"

"Oh, hell!" Dion said.

There was a silence between them. Candace thought that silence was never going to end. She didn't dare move away. In that profound stillness, they would have heard her, surely.

Laurel laughed suddenly. It was an abrupt, jerky, nervous

28

sound. Entirely mirthless. Sadder, Candace thought, than crying would have been.

"Look, Di, honey," Laurel said, "how come we're ruining a fine night like this one quarrelling over something that's not even likely to happen? He's still loony; and you—even though you're not worth the powder'n shot it would take to kill you—are all I've got. So the main thing I've got to do now is to see that this Yankee witch doesn't get her hooks into you, too. . . ."

Dear Laurie, Candace thought; I've got a surprise for you: I don't want him. You couldn't give him to me. Not even if you wrapped him in tissue-paper and hung him on the Christmas tree. But, if I'm to understand by your cryptic remarks about Paris that you're willing to give *him* up— No, don't. Henry might object, Henry, and my New England conscience. . . .

"Don't you worry your pretty little head about that none at all, Laurie," Dion said. "That is, if you don't let this poor horny child get too hard up for a little loving. Goddamn! This really ties it! We can't go to your house 'cause you're afraid she'll find out. We can't go to the hunting lodge 'cause your loony husband is there. And we can't go to my house 'cause Barry's home all the time now since he fell out with the widow Sims. . . . Lord God, Baby, where *can* we go?"

"Di——" Laurel's voice sank almost out of sound.

"Yes, Baby?" Dion said.

"It's—mighty pretty right here," Laurel said.

Candace turned then. Tiptoed through the woods. Came back to old Bess; mounted, tugged the ancient mare around, got out of there.

Why—I'm shaking! she realized. I'm quivering all over like crab-apple jelly when you spoon it out of the jar. Why? What's it to me?

Then she felt the stinging behind her eyelids, the scalding rush, the flood.

It'll come to me in a minute, why, she thought; and I

don't want it to. Please don't let it. Our Father which art in heaven, don't let it. Don't make me acknowledge, admit— Don't humiliate me this way. Let me keep this one crumb of comfort, this last scrap of pride. If You care about me. If You've ever cared. Or——

She pulled Bess up, aware suddenly that there was no more light; that she had ridden now beyond, or perhaps even behind, the moon. She sat there thinking about that: about what it meant. Then she flapped the bridle against the old mare's neck.

"Let's go, Bess," she said gently; "you and I had better be getting on home. . . ."

Then she added in her mind: if we have a home. If any one ever has. . . .

3

"PARIS," Candace said; "do you know where Hector lives?"

"Yes, Candy—I mean, Candace," Paris said. "Why?"

So he was in one of his lucid periods, Candace realized. Today, this morning, now, he was among those present, or very nearly so. But she had already learned to bar the door against hope on such occasions. She knew that tomorrow, surely, this afternoon, probably, even within the hour, possibly, he would have slipped back again, into vacancy, into absence. Another thing she had learned was that the quickest way to make him retreat out of consciousness, out of clarity, was to ask him questions about the past. He seemed perfectly willing to live in the present; there were hours, even occasionally an entire day, when he was indisputably sane. She could talk with him about anything whatsoever, and his conversation was intelligent, even, at times, witty—as long as that anything whatsoever concerned the here and now. But ask him about the War, about his youth, his childhood, and she could see him slipping away from behind his eyes, leaving, terribly, that body of young Hercules, that face of Apollo, vacant, those blue eyes as opaque as coloured glass. Candace wondered if his periods of withdrawal didn't occur when he asked himself the questions she had schooled herself by now not to ask. And she was absolutely sure of one thing: Paris Griffin was the way he was because of something that had happened before the War began.

The fighting just gave you an excuse, didn't it, Paris? she thought; an excuse you'd been looking for a long time, in order to get away from something you couldn't face. I know that. I'm perhaps the person best qualified to know it, because I'm going through the same thing right now. There's a thing I can't face either, Paris. Or maybe a couple of things. And, believe me—it would be a relief to lose my mind. . . .

"Why did you ask me about Hector?" Paris said curiously. He was clearly puzzled at her long silence.

"Because I need to see him," Candace said; "I have to talk to him about something. Will you take me to his house, Paris?"

"Why sure, Candace," Paris said.

"Call me Candy," Candace smiled; "Nobody ever did before. I like it. . . ."

"What did folks call you before?" Paris said.

"The girls in the nursing home where I got my training called me 'Dace," she told him.

Paris frowned.

"'Dace," he said, "'Dace Trevor. No'm, I don't like it. Sounds too—too flip, somehow. Like—a lady gambler or——"

"Or a woman of ill repute?" Candace teased.

"Well—yes," Paris said firmly. "I wasn't going to say it, but that's just what it does sound like. . . ."

"How do you know I'm not?" Candace said. And then, at once, she was sorry. The joke wasn't funny any more, was not, in fact, the kind that a gentlewoman ever made in the presence of a man—belonged to the rather coarse genre of humour that the girls at the nursing schools indulged in to prove to themselves they were advanced females, emancipated women, strong-minded ladies, like Susan B. Anthony and Elizabeth Stanton, who had already rocked New York and Boston in the fifties by demanding equal rights for women in every avenue of life. But, beyond its obviously questionable taste, there was another thing wrong with Candace's "advanced" jest: the appalling echo it awakened in her own mind: How do *I* know I'm not? At least secretly, in my own mind?

Paris smiled.

"You're joking," he said.

"Maybe I—I wasn't," Candace whispered. "How does one know, really, Paris? Maybe I—I could be a bad woman if——"

"Never," Paris said firmly. "You've got goodness and

sweetness written all over you. That's why I call you Candy. Come on now, let's go get the horses. . . ."

They had been riding the road that skirted the river a long time when they saw the horseman coming towards them. Candace stiffened in the saddle. Him! she thought angrily. Laurel's—paramour. Dion—Cad—Cadwallader. He'll probably do or say something that will set Paris back for weeks, and——

The rider came on. Then Candace saw that he wasn't Dion, after all. He had the same build, the same great thewed strength; but he carried his big body with much more grace. And his face—Why! Candace thought, Cadwallader or not, this one is kind!

"Paris!" the man boomed. "Good Lord, boy! You're a sight for sore eyes!"

"Howdy, Barry," Paris said.

"You're looking just great," Barry said. "'Scuse me, ma'am—I reckon you're the lady who——"

"Who is supposed to be taking care of Paris?" Candace said. "Yes, I am. My name's Trevor, Candace Trevor. I take it you're Dion Cadwallader's brother?"

"Right you are, Miss Trevor," Barry said; "but I didn't know you and Di had met——"

"We haven't," Candace said; "Paris—talks to me sometimes. I know I've heard both your names——"

"Then," Barry said quizzically, "how did you know I wasn't Di? Oh, that's right, Paris called me by name. I must say you've done him a mighty heap of good, Miss Trevor. He looks just fine to me. . . ."

"He is—better," Candace said.

"Miss Trevor, ma'am," Barry said suddenly, "I hope you won't think me forward, but I've just got to tell you that to have a nurse like you, I'd gladly sit down on a keg of gun powder with the fuse lit, myself!"

"As a matter of fact, I do think you're forward," Candace said pleasantly; "but that doesn't matter. What I'd like to know is what the Widow Sims would think if she could hear you right now?"

"Milly?" Barry said; "Oh, she gave me up as bad rubbish a month ago—Lord God! How'd you know about *that*, Miss Trevor?"

"Maybe I'm a witch," Candace laughed, "a New England witch. Besides, it's my business to know things——"

"Miss Trevor—you aren't busy with Paris, here, all the time, are you?" Barry said.

"Yes," Candace said softly, "I am busy with him all the time, Mr Cadwallader. And it's Mrs Trevor, not Miss. . . ."

"Oh!" Barry said lamely. "I—I beg your pardon, mighty humbly, ma'am. I didn't know. And I'm sorry——"

"Don't be," Candace said. "It's nice to be mistaken for an unmarried girl. Means that the years don't show. . . ."

"No'm, they don't," Barry Cadwallader said. "And now I'm twice as sorry, mainly because I didn't see you first. My respects to Mr Trevor. He sure is one lucky man!"

"No," Candace said; "Henry isn't lucky. Perhaps he's one of the most unlucky creatures who ever drew breath. Well, goodbye, Mr Cadwallader. It was nice, meeting you. . . ."

"You mean that, ma'am?" Barry said.

"Yes, I do mean it," Candace said. "Come on, Paris; we'd better go on, now. . . ."

Without turning, she was aware that Barry was following her with his eyes. It was a strangely warming sensation. Barry was a fine man, she realized; and, what was more, a decent one. Then she let her shoulders sag. There were so many possibilities to life. Or there would be, if——

She turned then, looked back. Barry was still sitting there on the big grey stallion, like a man turned to stone. His eyes swept over her as though he were trying to memorize her face.

You're lonely, too, Candace thought. That's why you're giving this more meaning than it has. But don't. You must not. It's all wrong. I—am married to a man with a crippled body, and am more than half in love with a man with a crippled mind. So don't, Barry Cadwallader—there can be no beginnings among things that have no end. Things like sorrow, and the non-existence of choice, except between

34

evils. Better that you stop what you're thinking right now, for you won't see me again—not if I can help it. . . ."

"Candy," Paris said, "come on. . . ."

Hector's house was exactly what Candace had expected it to be: a long, low bungalow with a veranda running all the way across the front of it. Also, just as she had expected, it showed no signs of ever having been painted; and one side of the veranda was filled up with saddles, harnesses, sacks of cotton seed, a broken wagon wheel waiting to be mended, ears of corn hanging from the ceiling to dry, and children playing cheerfully amid all the dirt and disorder. She had expected it to be the way it was, because ninety-nine and some hundredths per cent of all planters' houses looked like this. Neo-Grecian mansions had been rare, even before the War. As rare, actually, as the people who had owned more than one or two slaves.

They had come close enough by then to attract the attention of the children.

"Uncle Paris!" one of them shrilled. Then all four of them came flying down the stairs.

And Candace sat there frozen. Sick with shock. Because two of those four children weren't white. And the other two? About the eldest, a girl some thirteen or fourteen years old, Candace couldn't tell. There was no way to. Her hair was a shade darker than blonde, about the colour of old honey, Candace decided; and her eyes were blue. One of the boys, the oldest one, was as white as his sister, and, if anything, blonder; but there was a fullness about his lips, a flatness about his nose that, under other circumstances, Candace would have found adorable. The other two were clearly tar-brushed: the boy, one of those mulatto types that are an improvement over both the parent races; and the little girl, coppery brown, kinky-haired, negroid, vivid and alive. . . .

But Paris had climbed down and gathered them into his arms. They kissed him, wriggling like puppies from pure delight; and she, Candace, now that the shock had passed, sat there equally frozen; but this time from shame.

God forgive me, she thought; and you, too, Papa. You

35

taught me that this kind of a feeling is a sin. It is—I know it is. But so is intellectual pride, and you encouraged me in that. I wish you could have come down here before you died. I'd have liked to have seen it. The Reverend Llewellyn Matthews set down in this sea of black humanity. Oh, you'd have borne up nobly, telling yourself that all men are created equal and in God's image. I know that, too. But, Papa mine, up there in heaven, sitting, as you were sure you would, on the right hand of God Almighty, what good is knowledge against this—this revulsion? This repugnance? These children, now: my mind tells me they're beautiful children; but the message doesn't get through to my heart. I can't see them because my brain is too busy painting shocking pictures: a man like Hector, a fine man like that, lying naked in a black woman's arms. . . .

What good is intellect against these—visceral feelings? Against these fears, this recoil, this rejection implanted in the hairy thing that was our ancestor *before* he had become man, or developed a mind? I know you didn't believe in Darwin's teachings. But I do. I know how close the ape is to the surface in every one of us. How does one tame him, Papa? What shall my penance be? Hair-shirts? Self-scourgings? Or——

Slowly she dismounted, knelt beside Paris. Put out her arms.

"My turn now," she said.

They came to her shyly. Candace kissed them, one by one.

"Now, tell me your names," Candace said. "You, dear?"

"Rachel," the oldest girl said gravely, "and this is Hubert, and this——"

"I'm Matty," her sister giggled, "and here's our baby brother, Billy. He's silly. There, I made a rhyme! Silly Billy! Silly Billy! Sil——"

"Oh, shut up, Matty!" Hubert said. "You want him to start bawling?"

"Paris——" Candace began; but then she stopped; the slow tide of anguish rising in her with the recognition that he had gone again, had departed, escaped, while physically present

36

still, out of the here and now, swum backwards, perhaps, against the swift-running current of time to—where?

"Ain't no good to ask him nothing, ma'am," the boy, Hubert, said; "he won't even hear you. . . ."

"I know," Candace whispered. "Hubert—can you find your father for me? Tell him that we're here?"

"Why sure, ma'am," Hubert said; and was off.

Rachel took her uncle's arm.

"C'mon, Uncle Paris," she said, her voice soft, compassionate, tender. "Let's go sit on the porch, in the shade, 'til you feel better. . . ."

"Lordy!" Matty giggled. "He's gone loony ag'in!"

Rachel whirled upon her.

"You shut up, Matty!" she said. "Shut up, or I'll slap you!"

"Matty," the woman's voice came from the doorway, "you'n Billy run along and play. Howdy, Miz Trevor; won't you come in and sit a spell?"

Candace saw her then, saw the tall slim woman, who looked as if she'd been cast of old copper; whose hair was Indian straight; whose face was a monument to warring tribes: French and Ashanti and Creek.

"Thank you, I will," Candace said; "You're——" She stopped short, her face mirroring her confusion.

"Don't fret, ma'am," the woman laughed; "Just you call me Roberta. . . ."

"Roberta?" Candace said. "That's a pretty name. . . ."

"You think so, ma'am?" Roberta said, and pushed forward the big rocking-chair.

Candace saw, as she sank into it, the pitiful spectacle of the girl, Rachel, leading Paris along—just as one leads an ox or a sheep.

"Now, Uncle Paris, you sit down, like a good boy," Rachel said. "Take off your coat. It's too hot to keep it on. I'll go fix you and Mrs Trevor some lemonade. . . ."

"Isn't she grown up!" Candace marvelled.

"Yes'm," Roberta said, and drew up a straight chair beside Candace. "Rachie's a sweet child. Never did give me

37

the least bit of trouble. And Hubert, my oldest boy, not much. But Matty—Lord Jesus!—that there child purely invented mischief! 'Sides which, she's spoiling Billy, too. . . . But right now, Miz Trevor, I want to thank you for what you did. . . ."

Candace stared at her.

"I don't remember doing——" she began.

"I mean the way you behaved so natural with them kids," Roberta said. "I know it cost you a struggle, but that's just why it was mighty fine. So, thank you kindly, ma'am."

"It didn't——" Candace started to protest, but then she saw that it would be both useless and a mistake. There was no point in lying to this woman, even for politeness' sake. Roberta had lived past lying and even the need for it. "Yes," Candace said firmly, "you're right. It did cost me a struggle. Not because they aren't clean and pretty, for they are. But because I was still shocked at seeing them. You see, I didn't know. Nobody had told me. . . ."

"That Mr Hector lives with a coloured woman, and has four yard children to boot? No'm—naturally not. Ain't a thing that folks down here would care to talk about to a Northern lady like you, ma'am. And they'll never forgive Mr Hector for it. . . ."

"Why not?" Candace said. "I don't see what business it is of theirs. . . ."

"It is, though. Not the children. Half the rich planters in this here country have yard children, and nobody pays it no nevermind. That's not what's wrong. . . ."

"Then what is?" Candace said.

"That he treats them like they was got in lawful marriage, educates them like they was white, lives with them and me, right out in the open, and won't even make like he's shamed of it. Worse than that, he tells anybody who asks him that the only reason we ain't married legal is because the laws of this state won't let him; and that, long as he's kept from doing what's right, he don't even see how come the way we're living is a sin. . . ."

38

"Put that way, I don't suppose it is," Candace said. "You know, this is a pleasant house. . . ."

"It's plumb nigh a shack," Roberta said calmly; "but you're right about its being pleasant, ma'am. Any house where love is, is pleasant, whether it's spick and span, or no. . . ."

And any house where it's absent is hell, Candace thought. But when she spoke, she said impulsively: "I'm glad I came. I feel so—so at ease, here. . . ."

"I hope so," Roberta said. "Womenfolks are more alike than different, no matter what colour they be. And ain't nothing finer sometimes than being able to let your hair down, kick off your shoes, and talk. . . ."

"Now, isn't that the truth!" Candace laughed. Then she saw Hector coming through the gate with the boy, saw, in that instant, his face slacken with pure relief at the sound of her laughter. He came up the walk, one hand resting affectionately on Hubert's shoulder. At the foot of the stairs, he took off his hat.

"Howdy, Mrs Trevor," he said; "Paris bring you here?"

"Yes," Candace said; "I asked him to. And I've been having a perfectly wonderful time. . . ."

"So it seems," Hector said, watching her eyes. "And I'm glad, Mrs Trevor, ma'am, you just can't even imagine how glad I am. You see, I was afraid——"

"That I would join your accusers?" Candace said. "You needn't have been. If I've learned any one thing since I came to Griffin's Way, it's what the precise qualifications for stone throwing are. And that I, personally, am not entitled to toss a pebble, not to mention a rock——"

Hector stared at her.

"There're two quotations that would fit what you're saying, ma'am," he said; "and blamed if I can figure out which one you mean. Is it: 'People who live in glass houses shouldn't——'?"

"No," Candace said, "the other one, Hector—Oh, I'm sorry! But it does seem I've known you all my life. . . ."

"You go right on calling me Hector, ma'am. I like it,

especially coming from you. Then it's the other quotation? The one from the Good Book?"

"'He that is without sin among you, let him cast the first stone'," Candace quoted softly. "That one, Hector. And I can't even finish it. I haven't the right. Who am I to say, 'Go and sin no more——'?"

"No'm," Hector said, "I won't buy me even a little bit of that one, ma'am. You haven't got it in you to be sinful, and it shows."

Candace looked down. Looked up again. Faced him, knowing that he would see the tears in her eyes.

"You're right, Hector," she said; "and that's rather awful, isn't it?"

Hector stood there.

"Don't reckon I follow you, ma'am," he said.

"I don't suppose you do," Candace said. "It's quite complicated. Let's say that courage to resist temptation is—admirable. And as rare as it is admirable. But what keeps most people out of trouble, certainly isn't courage, Hector——"

"Then what is it?" Hector said.

"Several things, none of them very worthy," Candace said. "Things like fear—of the consequences, of gossip, of—even losing the desired object completely by taking that irrevocable first step. Fear of being ashamed afterwards; after one has come to one's senses, I mean. Perhaps, more important than being afraid is the lack of any real opportunity. I strongly suspect that all virtue is cloistered, or it doesn't remain virtue very long. And, worst of all——"

She stopped short, aware of the shocked astonishment in his eyes.

"Oh, I am sorry!" she said. "I'm being a good bit too candid, am I not?"

"You go right ahead, Honey," Roberta laughed. "Sure is refreshing to listen to a woman telling the truth for change!"

Hector smiled.

"It is refreshing," he said; "Tell me, what is worst of all —Candace?"

Candace looked out over the woodlands before the house.

"The realization," she said softly, "that even the temptation isn't very strong. That one has been over-trained, reduced to a curious kind of bloodlessness, the whole horizon of one's life diminished into flatlands with no mountain peaks even in the distance, nothing but sameness, sameness, sameness—because one hasn't even enough spirit to be bad!"

She felt suddenly a hand on her arm. Looking down, she saw that hand was brown.

"Honey," Roberta said, "you know you need help, don't you?"

"Yes," Candace said, "that's what I came for. Hector, could you spare a couple of days from your work—to go get my husband—and bring him here?"

Hector didn't answer her at once. But when he did, what he said was overlaid with meanings.

"Even if I couldn't spare the time, I'd go fetch him all the same," he said.

But, before Candace got Paris back to the hunting lodge again, there was one more thing. The man and the boy whom she was going to identify in her mind forever as the troglodytes, even after she had learned their names, stepped out of the underbrush from both sides of the road, were reaching up, jerking her mount and Paris's to a stop before she had got over her astonished disbelief that they were even partially human. The man was covered with hair, his bullet-shaped head black-thatched to the eyebrows, bearded, not by intention, but by neglect, because the swarth of blackness around his mouth and covering his jaws was too short to be anything more than four or five days' lazy disinclination to shave; his barrel chest, furred like a bear's, showing through a shirt that hadn't a button to its name, and, below that, his great, protruding belly hung over his belt like a hogshead of dirty lard that somebody had stirred horsehairs into. The boy was a smaller duplicate of this outrageous caricaturing of mankind, this beady-eyed thing that was but dubiously *homo*, Candace thought; and most certainly not *sapiens*!

41

"Now ain't he sweet?" the man cackled, showing fangs innocent of brushing since their first appearance in the cavern that served him for a mouth. "Baby boy out riding with his nurse! Git down, you loony bastid! You warn't loony when you kilt poor Hil—an', by heaven, this time I'm gonna make sure of you man to man, not like that it was that fool kid 'stead of you in that boat I shot a hole in and sunk. . . ."

Then he rolled Paris from the saddle with a blow that no other man could have managed, because even that required his ape-like length of arm.

Candace saw him lift a booted foot, heard Paris's rib go when it landed. That was all he had time for, because, by then, she was using her riding crop. The monster's howls echoed through the trees; but he came on in, got those arms of his around her waist and dragged her down from old Bess. She went on hammering at him, raking his face bloody with her nails, but not crying out or weeping, just fighting in a silent concentration of fury until the man threw her to the ground so hard that all her breath left her, and blackness roared down upon her from the dark-topped menacing trees.

But it began to lighten at once, and she heard the boy, his voice husking, beginning to shake:

"Pa—kin I have her? You said you was gonna take me to Lou's Parlor House the next time we go into town. . . . I ain't never had me no woman and here I am nigh onto fifteen!"

"Why you mannish lil' bastid!" the man chuckled. "Why sure, son. Skinny Yankee woman like this un won't be no fun, but leasewise it's for free!"

"Pa," the boy croaked, "I—don't know how!"

"Pull up her dress, you li'l jackass!" the man guffawed. "And see what you kin find. Then you plays around 'til I gits finished with this loony son of a bitch, an'—an' I'll show you how, myself. . . ."

Candace came up then, jackknifing into a sitting position; and the little monster snarled at her:

42

"Jes' you lay back down, damn you! Pa said I could have myself a piece of you, he said——"

Then she slapped him, hard across the mouth. Which was a mistake. Because the boy doubled a fist already as big as his father's, sent it whistling into her face; and all the trees bowed inwards towards her, their dark tops running together into total night, through which there lifted, thin and faint, the edged, shrill, choked-off echo of her scream.

She was aware that someone was bathing her face. She opened her eyes, but they wouldn't focus, so she closed them again. From some immeasurably immense distance, she could hear a man's voice cursing slowly steadily profanely. Her eyes jerked open. The green masses slowed their dizzy whirl, came to a reluctant halt, separated into individual trees, even into leaf and branch. Closer, the man's face was an enormous blur; then it, too, cleared. Clean-shaven, pleasant, or it had been before——

She put up a slim hand, touched that face.

"Don't worry, Barry," she whispered; "I——"

"Lord God!" Barry Cadwallader said. "You—you're all right, Cand—Mrs Trevor?"

She smiled at him, but her smile was sadder than all the tears on earth.

"I don't know," she said; "Perhaps you'd better tell me that, Barry. Am I—all right?"

"Yes," he said, "I got here in time, if that's what you mean. Likely because that little cretin hadn't figured out just how you go about it, and his apish Pa was too busy with Paris——"

"Paris!" Candace said. "Oh, my God! They——"

"They've damned nigh killed him," Barry said. "And to think they're my cousins. My first cousins——"

"Where are they?" Candace said faintly.

"Gone. I pistolwhipped the two of them bloody and sent them off a-howling. Please, ma'am, you—you aren't hurt bad, are you? 'Cause now I've got to look after Paris some. . . ."

Candace sat up, then. The trees started to whirl again, but she hung on until they stopped.

"Help me up, Barry," she said.

She had to cling to him through the black shuddering, the vile green rising, the crazy upending of earth and sky. She was about to go down again, to give up, when her eyes came clear, momentarily, locked upon Paris's face. The rage that exploded in her middle, that went whistling like shrapnel along her veins, her nerves, was then, at that moment, precisely what was needed. She moved towards Paris, step by slow step, sleepwalking actually. Without knowing how or why, she was on her knees, suddenly, cradling that broken, bloody head in her two arms, pressing it to her breasts, crying:

"Paris! Oh, my darling, they've hurt you so!"

And, even when she looked up into Barry's face, she neither recognized nor understood the reason for what was in his eyes. Which was just as well. The task before her was major, requiring no diversion of will, no division, however momentary, of feeling. Even for pity, now, there was no time.

44

✶ 4 ✶

Dr Harley Benson looked up at Candace.

"You've done a fine job, Nurse Trevor," he said. "Haven't left a blamed thing for me to do. . . ."

Candace could hear the note of resentment in his tone. Army, she decided. Conservative, like most Rebels. One of the kind who let hundreds of boys die in filth and misery almost up to the end of the war before they'd accept women nurses in the hospitals. Who wrote in the newspapers, "Only women of dubious morality would be willing to perform the intimate services for the wounded that a nurse must undertake daily. . . ." Who only gave in when, as at Vicksburg, they couldn't help it. Who only took us when even those dirty, stinking, clumsy, oafish cowards they were using as male nurses finally had to shoulder a musket at the end.

"Thank you, Doctor," she said crisply; "but there is one thing you can do; you can check him over again and find out why he's still unconscious."

Barry Cadwallader stared at her. He had caught the acrid timbre of her voice. And now, looking at the doctor, Barry could see him bristle.

"He has three fractured ribs," Dr Benson said. "His face is a mass of bruises and cuts. What does that suggest to you, Nurse?"

"It doesn't suggest anything to me," Candace said.

"You, I've been told," Dr Benson said testily, "were an army nurse. You mean to tell me that you've never seen a case of concussion before?"

"I've seen hundreds of them," Candace said; "I've even suffered from it myself, twice, in Vicksburg during the siege. That's why I know that this is *not* concussion."

"You question my judgment, Nurse?"

"No," Candace said. "To question a thing, there must be an element of doubt. Here, there is none. Paris has been

45

unconscious for all of five hours, Doctor, while Mr Cadwallader, here, was riding all over the country trying to find you. Have you ever heard of a mere concussion case staying out that long?"

Dr Benson glared at her.

"I've known men to stay in a coma for days!" he snapped.

"Yes. When there's skull fracture or brain injury. And then there are always external signs of it: bleeding from the mouth, nose, ears. Use your eyes, Doctor. There are no cuts or bruises on the forehead or cranium. His face has been fearfully battered; but I find nothing wrong with his head."

The doctor bent over Paris again. Examined his jaw, his face, his neck with great care. Straightened up. Barked:

"Concussion!"

"But five hours, Doctor?" Candace said.

"Well——" the doctor said; "maybe, since that explosion he was in before, he's become especially sensitive to it. I'll look in on him tomorrow. If he hasn't moved or spoken by then——"

"What, Doctor?" Barry said.

"He'll die," Dr Harley Benson said.

After Dr Benson had gone, Candace bent over the bed.

"Paris!" she called softly. "Paris! Can't you hear me? Paris, please——"

"It's no good, Candace," Barry said gruffly; "He's still out. I only hope——"

"That Dr Benson is wrong? No, he isn't, Barry. When they stay in a coma that long, usually they die. . . ."

"You're taking this mighty calmly," he said.

Candace shook her head.

"Just because I don't give way to hysteria, doesn't mean I'm calm," she said. "But it's not brain injury, Barry. It's not! It can't be!"

"You're talking like a nurse now, Candace?" Barry said. "Or like a woman?"

"Like a woman, I'm afraid," Candace whispered; "still——"

46

"Come over here and sit a spell," Barry said. "You can watch him sitting down, and it's no use wearing yourself out."

"All right, Barry," Candace said.

They sat there without saying anything for a long time. Then Candace said:

"Tell me about your cousins, the troglodytes. . . ."

"Troglodytes?" Barry said. "That's a good one! They do look like they came up from the caves, don't they?"

"Or from the bowels of the earth," Candace said. "And they should be sent back there, from my way of thinking."

"Mine, too," Barry said; it's no fun having people pointing them out and a-snickering: 'Them there are Barry and Di Cadwallader's first cousins! Always did say that that there family ain't rightly human!' "

"It is strange," Candace sighed; "You Cadwalladers are handsome men, while the troglodytes—what are their names? I can't go on calling them that——"

"Hank—for Henry; and the kid's called Ernest. Last name's Thurston. Hank's pa was my uncle. My own mother's brother."

"Don't tell me *he* looked like that!" Candace said.

"No, he didn't. Uncle Dan was a mighty good-looking fellow. Tall, dark, real handsome. And to think those apes who attacked you and Paris are his son and his grandson!"

"But why, Barry?" Candace said, listening with half an ear, the other straining to catch Paris's slightest groan.

"Don't know. It's beyond medical science. My aunt was a pretty woman, too. Doc Benson swears it was some taint in the blood, resulting from the way Uncle Dan lived. He was a gay dog, Candace; couldn't leave either women or the bottle alone. So Doc says it's a case of the sins of the fathers being visited upon the sons down to the third generation. Funny thing, all his kids weren't apes. The first boy, Hiliary, *looked* all right. Better looking than Uncle Dan, even. Hil was blond like his ma, only—"

Candace was facing him then. Something in her face stopped him.

47

"What's the matter?" he said. "Why are you looking at me like that?"

"Hil——" she whispered, "you said—Hil. And they——"

"They what?" Barry said.

"They said that—that Paris killed him!"

"Well——" Barry said.

"Did he, Barry?"

"No," Barry said flatly. "They fought a duel all right. But from every reliable account I ever heard about that stupid mess, Hiliary actually killed himself."

"Barry——"

"Yes, Candace?"

"What did they fight over? Or rather—whom? Was it—Laurel?"

"Don't you think you'd better have a look at your patient? Seems to me I heard him groan, just now," Barry said.

Candace smiled.

"You are a dear," she said; "I've never been told to mind my own business more politely in all my life. Why won't you tell me, Barry?"

"It's—family history, Candace," Barry sighed; "and it's messy. Don't figure I've got the right to go washing linen *that* dirty in public. Paris can't even defend himself and Laurie——"

"There!" Candace said. "Thank you very much, Barry Cadwallader; I—Oh, thank God!"

Barry was across the room in three strides, bending over Paris. But, quickly as he moved, Candace was there before him.

Paris twisted on the bed. Sweat beaded his forehead. His mouth came open, whispering: "Candy! Candy! Are you —here, Candy?"

"Yes, Paris," Candace said, her voice choked, hushed, drowned.

"All right," Paris said, "always all right—you—here. Sleep now, Candy. No more dreams—— No more—being afrai——"

48

His voice sank away into nothing. But his body was relaxed now, no longer inert, but slackening into sleep, the rise and fall of his breathing plainly visible.

Candace looked at Barry, and her eyes were liquid silver, brimming.

"He's going to be all right now," she whispered; "Oh, thank you, God!"

"Candace," Barry said, "it's none of my business, but you —you love Paris, don't you?"

She took her handkerchief out, dried her eyes.

"Yes," she said simply, "I love him, Barry. But I don't know how I love him, or even if I'll go on loving him after he's well again. Now, I love him like a mother loves a backward child: with pity for his helplessness—with a determination to protect him from the world that's rather fierce. And that—that's all right now. It fits the existing circumstances. But, later——"

"Later——" Barry said.

"I may come to love him as a woman loves a man, if I can bring back all I think he was, before. I believe he must have been an extraordinary person. . . ."

"He was," Barry said. "Paris was—a saint."

She stared at him, seeing at once that there was no contemptuous mockery in his use of that word. But her own confusion, her own pain made her answer him tartly:

"A saint—who fights duels? Who got involved with a woman like—Laurel?"

Barry smiled.

"Who ever told you the saints were sinless, Candace?" he said. "All I meant was that Paris was closer than most folks are to nature, and hence, to God. He could ride a horse nobody else could come nigh. I saw him once myself patting those bull mastiffs that crotchety old Zeb Wilkins had trained to tear any stranger to pieces; and they, though they'd never seen him before, behaved like puppies. And people, Lord God! Everybody loved him——"

"Everybody, Barry?"

"Except those who hated him for being what he was. And

49

there're always a mighty heap of those: folks to whom simplicity, goodness and purity are a slap in the face. Always have been—or so many of the saints wouldn't have been martyred."

He looked at her, then said, very quietly:

"And you, Candace? If you do come to love him, what will you do?"

"Run like a rat," she said bitterly. "I am still a married woman with a husband worse crippled than Paris. So I have always to—prevent the future, Barry. I have to keep anything, anything at all, from getting started that might upset the even tenor of my way. Do you understand that?"

"Yes," he said soberly. "Reckon I'll get along home, now. And Candace——"

"Yes, Barry?"

"Shall I drop by tomorrow?"

"Why, yes," Candace said. "Yes, of course! I enjoy your company so very much. . . ."

"Yes," Barry said, "and that's the hell of it!"

"What—if I may be so unladylike as to quote your profanity—is the hell of it, Barry?"

"That you *do* enjoy my company. That I don't bother or trouble you in the slightest," Barry said. "'Bye now, Candace. If you need me for anything, you just send Samson over, and I'll——"

"I'll do that," Candace whispered; "thank you, Barry——"

"Thank me?" Barry said. "For what——"

"For restoring my faith in humanity," Candace said.

She had sent Samson to Hector's plantation, less out of any pressing need to notify Hector of what had happened to Paris than from the acute realization that bringing her husband to Griffin's Way would very definitely have to be postponed until Paris was up and about again. Now, Barry Cadwallader had scarcely got out of sight, when she saw Hector pounding towards her. He was mounted on his big dun gelding; and the poor beast was blown. She knew from the very little time that had elapsed since she'd sent Samson on his errand that Hector must have galloped his mount all the way.

He drew the heaving, foam-flecked animal up. He had a pistol in his belt that, mounted on wheels, would have made a convincing fieldpiece, Candace thought. And his eyes were red-streaked, glaring, wild.

"Which way did they go?" he barked. "Just you tell me that, Candy! By heaven and hell, I'll——"

"You'll get down off that horse," Candace said crisply, "and come see how your poor brother is. You can chase the Thurstons tomorrow, if you still feel like descending to their level of savagery. Besides, I see Samson forgot to tell you they've had a six-hour start. You heard me, Hector; get down!"

"Yes'm," Hector said. He swung down from his mount. Stood there staring at her. Slowly he smiled.

"Durned if you aren't the beatingest female, Candy!" he said.

"I know. Now you tell me one thing: where'd you get that Candy business from?"

"Oh," he said lamely, "Samson told me Paris always calls you that. I was thinking how much it suits you, so I reckon I kind of got to calling you that myself in my mind. I'm sorry—if you don't like it, I——"

"I like for Paris to call me that," Candace said pointedly; "but I'd prefer that all the rest of my friends call me Candace. Now, come on in. He's not fully conscious yet, but I don't think he's in danger any more. I find this unconsciousness—strange. So does the doctor, though he won't admit it. It's as though Paris has entered into a state of—of well—shock. But emotionally, I mean, not physically. As if the Thurstons' attack reminded him of something; maybe made him recognize something. None of Paris's injuries account for it. There's no evidence of skull fracture or even concussion, so——"

Hector looked at her.

"Is that good or bad, Candace?" he said. "I mean this shock you're talking about?"

51

Candace stared at Paris's silent form.

"Truthfully, I don't know, Hector," she said. "But I—I think it's good. Which is just a feeling I have, nothing more. I believe—or want to believe—that he's returned to that other time. That he's taking a second look. A good, hard look at what happened to him, then. And when he comes back this time, maybe. . . ."

They bent over the bed. Paris lay there with his eyes closed, unmoving. Then suddenly, startlingly, he said:

"Ulysses! Ulie, boy—he's dead! He's dead and I killed him! I killed him! I——"

Then his voice trailed off into a broken jumble of sound.

Candace looked at Hector.

"Ulysses?" she said.

"Our kid brother," Hector whispered. "He was seventeen when he died. Drowned. Boat he was in turned over in the middle of the river on a dead calm night. . . ."

"Couldn't he swim?" Candace said.

"Like a fish. Reckon he must have got cramp. It was late fall, and that water was mighty cold. Paris—found him. . . ."

"And now says that he killed him. Why?"

Hector stared at her.

"Blamed if I know," he said. "He wasn't even there when it happened. I know that because he was helping me look for the kid, himself. . . ."

Candace looked at him. Opened her mouth. Said: "Why?"

"Now look-a here, Candace;" Hector said. "Don't crowd me into agreeing with Laurie!"

"That I ask too many questions? Hector, listen to me: No bomb-burst damaged Paris's mind. All that shell did was to open a door for him to leave through—or a hole for him to hide his head in like an ostrich—from the things he couldn't face any more. Nobody knows anything about the human mind, not even the doctors, so I'll stack my guess up against theirs any day. Hector, you've got to tell me! Don't you see that knowing, I might be able to reach him, bring him back, and then——"

"And then?" Hector said quietly.

"Nothing," Candace said; "but we've got to, Hector. We must! If it's at all possible. So tell me, why does Paris think he killed Ulysses? And why did those troglodytes accuse him of killing Hiliary Thurston? It appears that he killed nobody; so why, Hector, why?"

"I don't know," Hector said, "honestly I don't, Candace. It happened right after the duel. Ulie saw that obscene farce. He—he ran off. Seems like it upset him a sight more than it ought to have, so——"

"So now Paris thinks he drove his little brother to his death?" Candace said.

"Could be that," Hector said slowly. "But that's still mighty far-fetched to my way of thinking. That Ulie was upset at the sight of a man dying, 'specially that bad, ugly way that Hiliary died, was understandable. But that Paris should blame himself, just isn't. He tried his damnedest not to kill Thurston. Fired into the air six or seven times. . . ."

"But he did kill him, finally?"

"No! Hiliary killed himself. Came running up to Paris, a-screeching like a woman: 'Kill me, Paris! Shoot, damn you! Can't you see I want to die?' "

Candace's eyes were very wide and dark.

"And *then* Paris obliged him?"

"No! Goddammit, Candace, I told you——"

"Tell me again, Hector—without the profanity this time, if you please. What did happen?"

"He grabbed Paris. He was a big fellow and mighty strong. All I could see was them wrestling together, and then I heard the shot. The smoke came drifting up from between them so that nobody could tell which one of them was hit. So we all ran towards them. Got there in time to ease Hil down on the grass. He said a funny thing: 'Thank you, Paris. Thank you, dear, dear boy. . . .' "

"Hector," Candace said. "I'm going to ask you again: why?"

Hector looked at her.

"Reckon you'd better ask Laurie that," he said.

53

"Would she tell me?" Candace said.

"She—she just might. Been preying on her mind too, I'd suspect. . . ."

"That and a few other things," Candace said.

Laurel sat outside the hunting lodge in one of the chairs that Samson had brought. Candace could see her mouth growing more and more sullen, and her blue eyes turning greyish, like smoke.

"'Tain't none of your business," she said.

"Oh, come off that field-hand dialect," Candace said. "You can talk properly; I've heard you. And it *is* my business. I took the job of caring for Paris——"

Laurel smiled.

"Caring for is right," she drawled; "and I bet you don't find it a chore, now do you?"

"I meant 'taking care of' as you well know. But, just as you said, 'caring for' is right, too. Who wouldn't? Paris is one of the nicest, kindest human beings I've ever met. Even when he's sane, as he quite often is, that aspect of him doesn't change. You were his wife——"

Laurel went on smiling.

"Don't like your grammar none at all, Mrs Trevor," she said. "Funny thing, you're usually so precise. But right now, 'pears to me you're getting your tenses mixed up: I *am* Paris's wife. . . ."

Candace looked at her.

"Are you?" she said.

Laurel stopped smiling.

"Now, just what the devil d'you mean by that?" she said.

"You figure it out," Candace mocked. "You look mighty smart to me. . . ."

Laurel's eyes were pale grey now, wide with speculation.

"If I was sure you meant, what I think you mean——" she said.

"Don't think," Candace said; "you'll only get a headache. Besides, this stupid verbal fencing match has gone on long enough. What I started to say before you interrupted me was

54

that I took the job of taking care of Paris with the understanding that I'd be allowed to try to cure him. And I believe I can. But you've got to help me."

"Why should I?" Laurel said suddenly.

"One reason: I happen to know that, in spite of the way you act, you love your husband. I'm quite certain that if he were to regain his sanity, you'd come back to him. Am I right?"

Laurel looked away from her. Stared at nothing for a long time. When she turned back again, that wood-smoke banner of rebellion was gone from her eyes. They were their own pale blue again; and Candace was almost sure that a faint tremble tugged at the corners of that sulky mouth.

"Yes'm," she said; "I do love Paris. Reckon he's the only man I ever have loved, or ever will. And you're right. I would come back to him, if for no better reason than to get him out of your clutches, Nurse Trevor!"

"He's not in my clutches, Laurel," Candace said quietly.

"You mean you're not in love with him?" Laurel said. "Damned if I believe that!"

"I don't know whether I'm in love with Paris or not," Candace said. "You see, I don't really *know* Paris. It's difficult to love a man you can't even talk to most of the time. . . ."

"Between a man and a woman, talk ain't really necessary," Laurel said. "And I happen to know that not even thunder'll wake Samson up, once he gets to sleeping sound."

Why, she's jealous! The thought went dancing through Candace's mind, piping its high, discordant note of astonishment. In spite of what she's doing with Dion Cadwallader, she's jealous—and of me. Lord, how good that feels! Only I can't—I can't——

"I should slap your face," she said with icy calm, "but I won't do you, or your insinuations, that much honour. I'm going to explain a few things to you, Laurel Griffin. To begin with: judging everyone on earth by the way you, yourself, behave is a mistake. I, in very similar circumstances to yours, did not leave my husband. I have never been

55

unfaithful to him. I never shall, as long as he lives. Now, if
you judge me by yourself, you won't believe that; you may
not even believe it's possible. Only, I'm not you. I'm not
even anything like you. And I think you know me well
enough by now to realize I don't lie. So your husband is
perfectly safe from me. He'd still be, even if I were in love
with him. We're both grown women, and we're alone, so
I'll go even further. It is entirely possible that I might want
Paris one day. I might want him very badly. But I won't do
anything about it. Not ever. Is that clear?"

Laurel's eyes were very wide.

"Yes'm," she said, like a child.

"Very well," Candace said; "I want you tell me everything
you know about Paris—even if it's discreditable to him, or
to yourself. You have my word that I'll never breathe anything you've told me to a living soul——"

"You wouldn't have to," Laurel said sadly. "Folks hereabouts know a powerful sight too much about me, now; or
they think they do. That's not the point: why should I give
you a stick to beat me with? You manage to make me feel
like something the cat dragged in half the time without even
trying. . . ."

"And the other half?" Candace said.

"As if my soul was showing, or my conscience, like a
petticoat that's too long, ragged around the edges, and dirty
to boot. . . ."

Candace put her hand on Laurel's arm.

"Listen to me, child," she said; "I don't want a stick to
beat you. I don't even really want to know the things you've
done. But I have to know them, just as a doctor has to know
where in a man's body the bullet is, so that he can dig it out.
I can't find out what it was that caused Paris to retreat, to
run away out of life and close the door behind him, from
Paris himself. You see, he's got that door shut too tight
against the past, against remembering. Maybe he has even
bricked it over by now. But if I *knew* what it was he is
walling out, what thing so horrible that he has locked his
very mind against thought, so he won't——"

"But I thought you knew," Laurel said; "Paris was blown up by a bomb during the War. . . ."

"That's nonsense!" Candace said. "That bomb-burst was the door, the way out he'd been looking for for a long time, Laurel. He said to himself, 'I've been blown up, and my head is hurt, so now I don't have to think about *that*, any more.' Not so consciously, of course; but I'm sure that was the way he felt. We know so little about the mind, Laurel. I'm not even sure that my guess is right. But I've got one big advantage over the doctors: the same thing almost happened to me. . . ."

"You mean you lost your mind?" Laurel said.

"No. I mean I tried to. Almost deliberately, and very nearly consciously. I think that my father's stern Christian teachings saved me. I couldn't do it. I kept coming back to the realization of my responsibility to Henry. I kept remembering that the vows I pledged in the church are not only some of the most beautiful words written by man; but are as nearly sacred as any words can ever be. So I recognize the process in Paris. Of course, the stress was greater: shell-bursts, men screaming, bayonet attacks—and because of that it was so much easier for him to give up. But I believe I can bring him back from wherever he is, illuminate the cave in which he is hiding, unlock that door he has closed against the world. Only, to do that, I need the key—the key that you most likely have. . . ."

"I don't have any key," Laurel began; then: "You mean that I—that I *know* what drove him loony? You're wrong; I don't. I don't at all. But it wasn't me, Mrs Trevor! It wasn't me!"

"No," Candace said, "you don't know. That's why you have to tell me everything. Because out of what you say I might be able to pick that key, while you wouldn't recognize it. Will you trust me, Laurel? It's for Paris's sake. As God is my judge, for his sake and nothing more. . . ."

"All right," Laurel whispered; "can't do any harm. . . . Folks 'round here think I'm a bad woman——"

"Go on," Candace said.

57

"But they're wrong!" Laurel said. "I never wanted anybody else but Paris all my life. And if they'd have let me marry him from the first, I'd have been as faithful and true to him as you please!"

Candace's eyebrows rose.

"Please go on," she said.

"All right, you don't believe me. Nobody does. But you tell me one thing, Mrs Trevor: you ever heard of anybody who wasn't hungry breaking into a bakery or a grocery store?"

"You've a point there," Candace said quietly; "Of course, there are people who'd starve first. . . ."

"Name one!" Laurel hooted.

"Me," Candace said; "I'd starve first. But we're getting off the track. Who were 'they'? And why wouldn't they let you marry Paris?"

"Old man Griffin. And Paris's ma, too. They figured I wasn't good enough. No white trash, clay-eating filly from upstate Louisiana was going to marry their son, no sir!"

"Clay-eating?" Candace said.

"Yes'm. Up where I came from, in the Red River Valley in north Louisiana; some folks are so poor that they have to eat dirt from time to time to keep their bellies full. Some of 'em acquire a taste for it. You can see 'em chewing on that old red clay just like it was side meat swimming in gravy. But we weren't that bad off, not by a long shot. Of course I didn't have any book learning, I mean education. Hil taught me to read and write and to talk like a lady after we were married. . . ."

Candace stared at her.

"Hil?" she said. "You were *married* to Hiliary Thurston?"

"Yes'm. Don't tell me you didn't even know that! Reckon folks have got tired of talking about poor little me. . . ."

"You were married to Hiliary Thurston. But you were in love with Paris. Therefore you arranged matters so that Paris would have to meet your husband in a duel—you took a chance that it would be Mr Thurston and not Paris who'd be killed. Is that it, Laurel?"

58

Laurel's eyes went smoky.

"Listen, Mrs Trevor," she said slowly; "no good I may be; but a cold-blooded, calculating filly is the last thing on earth I am or was. Things just happened, that's all. Old man Phenias Griffin sent Paris off to Princeton College way up North somewheres to get him out of my way. And I was so upset, so mean mad and hurt that I got mixed up with Di Cadwallader——"

She saw Candace's eyes.

"So," she whispered, "you—you know!"

"Say I'm guessing," Candace said evenly; "and don't admit anything about right now, today, even to me. I'm not interested in now. I only want to know what happened then—before Paris went to war, at the time he actually lost his mind. . . ."

"You know," Laurel said; "you're likely right. Paris was a mite too sad, too mixed up to stand fighting. Only if you think I'm the cause of it, you're barking up the wrong tree. Paris didn't know about Di and me. He didn't even know I had to marry Hil. . . ."

"You got mixed up with Dion Cadwallader, so you had to marry Hiliary Thurston," Candace said dryly. "This gets clearer by the minute. . . ."

"Yes'm. You see, Hil wanted to marry me, or at least he'd told me two dozen times that he did. Maybe he was joking, I don't know. I think he really did, then; that he didn't know——"

"That he didn't know what?"

"Nothing," Laurel said; "let's say he really did want to. And he didn't have any parents to stop him. And Di was over in Louisiana hiding out to keep folks from hanging him because they thought he'd shot Phil Jurgens in the back——"

"Which of course, he hadn't?" Candace said.

"No'm. Di's got a lot of faults, but being yellow isn't one of 'em. They should have known better. Di would have shot it out face to face. . . ."

"I don't suppose it's really relevant," Candace sighed, "but who did shoot Mr Jurgens?"

"Why his wife, Tessie, of course. That's why people were so riled. They figured any man who'd shoot the husband in the back after he'd pleased himself with the wife had a big, fat hanging coming to him. Only they didn't realize that Tess blasted Phil so she'd be free to marry Di, that's how stupid she was, or that shooting a fellow from behind just wasn't Di's style, or even give him credit for being gallant enough to take the blame to save Tessie's neck, and what was left of her reputation, which wasn't much. . . ."

"I see. No, I'm wrong. I don't see. Would you mind explaining what all these Mississippi melodramatics had to do with your marrying Hiliary Thurston?"

"Yes'm. I'm getting there. You see I—I'd got caught. And Paris was 'way up North. And I wasn't sure that Di was ever going to be able to come back to——"

"Do the right thing by our Little Nell?" Candace said.

"Nell? Oh, you're joking. Nell's somebody in a play. I saw it. It came to Vicksburg. Funny, it *was* kind of like that play. Anyhow, it was a sure thing that even if Di did come back, it would have been long after it had started to show. So that left Hil——"

"And you arranged matters so that Mr Thurston would have reason to believe himself the party responsible for your —interesting condition?"

"I did not!" Laurel flared. "I told him the truth—well, not exactly the truth. I told him the baby was Paris's. . . ."

"And that made a difference? Perhaps I'm even denser than usual today, but I'm quite sure I fail to see why the identity of the father of your natural child should have changed matters at all. The average man would have left you flat in any case. . . ."

For the first time since she had started talking, Laurel smiled.

"Funny thing," she said, "how often folks just jammed packed with book learning can be dumb, downright ignorant when it comes to judging other people. Take Hil, now. I'd have told him it was Di's, he *would* have left me flat. He hated Di; always said he was coarse. But he rightly admired and respected Paris. Nothing Paris could do was wrong, far as Hil was concerned. Only trouble I had with him was to keep him from sending Paris a telegram asking him to come back. . . ."

"Why wouldn't you let him?" Candace said. "Wasn't marrying Paris exactly what you wanted to do?"

"Yes'm; that's right. Only you explain one thing to me: what does a girl say to a fellow who's just got a telegram asking him to come back and marry her on the basis that he's the father of the brat she's going to have, when she knows perfectly well that beyond a mighty sweet kiss or two, that particular fellow hasn't hardly touched her hand?"

"That would be difficult, wouldn't it?" Candace said crisply. "So here we are again on your private merry-go-round. Back to Hiliary Thurston, right?"

"Yes'm. I gave Hil some mighty sweet talk about how I'd always liked him, even while I was going with Paris, and about how Paris and I had fallen completely out before I knew I was like that; and that, under the circumstances, he'd think it was a trick, and nobody could blame him from thinking so, and, after all, a girl had her pride and, besides, I was sure from what had happened that Paris and I weren't suited for each other anyhow and——"

"So forth," Candace said dryly. "You mean to tell me that Mr Thurston was stupid enough to believe all that?"

"No, he wasn't," Laurel said. "But when it comes to getting their hands on what they've been pining for for a mighty long time, you'd be surprised at how many men-folks are willing to play awful dumb!"

"This is the second time I've been inclined to send you to the head of the class," Candace said. "Tell me about Mr Thurston. What was he like?"

Laurel frowned.

"You know, that's a hard question, Mrs Trevor. He was tall and real slim. Blond. Had a way of walking that was more graceful than most women ever manage——"

"You mean he walked like a woman?" Candace said.

"No," Laurel said thoughtfully, "no—of course not. But

61

then neither did he clump along like most men. Everything he did was like a motion in an old-fashioned minuet. And his voice was just beautiful: low and husky and sweet. Leasewise 'til he got excited. Then it would keep on getting higher and higher. . . ."

Candace stared at her.

"Go on, Laurel," she said.

"He was so nice. Wouldn't touch me while I was carrying the baby, though I wasn't that far gone; and I was mighty curious, I can tell you. Then I got the fever—the same epidemic that carried Paris's pa and ma off—and lost my baby. A woman's a funny thing, Can—Mrs Trevor——"

"Call me Candace if you like, child," Candace said; "I don't mind at all."

"Besides which you can't be even two years older than I am," Laurel said.

"Fishing?" Candace laughed. "Then you'd better learn how to cut bait better than that. You were saying that a woman's a funny thing——"

"Yep. I damn near died of grief from losing that brat who had almost wrecked my life——"

"Just a minute," Candace said; "I'm afraid I can't allow you that one. The brat, as you call it, had nothing to do with it. It certainly didn't conceive itself. You almost wrecked your own life, Laurel, by indulging in certain activities that society has always demanded be sanctioned by the church and hedged about with law. And, had your child lived, its life would have been wrecked by your thoughtlessness and lack of restraint. End of the sermon; please go on. . . ."

"You're right, Candace," Laurel said. "Anyhow, once I was well again, I started longing for another kid. And Hil——"

"Wouldn't co-operate?"

"Well—oh, I don't know! I started to say 'couldn't'. But that's not right, either. He could. Wasn't anything wrong with him that way. He was a natural man, only——"

"Only what, Laurel?"

"He—he just didn't like—doing that. Or else he didn't

like me, maybe. Anyhow, he was always too tired, or he didn't feel good, or—oh, heck! I even tried getting him drunk. That worked, sometimes. Once or twice, drunk, he was all right. In fact, he was just fine. But, if I gave him too much to drink, he'd be useless. It got to be too much of a chore thinking up things to celebrate and trying to figure out to the drop just how much he ought to have, and waking up the next morning sick at my stummick and with a splitting headache on top of that. So I gave up, 'specially since Tess Jurgens had the fever the same time as I did, and while she was raving she let slip that *she* shot Phil 'stead of Di. When she came back to her senses, she confessed all over again and begged them to hang her. But they only gave her seven years, and Barry let Di know he could come home again——"

"And that, as the poets say, was that?"

"Yes'm, though I don't know what a poet had to do with it. Paris was home, too, by then. But Paris was so blamed honourable. I was a respectable married woman to him, darn it. Besides, he'd just buried his folks, and was in mourning. I only saw him off at a distance once in a while. Then he went back North to finish college. So I sort of drifted back with Di——"

"And Hiliary found out?"

"Yep. But not right then. Not 'til two summers later, after Paris had finished Princeton College and was home for good. Then he found out. Only he wasn't sure who it was I was sneaking out to see——"

"The bad penny," Candace said.

"The bad penny?"

"Yes. The one that always turns up as the old saying goes. Especially—when something goes wrong. Or, when pleasure is to be had without responsibility. Sorry. That wasn't at all nice of me. Please continue, dear."

"He tried to get it out of me. Only I'd got so I hated him by then. So I told him—it was Paris."

Candace stared at her.

"Again?" she said.

"Again. Because I knew nothing would hurt him worse. And, even though I hated the poor fool, I didn't hate him bad enough to want him dead, which was purely what would have happened to him if he'd challenged Di, and he was hysterical enough by then to do even that. But I knew he wouldn't challenge Paris——"

"Yet, he did."

"No, he didn't. Not right then. That was six weeks later, after he'd come back. He did exactly what I'd figured he'd do: ran off, left me. So I loaded my lady's pistol with powder, but left the balls out, put some rock salt in instead——"

"Hasn't it ever occurred to any of you," Candace said wearily, "that you Southerners have a somewhat excessive fondness for gunplay?"

"I know. But you're forgetting that Hil had a brother. Name of Hank. And you oughtn't to. I've heard tell you— well, entertained him and that boy of his, socially—the day Paris got hurt."

"You win this exchange," Candace said, "although one could hardly call your tactics sporting. All right, what about your beautiful brother-in-law?"

"Beautiful? That ape! Oh, you're joking again. Well, I don't need to tell *you* that he was trying to crawl through my window every time he even thought Hiliary wasn't there. Funny thing, Hank was really fond of Hiliary. Looked up to him. But that didn't keep him from trying to grab me every chance he got. So I knew he'd try it in earnest soon as he found out that Hil had left me. I was right. He followed me the first night I set out for Griffin's Way——"

"You—set out—for Griffin's Way?"

"Yep. What did I have to lose by then? My husband had left me; every old biddy in the county was calling me a five-letter word, and even saying I'd got rid of my baby on purpose so that poor, dear Hil—now, I can make you see what he was like! He was exactly the kind of fellow that women over fifty go stark raving mad about, a-wanting to mother him, and to rock him to sleep, and——"

"You needn't go on; I've gotten the picture of Mr Hiliary

64

Thurston long ago. They said you'd performed an abortion on yourself so that Hiliary wouldn't find out the child wasn't his. Unnecessary details, Laurel: I also know women. So, on that basis, you decided to take Paris by storm?"

"Yep. And I did. Paris is only human, and he loved me. Besides, when I got there I was crying and all upset——"

"And with your attire in a most charming disarray? Let that pass. What were you upset about?"

"Hank. He grabbed me so quick that I thought I never was going to get my gun out. Funny—I've still got that lady's pistol. Ever seen one? It's a tiny little thing, but it sure Lord can do a lot of damage. They used to call 'em virgins' pistols; but I reckon somebody must have noticed that the girls who packed 'em never managed to stay that way, so they changed the name. I keep it in my bureau drawer. Loaded. Paris lets me keep it in case somebody—a strange nigger, or a tramp —tries to break into the house when he's not there——"

"But you did manage to draw your misnamed weapon finally?"

"Yep. I got it out and blasted Hank three times so close I powder-burned him. He dropped to the ground and lay there a-bellowing that I'd killed him; and I got going fast before he found out it was only rock salt instead of lead. . . ."

"But that duel?" Candace said.

Laurel looked away. Looked back again.

"Wasn't a duel," she said. "It was suicide. And Hil died happy—damn nigh kissing the hand that pulled the trigger. Because, you see, he wanted to die. Probably would have done it, himself, anyhow; but then he had this glorious idea. He'd make Paris do it! Get back at him for——"

"Stealing you?"

Laurel's eyes were very still and sad.

"You know better than that," she said. "No—for neglect. For not corresponding. Because Paris was the only human being on earth that Hil truly loved. And, like they say in that book, 'Hell hath no fury——'"

" 'Like a woman scorned,' " Candace finished the quotation for her. "But you said he wasn't——"

"Like that? Well, he was. Only he didn't know it, himself," Laurel said.

They sat there, watching the dusk gathering, the light spilling out of the sky. And Candace held her voice under perfect control, making it flat, calm, casual, as she risked her final, tremendous gamble. Risked it and lost. For, when she said, quietly:

"And Ulysses?"

Laurel stared at her in a puzzlement both open and unfeigned.

"That kid? What's he got to do with all this? I hardly ever even saw him," she said.

5

LAUREL brought the two letters to the hunting lodge herself, instead of sending them by a Negro, as ordinarily she would have done. She was, Candace guessed, trying to be more friendly. Or, perhaps, having given way to the relief of unburdening herself by telling her story, she felt that she was caught, that she'd better be nice to the woman who now knew a good bit too much about her.

Candace glanced at the letters, but she didn't open them. She had recognized the handwritings at once, so she knew that they could wait. One of the letters was from her friend, Ingra Holm; the other, from Henry's Aunt Bess, who ran a hotel for commercial travellers and steamboat captains in Natchez. That one could wait a month, or a year, because Aunt Bess would only be renewing her arguments that Candace and Henry should come live with her at the hotel, where Candace could be a big help to her, and Henry could be looked after properly. Both contentions were entirely just, Candace admitted; only they involved enduring Aunt Bess. And that, quite simply, she wasn't prepared to do.

"How is he?" Laurel said.

"I don't know," Candace said. "I think he's better. He keeps regaining consciousness for longer and longer periods. And when he does, he seems quite sane. Even when he's not conscious, he's not unconscious, really; but something more or less like asleep. I—I don't want to hold out too much hope; but I think it's a healing sleep. . . ."

"Can I see him?" Laurel said.

"Of course! Why did you think you needed to ask?"

Laurel turned away from her for a moment. When she looked back again, Candace saw the suspicious glint of moisture in her eyes.

"You—you said I wasn't his wife," she whispered.

"I said—what?" Candace said.

"Not in so many words. I reminded you once when you said I was his wife that 'was' wasn't right, that I am his wife, and then you said: 'Are you?'"

"I remember now," Candace said.

"By which you meant that I hadn't any more right to him, because I'd given him up, wouldn't care for him, and maybe even——"

"Let's skip that part of it," Candace said.

"All right. Only—I want to be his wife. It's the only thing I've truly wanted since I was old enough to think for myself. I can't help the way I am. And all I need to make me as ladylike and as good as you please is—him."

"Are you sure of that?" Candace said. "Mightn't Dion Cadwallader be more your style?"

"Yes. To both questions. I am sure of that, and Di *is* more my style. But, you tell me one thing, Candace: what's wrong with a girl's aiming far above herself? Di would suit me just fine if I hadn't met Paris, if I hadn't known him, if he hadn't sort of demonstrated to me, so quiet like, the difference between a gentleman and a pig. 'Cause Di is a pig. A shoathog rooting in the dirt. He hasn't even bothered to be faithful to me. Tess Jurgens wasn't the only one. But— he's always there, and——"

"And?" Candace said.

"There're those letters he wrote me when he was hiding out in Louisiana, and I wrote him back. I'd plumb given up all hopes of ever getting Paris then, so what I wrote Di then would be enough to convince Paris that I'm the worst slut on earth if Di ever showed 'em to him. And, after that, when they both went off to the War, Di started writing again. I'm not right bright, so I wrote him friendly like, figuring it wasn't any harm to write a letter or two to a poor, lonesome soldier boy who'd been an old friend——"

"Go on," Candace said.

"Only he, the smart cuss, asked me things that when I answered made it look like I was cheating on Paris, as well. . . ."

"And, weren't you?" Candace said.

"No! I loved the ground Paris walked on. Only Di would ask me things that, any way I answered, what I said would come out wrong. Something like asking a fellow: 'Have you quit beating your wife? Answer yes or no!'"

"I see," Candace said.

"No, you don't see. When he came back he tried to use those letters to make me leave Paris and run off with him. But when Paris turned up loony, that didn't work. I could argue that Paris wouldn't pay any attention to the letters, and that it was just too rotten to leave a man in Paris's state. So Di kept arguing that I ought to get Paris a nurse, so he and I could take a little trip down to Natchez or New Orleans. I wouldn't do that, which was why I was so mad when Hector went and found you. . . ."

"I must be out of my own mind," Candace said; "but for some unearthly reason, I believe you. Come on in, now. . . ."

Paris lay there, breathing quietly. The bruises had faded into yellowish splotches, and the cuts had healed into pale pink scars. He was still bandaged from just below the shoulders to the waist to immobilize his fractured ribs as much as possible. Laurel stood there looking at him, and very slowly her blue eyes filled up with tears.

"Turn your back, Candace!" she said suddenly, her voice coming out in a nasal snarl.

"Now, just a minute!" Candace began.

"Just a minute, nothing," Laurel said; "I'm going to kiss him, and I don't want you watching. Oh Lord, Candace, I just got to! Won't you please turn your back like I'm asking you to mighty kindly—please?"

Slowly Candace turned her back. Stopped her mind; which was hard, very hard, next to impossible; but she did it. Because she couldn't afford to think. She didn't want to analyse the way she felt then, realize fully that the end of life itself was very probably easier to bear than these partial deaths, and, worse, these dreadful little resurrections into vacancy, into pain.

She heard then Paris's voice, broken, incoherent, saying: "Killed him. Just like I turned that boat over myself.

Swim. He could. Only who took away his will to live?"

She turned then, saw Laurel's stricken face.

"What on earth is he talking about, Candace?" Laurel said.

"His brother, Ulysses," Candace said.

"Kind. He was," Paris said. "Made it look like—accident. So I wouldn't know, be sorry because——"

"Because what, Paris?" Candace said.

Paris opened his eyes. Smiled at her. At Laurel. Said:

"Candy. Laurie. Both of you, here? That's nice. My side hurts. Did Prince throw me again?"

"Prince threw him once," Laurel whispered; "busted a rib then, too. He got up off the ground and broke that devil of a horse so good that anybody can ride him now. . . ."

"I'm hungry," Paris said, then, "Will you fix me something to eat, Candy?"

"You go read you letters," Laurel said angrily, "and let me fix his victuals, Candace!"

"All right, Laurel," Candace said.

The words in Ingra's elegant Spencerian script kept swimming away across the page. It was decidedly difficult for her to concentrate. Something kept tugging at the edges of her mind. Something she had heard, something somebody had said. Then a line of Ingra's exploded out of the page, awakening appalled echoes in her mind:

"—so I'm going to bring Henry with me when I come. He's better off with you, Candace. The poor, dear man, he misses you so! And since I have to come there anyhow——"

Candace turned back to the first page of the letter. But that had nothing to do with Henry. It was an effusive and glowing description of one Bruce Randolph, who, it appeared, had been sent South by the Freedmen's Bureau and certain religious philanthropies to organize schools for the Negro children in the rural areas. To implement his work, he'd had to go into politics; but with scant success so far. Dr Randolph, according to Ingra, held the A.B. and the M.A. from Oberlin, and a Ph.D. from Harvard. He was the kindest, most cultured man anyone could possibly imagine; and his little wife was just too cute for words, and——

He has a wife, Candace thought a little mockingly; so why all the enthusiasm, Ingra, darling? Then she sat bolt upright in her chair, staring at Ingra's next startling line:

"And the best of it all is that he's as black as night. I'm so glad he's not a mulatto, because people always attribute it to their white blood when they're smart, But Dr Randolph apparently has no white blood at all, and a more brilliant man you'd never hope to see. He ought to be able to convince these bigots that intelligence is not a matter of colour——"

Sadly Candace shook her head. No, Ingra, dearest, she thought; he won't be able to. He won't be able to entirely convince even me. Because his only weapons are his intelligence, his logic, and even the logical conclusions to be drawn from his achievements, his life. And these weapons are worthless against feelings seated somewhere in our middles, not in our heads. So——

She turned back to the letter. As she might have guessed, Ingra had suggested the central part of Warren County as the best place to begin because of the admittedly selfish reason that it would enable her to be near Candace:

. . . you are the only real friend I have down here. I've tried and tried, but I simply can't get along with these simpering Southern females, especially since they're always trying to pry out of me the dirty details of my relations with coloured people—by which they mean coloured men. I've given up trying to convince them that I simply haven't any personal relationships with that poor, downtrodden race. To them I'm only interesting because of my alleged depravity, which darned if I don't believe they envy! Anyhow, I shall see you soon—actually in a month or less. I only hope I've given you sufficient time to get ready a place for poor, dear Henry.

Skold,
Ingra

71

Thank you, Candace thought; I should have put it off, found another excuse after this one of Paris's injury was finished, and another one after that until the end of time. Until lying to myself became a habit. Until I'd be unable to admit that I'm no better than Laurel; that I, too, have deserted the helpless, and in a fashion less honest than hers. Arrange a place for Henry? That's a matter of an hour's work, or less, for Samson. Only, tell me, Ingra, if you please: how does one arrange one's mind, one's heart?

She tore open Aunt Bess's letter. As she had thought, reading it was very largely unnecessary. Only one line was new: "Been feeling mighty poorly here of late. Reckon I ain't long for this world. So I had Ben Thompson in—he's my lawyer, you know—and made my will. I'm leaving the hotel, and the few pennies I've been able to save, to Henry and you. That way, since I don't have nary a chick nor a child, leasewise it'll stay in the family. . . ."

Poor old soul, Candace thought. And who knows? Maybe we'll need that white elephant of hers one day. . . .

Laurel came outside then. Her face, Candace decided, wore an almost beatific expression.

"He's fed," she said happily, "and asleep again. I washed his face. . . ."

"That was sweet of you," Candace said.

"Funny thing, soon as he went back to sleep, he started mumbling about Ulysses, again. Tell me one thing, Candace: you think what happened to that kid was what upset Paris's mind?"

"No," Candace said quietly; "Not *what* happened; *why* it happened. I was hoping you could help me there. . . ."

Laurel frowned.

"Well, I can't," she said. "Like I told you, I hardly ever even saw the kid. He was a nice little fellow, though. Once he gave me a bunch of posies he'd picked himself. Handed them to me, mumbling something like, 'Here, Laurie, I picked these for you. . . .' then he ran off like the devil was after him. Mighty funny he got drowned; he was the best damn' swimmer I ever did see. . . ."

"Laurel," Candace said, "can you think of any possible reason why—Ulysses just didn't swim that night?"

"Maybe he got a cramp," Laurel said; "the water was awful cold by then. . . ."

"And maybe he didn't. Paris thinks that Ulysses drowned himself on purpose. . . ."

"Lord God!" Laurel said. "What makes Paris think that?"

"If I knew that, I'd bet my last red copper that I could have Paris up from there in a couple of weeks, clothed and framed in his right mind."

Laurel looked Candace straight in the face then, and her blue eyes were very clear.

"Candace," she said simply, "I don't know anything about that, 'fore God I don't. So, if you think that asking me the same questions different ways, you'll dig it out of me, you're wrong. I'd tell you in a minute if I knew; but, honest, I don't. . . ."

"All right," Candace sighed; "but maybe we can figure it out between us. Ulysses could swim; but was he any good at handling a boat?"

"The best. Better than Paris, better than Di. Better than anybody. That kid was more at home in the river than he was on land. . . ."

"Laurel, does it make sense that an expert boatman like that should have turned his boat over in the middle of the river on a calm night?"

"Turned his boat over? Why he never! That boat of his must have hit an underwater snag. Why, there was a hole in it big enough to shove my fist through. . . ."

Candace looked at her. Said:

"How did you know that, Laurel?"

"'Cause—'cause—oh, heck! You know too much about me now, so you might as well know this, too: I was out swimming with Di—and he—and he found the boat——"

73

"You were out swimming with Dion *after* the duel, after Hiliary had forced Paris to kill him over you?"

"Yes'm," Laurel said sullenly.

"I don't think I need to ask you what sort of bathing costume you were wearing, do I?"

"No'm. Just what you're thinking: my birthday suit. And the water was cold as ice by then, damn it! Not that that made any difference to Di. . . . But I had to, Candace! I had to keep Di calmed down 'til I got a chance to marry Paris, or else he'd have spoiled everything. . . ."

"What made you think he'd refrain from spoiling everything *after* you were married?" Candace said drily.

"I didn't think that. I was certain sure he'd try to ruin my married life, too. Only I thought that once I got my hands on Paris, I'd make him so much in love with me that nothing Di said would make any difference. The funny part about it was that Di didn't do anything after Paris and I were wed. I kind of think that Barry stopped him. . . ."

"That's possible. Barry is a gentleman through and through. All right, let's drop your multitudinous amatory escapades and get back to the boat. You know anything about rowing, Laurel?"

"A little. Mostly it was the fellows who did it while I sat there in a big picture hat and trailed my lily-white hands in the water. . . ."

"Well, I do. And I'll tell you what I think: I don't believe it's possible for any man to oar an ordinary rowboat fast enough and hard enough to knock a hole in it, even if it did hit a snag!"

"Not even going downstream?" Laurel said.

"Not even going downstream, unless he were shooting some rapids or pounding through a millrace. And it was in mid-river, on a calm night. In water deep enough to drown in. An underwater snag? I just don't believe it!"

"Well, what else could shove a hole in a boat big enough to run my fist through? There was a hole that big in it, I tell you!"

"I don't know," Candace said; "besides, whether the boat

74

turned over or was shoved in makes very little difference. The real question is, why didn't Ulysses swim?"

"A cramp," Laurel said stubbornly; "he must have got a cramp. Cold as that blamed water was. . . ."

After Laurel had gone, Candace went on thinking about it. She had the odd feeling that she knew the answer, that it was floating there just out of reach in the back part of her mind. There was something, something she almost remembered; something she'd heard; something somebody had said to her.

But it was no good. At the end of a whole hour, all she had for her labours was a splitting headache. She got up and started to go back into the lodge. Then she stopped. There was a swaying in that thicket beyond the cabin. A motion. A motion in a thicket on a dead still, breathless day.

"Samson!" she called softly.

"Yes'm, Miz Candy!" Samson said.

"Come here," Candace said.

Samson came out of the lodge.

"Don't pay any attention to what I say aloud," Candace said, "only to what I whisper." Then, raising her voice: "Go saddle Bess, for me, Samson!"

Samson stared at her, doubt in his eyes.

"No," she hissed, "I'm not crazy. Head for the hitching rail, then circle around until you get to that thicket. There's someone in there, watching us!" Then loudly: "Don't you understand anything, Samson? Go get me Bess!"

Samson's big face split with a grin. She could see the gigantic muscles of his arms knotting in anticipation.

"Yes'm," he boomed; "I'll go git you yore hoss, Ma'am!"

She stood there, waiting. Big as he was, Samson could move like a ghost. She knew that. But what surprised her was how fast he got there, considering what a wide circle he had to make.

The thicket exploded into a thrashing roar. She heard a voice, clearly a boy's, because the timbre and the pitch were still uncertain, rasping:

"Take your hands off'n me, nigger! Ain't nobody never

75

learned you not to tetch a white man? Gawddammit, I——"

"You ain't no white man, boy," Samson rumbled. "Fact is, you ain't no kind of man. 'Pears to me you must of 'scaped from the circus!"

"Bring him here, Samson!" Candace called.

Samson dragged the struggling boy over to where she stood.

"Ernest the troglodyte," Candace said. "Just what were you doing in that thicket, boy?"

"Watching you," the boy grinned; "thought maybe I could git a chance to see you with your clothes off!"

"You want me to whup him, Miz Candy?" Samson said, outrage shaking his voice. "Just you say the word and I'll tan his hide for fair!"

"No," Candace whispered, no longer seeing the little monster, or Samson, or even the house, because nothing under heaven was visible to her through the great blaze lighting her eyes; "no, Samson, let him go. . . ."

"Let him go?" Samson said. Then seeing her face: "Yes'm, if you say so, ma'am. . . ."

But she had already whirled, was racing for the door. Inside the lodge, she stopped. Hung there, fighting the heart hammer, breath storm, delirium of joy in her, until they slowed, until she was in control once more. She tip-toed to the bed, knelt beside it. Before, she had made the mistake of waking Paris from his deathlike sleep, his terrible dreams; but now, she wouldn't make that error any more. She must enter that sleep, penetrate those dreams.

"Paris," she crooned, her voice music itself, flute notes, and tiny tinkling bells, "Paris, Ulysses—didn't drown himself. He was sad over what had happened, but not that sad. . . . Someone, an enemy—shot a hole in the boat—and Ulysses got a cramp; the water was cold. . . . Do you hear me, darling? It wasn't your fault. It was an accident, a mistake. . . . Someone, an enemy—shot a hole in the boat—the water was cold, was cold. . . ."

76

BOOK TWO

PARIS GRIFFIN

* 6 *

WAS cold. From the Duck River to the Tennessee, that December of 1864, all the marshes were frozen. Slumped forward in his saddle, Paris Griffin, who had ridden with Forrest's command for three full years now, could see the infantrymen swarming like buzzards over the carcase of a mule, while the wagons General Forrest had put them in, to save their poor feet from being cut to pieces by the flint-hard mud, waited. They weren't after meat, though mule steak could fill a belly mighty handily; what they wanted was the hide, which made a fairly tolerable pair of moccasins. There wasn't a hat left among the infantry, because, while a man's head could stand the sleet-filled winds, a man's feet left bloody tracks across the mud turned black ice, unless he wrapped them in something—and a felt hat made a fine warm covering for one foot. For every man who had both feet wrapped in felt, Paris knew you could count a comrade dead. Because Thomas, the Rock of Chickamauga, had commanded the Union forces at Nashville, with Wilson, the one blue-clad cavalry leader at least three-quarters as good as Nat Forrest himself, serving under him.

So now the Confederate Horse had slanted down from Murfreesboro to put itself between Hood's retreating army and Thomas's mighty paw. They were getting murdered piecemeal in a hundred brief, hopeless stands to hold off Thomas's army, Wilson's cavalry, long enough for the broken, tattered, bloody remnants of Hood's forces to get back across the Tennessee; and it was beginning to dawn on even the riders who boasted the highest *esprit de corps* in military history that a nation which had to send its infantry into battle barefooted in December, was on its last, distinctly wobbly legs.

But Paris Griffin wasn't thinking about that. To be precise, he wasn't thinking about anything. He no longer remembered when he had first succeeded in the difficult business of the complete suspension of thought, except that it had been a long time ago, certainly as far back as the summer of 1862, when they were driving Union General Buell crazy by raiding from their base at Murfreesboro over much of the same territory where they were now, two and a half years later; and, maybe, even in those dim days of antiquity when he'd ridden out of Fort Donelson with the then Colonel Nathan Bedford Forrest to go on fighting instead of staying and surrendering like the rest. There was a very simple formula for this easy evasion of the despair that was numbing his fellow troopers all around him; but it was a formula that couldn't be shared. It consisted of flight to regions of the spirit so far off that maybe it reached beyond the spirit itself into what was essentially a kind of death, since life is much more than the drawing of breath, which was all he was doing now.

It was cold, was cold. And the sleet came down in a grey hissing. He, Paris Griffin, listened to that hiss, letting it enter through his ears until all his mind was filled with it —so that there was nothing inside him but grey mist, sleet hiss rising, rising until everything else was crowded out, and he, finding it easier and easier to do this now, to fill up his mind—with nothing—with grey—with blindness— not because his eyes couldn't see but because the grey mist rising blanketed out the connection to his brain, while the sleet hiss went on murmuring, blending into softness, into silence, all the multitudinous variant sounds of an army on the march, so that his ears no longer heard them, any more than his eyes now saw the ragged, freezing beggars swarming over that mule.

But what was becoming harder and harder to do was to come back, to leave that sweet Nirvana—of nothing—no pain—no guilt—no sorrow. He had to force himself with greater sternness each time. Because he didn't want to come back; he much preferred that soft velvety purring nothingness; only he knew that in battle a man who was absent in fact, leaving only his mindless bumbling body behind, was a danger to his comrades—and he cared a great deal about his comrades, though about himself he cared not at all.

It was time now. He'd better start fighting his way back out of the sleet hiss wind whistle grey mist, before that tiny receding area of control of consciousness he somehow had always maintained up until now, that miniscule image of self that stubbornly refused to be dragged under—blotted out—drowned—vanished, was vanquished; and he, happily surrendering to the sensation of floating—of drifting—to the colour grey extending itself across the whole spectrum, would sink out of time, out of existence, into the soft dark womb of pre-life where nothing could ever hurt him any more or make him cry——

It was time; but, to his swiftly diminishing horror, he found that he couldn't, that the tiny gesticulating image of himself (that always before had clung to some infinitesimal portion of awareness, of identity) was no longer there, not even the little square light, of clarity, he'd always managed to preserve on the edge of the velvety nothingness, remained, except as a glimmer already fading.

Was cold. And, riding out into that cold he no longer felt, away from the freezing soldiers stripping the smoking hide off the mule, he moved forward half a mile until he came to where the battle lines momentarily and unexpectedly—not that he cared about that, either, or even recognized his danger—were. He kept on riding towards that little salient where Wilson's Cavalry had dismounted and were snickering away with their repeating carbines that never seemed to need reloading; but he, unaware of the ball whistle, bullet whine, bomb-crash, rode on, not even knowing that he had drawn his revolver, thus earning for himself the totally undeserved reputation of a martyred hero, until a forty-pounder Dahlgren, so far away that the Yankee artillerymen who fired it couldn't even see him, opened up and dropped a shell under him that eviscerated his horse. He went down into smoke-stink, red hell-fire, shattering thunder. Into blood-wet, gut-slime, hoof-thrash. Into the deepest womb of darkness. Into night. Into a soft, lovely, very nearly perfect counterfeit of death.

Was cold. In the Union prison hospital, it was cold. He came back there. There he remembered he was Paris Griffin of Griffin's Way; but when he tried to think about that, about what it meant to be Paris Griffin of Griffin's Way, instantly and at once the grey mist, without his even seeking it, rose up between him and memory like a wall. He knew he was Paris Griffin, knew that he was cold. But he knew nothing at all about the time before the prison hospital. He had a great and aching need to know. Only, when he tried to call it back to mind, the sleet hiss filled his ears and all colours ran together into grey. He learned very soon not to try remembering. For, as long as he did not make the attempt, he could stay in the here-and-now, suffer cold, claw with agonized fingers at the lice that devoured him, almost faint from hunger, wolf down the miserable slops that the North starved thousands of prisoners to death upon, and then conveniently forgot while making an epithet of Andersonville.

For, though he didn't know it, time had begun to work its healing in him. Now he feared and avoided his former refuge in the womb of no time, no life, nowhere. For the last three months before Appomattox he was almost continuously sane and conscious. He remembered his release from captivity, the endless train ride south from the prison camps near Chicago. He remembered the steamboat that brought him into Vicksburg. He remembered tramping towards the place he somehow knew was home.

Then the woman had come flying down the stairs to greet

him. He saw her face, her eyes, her warm and trembling mouth; and, for an instant, light flooded his brain, light so cruel bright that it was like staring into the sun; and the pain in him was a tearing of his secret flesh, a gut-ripping uprush of blood to his throat, so that he screamed:

"No! Don't touch me, you bitch! I——"

Then the grey mist rising blurred her very easily and quickly out of existence, the old familiar hissing whipped away her voice, murdered every sound.

He came back into a world of faces to which he fitted names. Hector. The Cadwallader brothers, Barry and Dion. Those simian sub-humans, the Thurstons. Roberta and Hector's children. Bigger now, oddly handsome. And he knew all about them, but something wouldn't let him think about it. He knew, too, that there were other faces that should be there, but weren't. In the night, in sleep, he could call those faces to mind. But, in the morning, waking with the salt of his crying on the corners of his mouth, he could no longer remember them, nor explain to himself the dull ache that his body retained from the anguish of the night, though not his mind.

Here, at home, he retrogressed. His life was like the flickering of a fire, now bright, now dark. More and more he sought the darkness now, took refuge in grey mist rising in sleet hiss, escaped out of the consciousness into the warm floating darkness, where he curled head against knees, doubled over, protected, safe.

Then *she* came. She who was all now, had no connection with hidden anguish, buried pain. She to whom he could not even fit a name, until she told him: Candace.

Candace. Who was all goodness, just as Laurie was all— but what was Laurie? That was one of the things he couldn't remember. No matter. Candy was here. And where Candy was, was sun—was light—was never more cold. . . .

So why was she saying that? Why did her voice come from so far, so far, saying, "was cold, was cold?"

He hurt. His chest hurt. He had fallen. Prince had thrown

him and Laurie was laughing. So he got up off the ground, remounted and——

No! It wasn't that. Hank Thurston had hit him! Hank Thurston, the hairy ape had struck him from his horse before Candy's eyes and now——

"Was cold," he could hear her crooning; "the water was cold, was cold. He caught a cramp. He didn't mean to die! Dion found the boat——"

Dion. Dion and Laurie, Laurie and Dion. It had to have been that. It must have been. Because Hiliary had been so sure, so sure about before. And there wasn't any before. There was only after. After poor Hiliary had run away, had fled——

"It had a hole in it you could shove your fist through," Candace was saying; "that was why it sank: why Ulysses couldn't cling to it and save himself. Because Hank Thurston shot at it in the dark. He admitted it in so many words the day he beat you up. Only he said 'that kid'—and it took me too long to realize he meant Ulysses, to remember how it was your little brother died. Hank shot at the boat. Holed it just at the water line. Ulysses didn't kill himself, Paris! He didn't and it was not your fault!"

Ulysses—Ulie. Baby brother Ulie. Good kid—gentle, tender. Unprepared in all ways to face life as it is, and men and women as they are. He looked through the window of the hunting lodge and saw——

"It was not your fault," Candace said. "All right—you hurt him unwittingly in some way I don't even understand. But, Paris, darling, life is a slow disease we always finally die of, and all learning is a hurt, a wound. . . ."

—how much lower we actually are than the angels. What shutters were invented for. Why lamps can, and should be blown out. Only we hadn't, Laurie and I, done either. The shutter stood gaping like an idiot's mouth, and we'd forgotten the lamp. And he, at that age when dreams are still untarnished, believing as he did in man's honour and woman's chastity, specifically and tragically in my honour and Laurel's chastity, was confronted with ugly fact, the

82

ugliest of all facts, that our lusts and filths are forever linked
—who was it who wrote that? With the brutal proof that
the highest of creation, with all things under his feet, can
only be continued in time by descending into his essential
animality; and, worse, that the descent is voluntary, without
even the continuation in mind. No. Not then. He probably
considered all that later in the boat on the dark Styx of his
own seeking. What he was concerned with then was shock:
the hammer-blow to his guts at the realization of what his
vestal was capable of—and his Galahad, his demi-saint, his
brother—at seeing adultery reduced from abstraction into
act, and piled upon murder, for a man driven to his death *is*
murdered, whatever the accidentalness of the method, to
boot. So he——

"Went out and drowned himself, you think?" Candace
said. "No. Went out into the river in his boat, rowed out
into the track of the moon to sit and think. To reconcile
himself with the existence of sorrow, which is a knowledge
that comes very hard to the young. But not to drown himself. Barry told me his body was found very close to the
shore. Which means he tried to save himself, but couldn't
quite make it. Besides, nobody ever chooses a form of death
they're familiar with. No swimmer would ever try to drown
himself; he'd know from having come close to it many times,
in his days of learning how to keep afloat, what an awful
way to die that is. . . ."

—went out into the river in any case, and did drown.
Because he had accepted Laurie's marriage to a creature as
gentle, as over-refined, as Hil Thurston as only a slight
tarnishing of the imaginary purity he'd invested her with;
but he was not prepared to accept both witnessing her
adultery, and the identity of her partner in crime. So, however he came to find himself in the black water——

"Let's say he thought of it. But doing a thing is an
altogether different matter from merely thinking it. And one
thing I know: you Griffins are fighters. So when he saw the
flash, heard the gunshot, felt that ball smack into the boat
at the waterline, however much he may have felt like killing

himself before, the idea that someone was deliberately trying to murder him must have brought all his natural
instincts towards self-survival leaping to the surface, must
have armed and nerved him with the decision to escape, if
for no better reason than to get the bushwacking coward
who was trying to get him. Only, as I said before the water
was cold. He got a cramp. But wouldn't you have reacted
like that, Paris? Wouldn't you?"

"Yes. I would have, and I'd have got ashore no matter
how, and——"

"Paris!" He could feel her voice. And what it felt like
was involuntary nakedness, so that listening to it was a
shameful invasion of her privacy; but he couldn't help
listening to it, as she said: "You heard me! You answered
me! And you——"

Then her arms were around him lifting powerfully for all
their white slenderness, crushing his face against her clean
warmth, her firm softness, and her tears were a spring
shower, a warm and healing rain.

He raised his face and stared at her. A long time. A very
long time. Then he said:

"So there are angels, after all. . . ."

He could almost see fear rising in her, black-winged and
ominous.

"Paris——" His name was the pale blur of her lips moving,
struggling, it seemed to him, to even form the sounds, "Do
you—do you know who I am?"

"Yes," he said; "you're Candace. I called you Candy."

"And do you—remember? I mean can you call to mind
what happened before the War? Can you, Paris?"

He considered that, seeing, out of the corner of his eyes,
her nostrils pinched; the sudden cessation of the rise and fall
of her breasts, the tension in every line of her, breath held,
waiting. He said:

"I think so, yes. Not all of it, though. You—you made me
remember. I guess I always did in my sleep, only you made
me do it out loud, awake, and——"

"Exorcized your demon," she said; "your quite imaginary

demon. But I'm afraid you have others. Let's have them out, shall we? I'll see if I can find a herd of swine to cast them into. Tell me, what are you torturing yourself with, now?"

But he couldn't tell her that. He had no right, no right——
So he said:

"I'm tired, Candy. Tomorrow. We'll talk about it, tomorrow. I want to sleep, now; sleep——"

Her voice came over to him like the colour grey. Like tiredness. Like sorrow.

"All right, Paris," she said; and left him there.

He could hear her in the other room, hear and recognize the intimate sounds a woman made undressing, even, now, being fully returned from the no place—no time—nothing where he had been, could imagine what she looked like doing that, the images in his mind being a bold revision in line, in colouring, from Laurel's midnight on snow to Candace's honey blondeness, from slenderness to slimness less accentuated, from slumberous sensuousness to crisp, accurate motion, made with absolute control. The images planted unease in him, awakened confusion. He could feel a slow curl of heat arising from his middle, he who, year in, year out, had known only sleet hiss, grey mist, cold.

It's no good, no good! he thought savagely; because, even if my bedding with another man's wife didn't drive Ulie into the river like I thought, there was still poor, gentle Hil. And she, this one, has a man. Crippled. She told me that— when? And I have Laurie. Or do I? Do I even want her, now?

He buried his face in the pillow.

"Laurie," he almost wept; "Goddammit, I——"

He didn't want to think about that. And, as always when he didn't want to think about a thing, he could feel the soft grey darkness rising, the silent, secret hissing entering his mind. But now, instead of welcoming them, he fought against them with furious horror, not quite thinking the words, "I owe it to Candace not to——" but feeling them,

85

struggling against the rising tide of amorphous nothing hour after hour until, near morning, he had won.

Won, but was utterly spent. He lay there very quietly until sleep washed over him, and he sinking down contentedly into the dark only to rise again like a chip into brightness, into smoke swirl, cannon roar——

And they, his company, pinned down in one of those innumerable skirmishes they were forced to fight dismounted, after having cut Sherman's railway supply lines (too late, for Atlanta was already gone) cut off, maybe even surrounded, and at his side the kid who didn't even look like but nevertheless reminded him of Ulie, his mouth and all his face black from powder soot and biting off cartridges; and they, those stubborn Yankee infantrymen who when hit didn't panic like he'd been taught Yankee counter-jumpers always did, and when hurt didn't run, coming forward lumpily, slogging forward, not even firing yet; and he, for all that he'd been telling himself for three years now he'd come to War to die, seized with a sudden horror of the physical imminence of that longed-for act of dying, and this, strangely, because it had been imminent almost daily for all of those three years, broke, crawled away from there towards the horses, got all of fifty yards away before it came to him what he was doing, and, cursing himself for thirty stinking varieties of coward, stood up and walked back, shooting as he came, miraculously unhit all that way until he got back to the others who, just as miraculously, beat off that attack and ten more, until it was dark enough for them to get the hell out of there. And he crying and cursing and firing without even aiming, because, even before he got back to them, the kid was dead.

"Dead!" He could hear his own voice woman-shrill. "Like every one I'm fond of, each brother that I love. . . ." Then he felt his grief in his throat like a tearing, tasted the brine and blood in his mouth. Only he couldn't stop it now, going on crying, his big body one long shudder, his breath a rasp, a strangling until——

There was that soft, faintly perfumed warmth around

86

him, lifting his head, pillowing it against softness unrestrained by more than a single layer of cloth, so that he could feel one of the infinitely tender firm, widely separated, twin firepoints probing into the flesh of his cheek with curious insistence, and he still crying, and, from somewhere in the warm blackness, the crooning murmur: "Don't cry, Paris! Please, please don't cry!" going on and on, dark anguished, humid with the tears he could not see but knew were there, and he without opening his eyes drew her down and found her mouth as salt as his own, as tear-wet trembling, and that too going on and on until his hand came up, pushing at the crisp cotton stuff of her gown until her warm resilience lay under it unresisting, only her voice saying:

"Don't, Paris. I'm asking you that. Neither begging nor imploring, just asking you not to destroy me——"

"Destroy you?" he muttered. "How——?"

"Destroy my image of myself. My idea of what I'm like. I—I couldn't stop you. My defences are down. And I——"

"And you?"

"I—I want you, too——"

"Then?" he snarled.

"What I want is unimportant," she said, her voice sad and almost infinitely calm, except that it rose on a spurt of breath, went a little ragged each time he touched her; "or what you want either. . . ."

"What is?" he mocked.

"Certain words we said to two other people. Certain promises we made that we have no right to break. Even that love itself is no excuse for swinishness; and some forms of human selfishness are just too rotten. You have Laurie——"

"Laurie!" he said. "She——"

"And your promise made before Almighty God. Whatever she may or may not have done does not free you from it, any more than Henry's being crippled releases me. So now, Paris, let me go, I ask you—please!"

And he was lost, perhaps because something in her voice got through to him; perhaps because he had in him too much remembered shame. Carefully and slowly he released her; said humbly:

"I'm sorry. Don't go. I—I promise that I——"

And she letting that sad, slow laughter bubble up:

"You do. But *I* don't. Allow me to take this treacherous starved beast of a body of mine out of here, Paris. . . ."

"You'll come back?" he said; "I—I couldn't sleep now. . . ."

"Later. Fully dressed, and clothed and framed in my right mind. And I'll sit over there in that chair a long, long way from you; and we'll talk. . . ."

"All right," Paris said.

But she didn't come for too long a time, so that the transitory darkness rose and engulfed him, and he again floating effortlessly free of it swirled up into lamplight, the room unchanged except that his own voice far off and faint was saying, this is wrong, Laurie, wrong, and she coming towards him out of the darkness, her hair blending into it and her body's terrible whiteness like a cry against it except where that whiteness itself bore the shadowed reminders of the race's ancestry, its essential animality, and he crying, No! Not right, and raising his head in that interval of no time that absolute continuation of now, saw Ulie's face at the window yellow-washed by the lamplight, horror-twisted, and Laurie's husk-whispered: What'd you quit for, this is no time to stop Paris what d'you think a girl's made out of anyhow you big damn' fool?

And the night dissolving in bleak anguish into shame into tears and he crying perhaps silently because there was no evidence that she heard him, her blue eyes turned inwards, lightless and intent—Ulie! Ulie! Don't go, I——

Then the other voice was saying softly, sorrowfully:

"O God, not again!"

And those other arms were around him, holding him against a great many layers of cloth this time, and he, finding the feel of it distinctly unpleasant, twisted a little, murmured, "Candy—" and slept. Peacefully now. Like a child.

"Mighty pretty!" the voice said.

Paris's eyes felt as if they were glued shut. He forced them open. There was a vague blur in the doorway. He lay there, blinking at that blur until it cleared, acquired definition, form, edges—though the edges were mostly curved.

"Mighty pretty," Laurel drawled again; "but, believe me, Candace, it's more fun with your clothes off. . . ."

He felt the surge at his side, saw Candace surge up into a sitting position; saw, astonished, that she was fully clothed except for her shoes, then he remembered how that had happened too, thought: she came back after I was dreaming again—about Laurie, about Ulie, and I——

"I must have fallen asleep," Candace was saying calmly.

"Does leave you worn out," Laurel said. "Don't reckon I've got any real right to complain, since I left him in your clutches. But now you see the difference between us. I've been no good. Maybe even bad. Only I drifted into things——"

Paris saw Candace's penny-brown eyes, then. Saw how wide they were, how stricken. Heard the desperate urgency in her voice as she said:

"Laurel, he can hear you!"

"What difference does that make, loony as he is? I never planned things. Never calculated. Never was—dirty. And this is—dirty, Candace. Mighty, mighty dirty!"

Paris could feel what it was that shook Candace's throat now, quivered the corners of her mouth. Pain. Stark naked pain.

"Laurel, wait!" she was saying. "Don't say those things! He—last night—he came back! He was entirely sane. He—he remembered everything——"

"Which you took advantage of——" Laurel began; but Paris stopped her with his eyes.

"Laurie," he said; "Hil said 'before' the day I shot him and he was dying. He meant before he ran away. And you know damned well that I never came near you, before. So, who was it, Laurie? Who was it that Hil thought was me? Tell me, was it—Di? Was it, Laurie?"

"No," Laurel screamed at him, "it wasn't anybody!"

She bent over him suddenly, her voice rising, into that fish-wife shrillness he never had been able to bear, her teeth bared in a snarl so animal it destroyed her very considerable beauty, reduced her out of humanity into something that he, tired now, very tired, sick still, his invisible wounds only beginning to heal, found absolutely insupportable, so that he saw gratefully the colour grey rising around her, enveloping her as she screamed, "It wasn't anybody! Hil was crazy, too! As crazy as you are, you lunatic! Crazy! Crazy! Cr a a a zy! You're——"

Candace's motion tore the grey apart, halted momentarily the hiss. She came up from beside him alert, intent, sure and her arm swinging made a whitish blur in the half-light of the room, and he felt in his own flesh more than saw her hand exploding, open-palmed, across Laurel's face, jetting bright tears from both blue eyes——

But that was unbearable, too, and deliberately he called up the grey mist, the hissing like sleet, only they came slowly, so he could see Laurel standing there, unmoving, her own slim fingers touching the dead white stripes Candace's had left across her face, that were only beginning to turn red, her whisper, dead-voiced:

"You hit me. . . ."

And Candace's voice answering, flat-toned, grim:

"Yes. At that you're lucky."

"Lucky?" he heard Laurel say. And Candace:

"That I didn't have a gun. Look at him now, Laurel!"

And Laurel's face coming clear in that instant, startlingly clear so that he could see her wide, sullen mouth beginning to shake, hear the utter, pitiful, childlike, choked shudder of her voice as she said:

"Oh! Oh my God!"

Then gratefully he saw them both shading off into smoke, becoming tenuous, losing their outlines, fading; the sleet hiss invading their voices so that he could no longer hear them either, and he sinking down, down into the dark, into the warm, safe, lovely dark.

There were voices. No, one voice. It kept saying "Paris Paris please Paris you must come back you must fight you are not crazy Paris not crazy not."

Night day night daynight Not cold not cold warm. Warm soft softwarm warmsoft safe safe

Only that voice coming through breaking the darkness destroying the warmth the safety letting in the trouble the pain. No. Can't face them. Don't want to, can't

Hil. Dead. Dead self-murdered running towards me screaming Kill me kill me can't you see I want to die? clawing at the trigger of my gun the shot the shot smoke drifting up between us and he——

"Paris, you mustn't! Please believe me, you are not mad!"

—sinking down saying Thank you Paris Thank you dear dear boy. . . . Why thank me? Because I ended his trouble, killed his pain but nobody will do that for me nobody not even Candy she wants to drag me out of my warmth out of the soft darkness into the cold the trouble the pain——

—into knowing. And I don't can't won't

"Paris!"

—won't

"Paris, listen to me! You can run away to wherever it is you go; play hide-and-seek inside your mind. But I—I've nowhere to go, no hiding place; and no inclination whatsoever towards children's games. I don't even have the strength any more to run and poke into corners, hoping you'll be there. Paris, Paris, baby boy sulking in your corner in the dark, must you make me suffer so? Must you rip my insides to shreds with pity, make me cry 'till I've no tears left and, even after that, go on crying until my eyes are swollen shut and my throat feels like it's full of sand? Can't you even for one minute stop thinking about your sorrow, your pain, and give mine a little attention? I'm a woman, Paris! I wasn't meant to be leaned upon, but to lean! Oh God, I——"

He stared at her, seeing her face blurring through the mist, coming clearer. Now it was all clear and he saw what it was like now, saw what he had done to her. He said:

"I'm sorry, Candace. I won't, again. How long was I—out, this time?"

He saw the reluctant hope in her eyes, hedged about with fear. Heard her voice fighting for control, saying:

"Three weeks and one day Tell me: are you really back? If Laurel, or somebody else, comes in that door and shouts at you, screaming that you're crazy, are you going to run away? Are you going to leave me. again?"

He smiled.

"Any man who'd leave you, Candy, is beyond all salvation," he said.

He saw her two hands rising like white wings, felt them trembling along the slant of his jaw, holding him like that, prisoner under her gaze.

"Paris," her breathing rustled against his mouth, "are you fond of me?"

"Fond?" he said simply. "No. I love you, Candace."

"And I love you," she said just as simply. "So—since I cannot have more, grant me the consolation of staying in the same world with me, at least. Will you, Paris?"

He looked at her with eyes dark with trouble, sunken with pain.

"I'll try, Candace," he said.

"All right," she said crisply; "as a start, talk to me!"

"About what?" he said.

"About you. All about you. Start as far back as you can remember and tell me all your joys, and all your sorrows; everything you've been proud of, everything of which you've been ashamed. Talk them out, cast them forth—all the devils that have possessed you, and I——"

"And you?" Paris said.

He saw her penny-brown eyes go bright with mischief, a smile play about the corners of her mouth.

"I'll just sit here and substitute for those swine Our Lord cast the devils into. With the thoughts I've had lately, it won't be hard," she said.

7

"CANDY," Paris said, "what is it about talking over a thing that——"

"Helps? I don't know. Kind of a catharsis, I suppose. I don't know why it helps; but it does, doesn't it?"

He sat there, in one of the chairs in front of the hunting lodge, looking at her, studying actually; seeing her honey-blond hair framing a face that was clean-lined, incisive, crisp, its sure intelligence betrayed only by the warmth of her oddly contrasting dark eyes, by the rich fullness of the mouth that, though pale, suggested that her stern code had not been easily come by; that it, like all the attributes of her personality, was the result of a self-discipline, which, in somebody else, would have seemed forbidding, but in her was wholly admirable. Like all of her, he thought.

"Candy," he began; "I——"

But Samson's bass rumble, rolling down from the wooded rise above the lodge, cut him off.

"Miz Candy!" Samson called. "Here come some folks!"

Paris looked up and saw the wagon coming towards the lodge. It was a sort of Conestoga wagon, or maybe even a prairie schooner, only it was a good bit smaller than either, so that it could be drawn quite easily by a pair of mules instead of the four, six, even eight that the bigger covered wagons required. He stood up, aware as he did so that Candace had got to her feet and was holding on to one of his arms. The gesture was protective, maternal, tender.

The wagon was close enough now for him to see the Negro driver and, beside him, the shaggy, unkempt wrack of skin and bones that had once been a man; and, beside him, the tall blonde who seemed to be made of Dresden china, and who was so perfect that even looking at her he still didn't believe her, and decided in the next instant that he really didn't care whether he believed her or not, because, with all her Norse goddess's perfection, she still wasn't Candace; but then, who was?

"Henry!" Candace said; "Ingra!" and surged forward.

"Whoa there!" the Negro driver said.

The tall blonde leaped from the wagon and caught Candace in her arms. She dwarfed Candace absolutely; because, Paris saw, this one could look him or Barry Cadwallader or Hector straight in the eye, and all three of them were over six feet tall in their stocking feet.

"Oh, Candace, how fine you look!" she said in a velvety contralto that matched the rest of her. "Somebody must have been treating you awfully well!"

"Now you've said it!" the almost skeletal creature on the wagon snarled. "I take it this is your patient, Candy? Damned if I see anything wrong with him!"

"There—there isn't—now," Candace faltered. "Please, Henry——"

"Please what?" the man said. "Don't see a goddamned thing to be pleased about. He ain't crippled; and you——"

"Henry, will you behave yourself?" Candace said wearily. "Mr Griffin has been awfully sick, and——"

"You mean loony, don't you?" Henry Trevor said. "That why you had to hang on to him so affectionate like while we was riding up? To keep him from wandering off and getting himself lost?"

"Oh, Henry, for God's sake!" Ingra said. "Your heroic war wounds are no excuse for jealous tantrums. You've no right to insult Candace. You should be eternally grateful to her——"

"I am," Henry said, "oh, I am. Never asked her too many questions. Long as she didn't fair rub my nose in what she was doing. I didn't pay no attention. But hanging on to him that way——"

Paris could see that Candace was crying. She didn't make a sound. She just stood there and let the big tears roll down her face, so that he could almost feel her hopelessness, the resignation that trembled on the brink of rebellion, but

94

held back, mainly because there really wasn't anything to revolt against, because given the existent circumstances and her sense of responsibility, to strike out against the kind of life she had to lead would have been shadow boxing with the moving air. So he stepped forward, and put out his hand.

"Good morning, Mr Trevor; welcome to Griffin's Way," he said.

Henry Trevor stared at the outstretched hand. He would have given anything short of his life to escape taking it, Paris saw, but he just didn't have the cold nerve that took. And it was glaringly evident that he had never had it, not even before he had been crippled. Misfortune didn't change a man, it merely brought out what was already there—or the lack of it. As I abundantly proved, Paris thought.

Limply Henry Trevor took his hand, shook it, let it drop. Then, as the weak always do, he had to bluster.

"Don't know about that there 'welcome' business," he began.

"Oh, yes, you're welcome here," Paris cut him off. "And don't get your back up on the score of pity. Say comprehension, rather. I've been crippled, too, friend; and you can take my word for it that a maimed mind is even less pleasant than an injured body. In fact, maybe I still am—I don't know. I've been sane before, and always slipped back. . . ."

"Oh, Paris, no!" Candace said.

"I don't believe you're going to slip back now, Mr Griffin," Ingra Holm said; "in fact, if I've ever seen a man who looked just all right, it's you!"

"Ingra," Candace said—a little tartly, Paris thought— "you aren't going to play the 'advanced woman' today, are you?"

"No," Ingra smiled; "I wouldn't dare. I'm Ingra Holm, Mr Griffin——"

"Mighty proud to make your acquaintance, ma'am," Paris said. "Sure is a funny thing to find two such pretty women being staunch friends. . . ."

"No," Ingra said, "it isn't. Always, of course, disregarding

95

the fact that you Southerners would call a scarecrow pretty if it were dressed in skirts. For me, it's an advantage. The men look at Candace first, and that gives them time to get over being shocked at the sight of a woman who's taller than a pine tree and bigger than a Jersey cow. Because, after she primly discourages them, they have to talk to me; then— at least those very, very few whose heads I couldn't eat off while they're standing up—sometimes discover——"

"That you're pretty as a picture, and that that mouth was made for kissing, even if a fellow has to climb up on the banisters to reach it," Paris said.

"Paris!" Candace said.

"I was going to say that they sometimes discover I'm tolerable," Ingra laughed. "Well, Candace, here we are!"

"Yes," Candace said, "and it's all my fault, I should have written you that Par—Mr Griffin was better, and not to bring Henry——"

"Ha!" Henry said.

"Because now I've got to cart him right back to Vicksburg. Only I——"

"Only you didn't dare," Paris supplied; "you weren't sure I wouldn't have another of my relapses. In fact, you still aren't——"

"Oh, yes, I am!" Candace said. "When a man begins flirting as outrageously as you were with Ingra just now, he's well, all right!"

"You sound like you're jealous," Henry began, again.

"Oh, shut up, Henry!" Ingra said. "Look, Candace, darling, you can't go back to Vicksburg, right now. To tell the truth, I'm hoping you won't have to go back at all. I've already got you a job with me at the new school; but first you have to help me find lodgings, and even help me locate a building that will serve as a temporary schoolhouse and——"

"Oh, dear!" Candace said. "Ingra, you're much too impulsive! Didn't you realize how difficult all that was going to be?"

"Why should she have?" Paris said. "Matter of fact, it isn't, not at all. Both of you—and Mr Trevor——"

"Thank you mighty kindly for remembering I'm alive," Henry said.

"Can be my guests at Griffin's Way——"

Candace looked at him.

"No, Paris," she said.

"Because of—Laurie?" Paris said.

"Because of Laurie," Candace said.

"Then how about right here?" Paris said. "The lodge isn't half bad; and I could send down some more furniture and bedding——"

"Oh, would you?" Ingra said. "That would be just wonderful. . . ."

"Look, Ingra," Candace said; "I'm not sure we should impose upon Mr Griffin's generosity that way. He *lives* here, and——"

"It's no imposition at all," Paris said. "Samson!"

"Yessir, Mr Paris?" Samson said.

"You and this boy lift the gentleman down. Be careful now. Put him in my room. . . ."

He stood there, watching the two Negroes lifting Henry Trevor down. They got in each other's way. One would have been enough. In fact, a sturdy child would have been sufficient. Henry Trevor was as nearly nothing as a man could be and still live, Paris thought. The only thing left of him was his irascibility.

"Goddammit, nigger, you're hurting me!" he snarled.

"Sorry, sir," Samson said.

The two Negroes carried him into the lodge. Paris turned back to the women.

"About your schoolhouse. I think we can arrange that, too," he said. "My brother Hector allowed the coloured folks to build a church on his place. On Sunday nights you can't hear your ears for the singing and the shouting. But I reckon if we sent Samson to find the preacher, we could arrange to use it week days. . . ."

"Mr Griffin, you're a magician!" Ingra said. "I'm sure it will only be temporarily, because we should be able to get the Lovegood people to give us the money for a new building; and Bruce has got friends of his in the legislature to make our school a part of the public school system and to vote us funds. The County Superintendent has already earmarked a part of the local property taxes for us. . . ."

"Paris—" Candace said; "you've put Henry and me in your room. Ingra will have to stay in the other. And there're only two. Where—where will you sleep?"

He smiled at her, seeing, as he did so, her face whitening, her brown eyes going black, not from anything so imprecise as intuition; but from an absolute certainty of what he was going to say.

"Home," he said, "home to Griffin's Way. We've decided what's important, haven't we, Candace? That the principal thing is not to hurt——"

"Those to whom we've given our pledged word," Candace said tonelessly. "Yes. But there is another thing that must be considered, Paris——"

"And that is?" he said.

"You."

"Me?" Paris said.

"Yes. Oh, I—I don't know how to put it! Because, now, anything I'd say would sound wrong, horribly wrong. Yet, all I'm trying to do is to protect my investment in a very superior type of humanity, the kind, it seems to me, the world very badly needs. . . . Paris, don't—seek unhappiness. You—you're not strong yet, and I——"

Paris looked at her.

"You mean," he said, "that I'm not to ask Laurie questions about what she's been up to while I was wandering around in my private fog; that my relationship with her must be straight ahead: all future and no past. All right. I'll accept that, largely because I don't give that much of a damn. And I don't have to seek unhappiness, Candy. I've already found it—from the only source that could affect me now. Good day, ladies; I hope you'll be quite comfortable. Anything you need, just send Samson up to the house for it. I'll drop by tomorrow and——"

He stopped short. For her face was naked again. Her eyes

were defenceless. And, having no words of comfort to offer her, being himself comfortless, he turned on his heel like a soldier and left them there.

When he got to Griffin's Way, Laurel was sitting on the veranda. The day was hot; she was fanning herself with a big palmetto fan. He dismounted, letting the bridle trail in the dirt, and started up the stairs.

Laurel didn't move. She stopped fanning. He could see her eyes getting bigger and bigger as he came up the stairs. Could see the fear in them.

"Hello, Laurie," he said.

"'Lo—Paris," she whispered.

He stood there, looking at her. She was very nice to look at, with her hair like resinous pine-smoke pluming from a steamboat's stacks, and her eyes like the far edge of the sky. He could see the trapped-animal darting of her gaze, and her breathing stirring that fine-drawn, racing-thorough-bred's body of hers. That very good, useful, exciting body that always before had been able to make him forget that he had no real communication with her out of bed, and that the possibility of any such communication scarcely existed —considering the type of mind she had, if it could even be called a mind.

It could, he decided; oh yes, it could. It wasn't even the mind of a child, but rather that of a peasant: very shrewd in small matters, like taking advantage, getting the best of a bargain, seeking the tiniest opportunity to cheat. But as hopelessly illogical in larger affairs as the peasant mind always is; attributing as cause of observed effect what was no more than random coincidence. Superstitious, common-place—even, sadly, vulgar. Insufficiently intelligent to even recognize intelligence in others—saturated with that curious feminine belief (also existing in far cleverer women, he had to admit) that her wiles were invincible, not even recogniz-ing that, to a grown man, female trickery is a game for girl children which he a little sadly pretends to be taken in by, for the sake of peace.

99

"Paris—" she ran a pink tongue over lips gone suddenly dry; "you—you feel all right?"

"I feel just fine, Laurie," he said.

"It—it's awful hot, isn't it?" Laurel said.

"Yes," Paris said.

"You—you aren't mad at me, are you, Paris?" she said. "Are you, Paris?"

He smiled.

"No, Laurie, I'm not mad at you," he said.

"Oh!" she breathed. "Oh, dear! What a relief. I—I thought——"

"That I'd come to strangle you, because, as you know, you deserve being strangled. Only I don't know what you deserve being strangled for. As long as you don't tell me, you'll be all right."

"But," she whispered, "if somebody else——?"

His smile broadened.

"I won't let them tell me," he said. "Mind if I sit down beside you? And I'd like a mint julep, if that's still possible. . . ."

"Possible? Of course it's possible, darling! I'll go ring for Sarah to make you one right now. . . ."

He held her with his eyes.

"Are you planning to run right out of the back door, Laurie?" he said.

"I—I——" she quavered. "Well, yes—I was! I—I'm so scared of you now, Paris!"

He put out his big hand and touched her hair.

"Don't be," he said. "I'll never harm you, Laurie. Never, no matter what you've done; no matter what you'll ever do. . . ."

She stared at him. Her blue eyes went light-filled, crystalline.

"Paris," she said; "would you please kiss me right now, this minute, please?"

He bent forward, touched her lips, so lightly that she couldn't even be sure that he had touched them, so she brought her two hands up behind his head and ground her mouth into his in an aching, fear-filled counterfeit of passion.

"Paris," she said, her voice a husk-whisper, breath-rustled, "let's go—inside, shall we?"

He wondered sadly why it was that every single time a woman offered herself, the element of whoring entered in? He supposed it was because in women passion was no instantaneous explosion along the nerves as it was in man. Rather, it was a still-born thing that had to be stroked, caressed into life. So, when a woman offered herself, it was always for reasons: like, for instance, trying to insure her safety, protect her cunning, undeserving hide by enslaving him through his dependable, easily awakened male lust. Only they never, never realized that, between a man and a woman, any reasons whatsoever were wrong. Wrong and as destructive to passion as an icy bath.

"No," he said; "let's stay right here. It's too hot to go inside. And I still want my julep. Go and tell Sarah; but come back, will you?"

"Yes, Paris," Laurel said.

He sat there, sipping the frosty drink. He could feel her eyes on him, wide with questioning.

"Paris," she said, in a tiny, little girl's voice; "why wouldn't you come inside with me? Don't you—don't you love me any more?"

Refuse them, he thought, even when the offer is falsely made, passionless, and a cheat, and you shake them to the core. To make a woman doubt her desirability is to kill her, living. Isn't it, after all, their extreme simplicity that makes them seem so complex?

He sipped the julep.

"Because I didn't want to," he said; "but mainly because you didn't want to, either."

He saw her stiffen, as women always do when confronted with the fact that a man is, or even can be, perceptive; a realization equivalent, Paris thought, to the crumbling of the dykes with which they shore up their world.

101

"Paris, you—you're all right now, really all right, aren't you? Tell me—what happened to—to bring you back to your senses?"

He smiled. What had happened wasn't a thing that went easily into words. He wasn't sure he really knew; he doubted that even Candace could entirely explain her miracle working. And he was certain that any explanation he could give, any attempt to pin down the force of anguished pity, the aching, naked will with which Candace had dragged him back to life again, would be beyond Laurel. So he said:

"Hank Thurston beat me up. Injured me pretty badly. I guess one sickness cancelled out the other, Laurie. . . ."

"Oh!" she said. "I—I've heard that. People getting hit on their heads, and losing their minds; then somebody hits them on the same place again, and their senses come back. . . ."

You've heard it, Paris thought; only, according to Candace, it never happens. Popular superstition; but, right now, useful, as superstitions often are.

"Something like that," he said.

"And, as long as you don't get hurt again, you—you'll stay in your right mind?" Laurel said.

"Yes," Paris said.

"Oh," Laurel said; "oh, Paris, I'm so glad!"

He heard, astonished, the unmistakable note of joy, shaking her voice; turning, he saw more astonishingly still, the tears trembling on her lashes.

"Are you, Laurie?" he said.

For answer, she slipped out of her chair, knelt, with curious humility, at his feet, took his hand and pressed it to her breast.

"Feel how it beats!" she said.

He could feel that muffled hammering under his hand; feel her breath going ragged, soaring, wild. She leaned forward, let her head rest on his knees, crying stormily, angrily, breathlessly, like a child.

"Oh, Paris, I've missed you so!" she said.

He put out his hand and stroked her hair.

She jerked her head away from his hand, looked up, and

her face was anguished. It wore, curiously, the expression of a person undergoing intolerable torture.

This, he recognized. This was real.

Her voice was uneven. It sounded hoarse. She said:

"Paris, *will* you come inside with me now?"

"Yes. Yes, now I'll come," he said.

★ 8 ★

WHAT it amounted to was that life had begun all over again
for Paris Griffin. Begun, curiously, like the small, trickling
thrust of a rain-swollen river, probing through a levee,
widening the breach once found, raging through with pent-
up, torrential passion, then spreading out over the lowlands,
slowly, placidly, becoming, finally, wide sheets of unbroken
quiet, mirroring the sky.

Which was what his life was now: quiet. Shoal waters.
The stagnation of old floods sinking into the mud of routine.
Nothing, it seemed to Paris Griffin as he rode out over his
broad acres, was happening any more.

To other people, yes. Barry, now. Barry and Ingra. That
was an odd relationship. Barry was squiring Ingra about
with marked attention; had been, in fact, ever since he had
met her shortly after her arrival at Griffin's Way. But what,
in the name of heaven, was holding him back? All a body
had to do was to look at Ingra while Barry was around—no,
less than that, merely to see her face when his name was
accidentally mentioned in her presence—to know who it
was who was keeping a tight grip on the reins. Heck, they'd
be home from their honeymoon and with a baby already on
the way by now, if Ingra had anything to say about it, Paris
thought. But old Barry's dragging his feet. Why? Scared of
matrimony, or——

Too fond of Candace, surely. Wonder if he plans to keep
poor Ingra dangling on that string in the forlorn hope that
the Good Lord will put Henry Trevor out of the way?

But that particular thought was far from pleasant, Paris
found. Barry was free, all but unattached; blamed good
looking. So, if poor Henry—Lord what a nasty disposition
he has! Can't rightly hold it against him though—if he were
to pass on, there'd be nothing whatsoever to——

He put that from his mind. He rode on, aimlessly, thinking a little worriedly about what was happening to the State of Mississippi, now. That bunch of carpet-baggers and scalla-wags in Vicksburg were ruining the State for fair. There didn't seem to be an honest man in the lot; but there were certainly some outstanding thieves. He'd repeatedly heard the name Crosby mentioned. Peter Crosby, a white man of unknown origins who seemed to have the knack of getting himself elected or appointed to a long series of minor offices, all of which had access to the State Treasurer's cash box. And Randolph—Bruce Randolph, Ingra's highly praised black paragon. Nobody could prove Randolph was stealing; but, for an honest man, he sure kept some mighty questionable company. . . .

Reckon I ought to ride down to Vicksburg and take a look around, Paris thought. Then, as usual, he rejected the idea. Vicksburg was exactly sixty miles from Junction Village, the nearest railroad station to Griffin's Way. Before the War, the Griffins had thought nothing of the trip to Vicksburg, because it involved nothing more than a forty-minute buggy ride into Junction, then two hours on the train. But now, over much of the South, life had retreated back over centuries, as far as the amenities of civilization were concerned. The railroads connecting Junction with Vicksburg were still impassable even now, five years after the shooting had stopped, the rails still bent around the telegraph poles, torn up, long stretches of the railroad destroyed, as a result of Union General Wilson's wartime raids. Those windy thieves in Vicksburg had talked about repairing it, of course. Had even voted money for its rebuilding. But that money had gone the way of all monies that passed through the hands of Reconstruction governments in the South: straight into the pockets of the august gentlemen who had voted the funds in the first place. A little work had been done—sparse, frequently interrupted, near-finished; but Paris suspected that somebody would have invented a practical flying machine and the rest of humanity would be flitting from cloud to cloud before the people around Junction Village would have a railroad again. Which meant that Vicksburg wasn't three hours away from Griffin's Way, now; it was closer to three days. To go, spend a day there, and return, would cost him the better part of a week. And he couldn't afford that week. A man had to keep his hands to the plough every minute now, just to stay alive.

He decided suddenly to ride over to his brother's place. He hadn't seen Hector and his brood in a coon's age. He was very fond of his brother's yard children, an emotion intensified by the vast and brooding pity that the sight of them always awoke in him. Poor little bastards. They were in no way responsible for their parents' sins; nor for the intolerance of a society that left no place for them anywhere, neither among the Negroes nor the whites. Hector would have to make some plans for them soon, get them out of the South, take them to some colder, more indifferent climate, where they would have at least a fighting chance for survival.

That was one thing. But the other reason he needed to see his older brother was more serious. Ever since his own duel with Hiliary, there had been bad blood between the Griffins and the Thurstons. He had promised Candace not to pursue the quarrel further. She had given him what he mockingly called a legitimate excuse for cowardice. That a man could, even ought to, risk his life over questions of honour was a point of view held by all men of his time, region, race and class without question; but nobody that he knew—except himself—had ever been confronted with the problem of what to do about honour when maintaining it involved a danger not to his life so much as to his sanity. I, Paris thought, seem to have put new meaning into that old, worn-out phrase: "a fate worse than death". Because, any way you look at it, it is. . . .

Candace had insisted upon the point. "You mustn't get upset, Paris!" she had said over and over again. "You must avoid situations that would make you get excited or angry. You've a wonderful mind; and troglodytes like the Thurstons simply aren't worth the risk of your losing it! Promise me, Paris?"

She had kept after him until he had promised. Done even more than promised: gone so far as even to conceal from Hector the facts about Ulysses' death. Because he knew what Hector would do the moment he found out that Hank Thurston had admitted his guilt in the accidental murder of their younger brother: hunt Hank down; blast him from among the ranks of the living—at any cost, including that of his own life, including even what would happen thereafter to his defenceless, pitiful, belonging-nowhere family.

But, it now appeared, even that concealment wasn't enough. Josh—the old Negro who had been their father's groom and stable-keeper, but who was a supernumerary now, too old to be trusted around any horse having a little spirit, so that, although he was allowed to keep the title of groom, it was his full-grown grandson, Duke, who did the actual work—had brought home a confused, incoherent account of a quarrel between Hector and Hank Thurston in Junction Village the other day. Josh hadn't been clear as to what the quarrel had been about; the only certainty in the whole affair being, as Josh put it, "If Marse Barry Cadwallader hadn't of stepped in betwixt 'em mighty fast there'd of been some fightin 'n stompin' and maybe a li'l' cuttin' and shootin', too!"

Paris pulled up his mount. Barry, now. Wouldn't it be better to talk to Barry first? Wiser, even, to concoct some scheme between them for keeping Hector out of trouble? Because, if there were anything sure in this world of sin, it was that Hector Griffin wouldn't listen to reason. When had he ever in his life?

A prime example was the new coloured school. It would have been more than sufficient for Hector to fall in with Paris's own suggestion about using the already existing Negro Baptist Church, a matter which would have come to the attention of the white Conservatives slowly enough to give them time to calm down. But that wasn't Hector's style. No. Nothing had suited Hector better than to ride into Vicksburg, sacrificing the better part of a week to do it, and legally and publicly deed five acres of prime land adjacent to the church to the Lovegood Fund and the State Board of Education for the site of the proposed school. And, as if that hadn't been enough, he had detached a sizeable portion of his hands from the ordinary labours of planting and put them to work erecting a kiln to burn brick for the construction with the already widely quoted remark:

"I'll give those bedsheet bastards something they'll catch hell trying to burn!"

No, caution was not to be expected of his elder brother. Hector's life had been one long assault upon the mores and conventions of his world. And he was too old a dog by now for instruction in new tricks. Better to have a chat with Barry; to arrange something between them—a sort of invisible picket line between Hector's idiotic idealism and the forces threatening to destroy both the idealism and the man.

But nothing was ever simple in life. To see Barry meant riding over to Walfen, the Cadwallader place, an act involving not the risk, but the near certainty of running into Dion. And to that certainty, he could add another: inevitable conflict with all the dangers that Candace had warned him of. He wasn't afraid of Di. He wasn't afraid of any man of woman born. But he thought of that sleet hiss, the cold wind rising, the colour grey spreading across the warm, vibrant, living, rediscovered colours of his world, and pulled up his mount.

I could send old Josh, he mused. Make some excuse—say I want to see Barry about buying a stallion and a mare of that breed of greys their grandpa established. Finest saddle horses in the state, those Cadwallader greys. Have to give them that. Barry says the old man crossed a white Arabian stallion with a grey Morgan mare and kept in-breeding until he had the strain fixed. Only Di would see through that in a minute. He'd know that Barry and I are close enough for Barry to have told me about the old man's will forbidding the sale of any of those greys as long as there's a Cadwallader left alive to ride 'em. So that won't wash. No, I guess I'd better wait until I run into Barry by accident. So now?

So now, do what I've been wanting to all along. Ride down to the lodge. See her. Torment myself seeing her. Oh, Lord, I——"

The first thing that Paris saw, when he came up to the lodge, was that the covered wagon was there, again. Samson and the driver were loading it: with valises and a trunk that had I. H. stamped on them; but, also, with others marked H. T.

He sat there on his horse, looking at them.

"Howdy, Mister Paris!" Samson boomed. "Did you come down here to tell your friends goodbye, sir?"

Then Candace came through the door and stood there looking at him, her brown eyes dark with pain.

Paris swung down from the roan.

"So——" he said; "you were going to run off, with-out——"

"Saying goodbye? No, Paris. We were going to stop at the big house on the way. I—I didn't want to tell you, before. I—couldn't. You see—it's too horrible. Poor Ingra's literally sick——"

"Over what?" Paris said.

"Our school. It was to have been part of the county's rural education programme. Bruce had got the Board of Education to grant us the funds, and——"

"What about those Northern philanthropies you told me he represented," Paris said; "didn't they have anything to do with it?"

"No. Of course not. They built the school in Vicksburg —the one where Ingra was teaching. That used up the entire grant. So this one had to be part of the Warren County public school system, and now"

"Now?" Paris said.

"The County Superintendent of Schools has—disap-peared; and all our funds went with him," Candace said.

"Good Lord!" Paris said.

"Amen," Candace whispered; "but—in a way—I'm glad——"

"In what way, Candace?" Paris said.

"Now, I won't have to see you every day. . . ."

"Oh," Paris said.

"I—I don't think you understand what I meant by that. Only, Paris—I'd rather you wouldn't ask me to explain it. In fact, I beg you not to. . . ."

"All right," Paris said. "Candy——"

"Yes, Paris?"

"Where're Ingra and Henry?"

"Ingra's lying down, nursing a headache. She's so disappointed, Paris. Both about the school and because this is going to take her too far away from Barry Cadwallader. You knew about that, didn't you?"

"Yes," Paris said. "And Henry?"

"Asleep. I didn't want to wake him up until we were ready. . . ."

"I see. Then how about us taking a little stroll through the woods—where we can talk, I mean. . . ."

"No, Paris."

"Why not? It's a lot cooler than here, and——"

"No, Paris."

"Look, Candy—even conventionality can be carried to ridiculous extremes. . . ."

"I know. Only you're wrong again. I wasn't even thinking about conventions. . . ."

"Then, what were you thinking about?" Paris said.

"About—you. About me. About us."

"Well?"

"About spontaneous combustion. There! Are you satisfied now, Paris? Or do you mean to go on tormenting me into being more indelicate still?"

"If I thought I could get you to be really indelicate——"

"Well, you can't. One: I'm not going walking in the woods with you. Two: I'm going back to Vicksburg to wear myself out with work and loneliness. Three: if I ever do see you again, I'll go on maintaining the correct minimum distance between us——"

"And that is?"

"About two yards. No, three. Closer than that is—too dangerous, Paris."

"I see," Paris said; "and now?"

"Now you're going to run along home like a good boy, and leave me in peace," Candace said.

9

LEAVE her in peace. Paris had occasions enough to call that phrase to mind in the next three years, and to wonder at the fact that he continued to do exactly what she asked. He made no efforts at all to see her, which had been fairly easy the first year after she had gone, when the difficulties of the journey into Vicksburg were taken into consideration. But at the beginning of the second year Barry Cadwallader had materially contributed to the total elimination of those difficulties. Barry called a meeting of all the neighbouring planters, which met at Walfen in January of 1872. There he proposed two solutions to the increasingly troublesome problem of their communications with Vicksburg. The first was that they buy a broken-down steamboat and recondition it, each planter to build his own docking facilities and to contribute towards both the purchase price and the maintenance of their own Warren County steamboat line; and the second was to contribute the labour of their field-hands in slack season, as well as the funds—to be administered by a committee chosen among themselves—to the rebuilding of the little spur line that had run the sixty miles between Junction Village and Vicksburg before the War.

Naturally enough, the second suggestion won. Too many of the planters had no acreage fronting on the river at all. And, once rebuilt, the original railroad company would surely see the advantage of re-incorporating the spur line into its system, and thus relieve the planters of the trouble of having to run it themselves. Best of all, it took the whole question out of the hands of those windy thieves in Vicksburg.

The speed and efficiency with which the job was done should have been an object lesson to the Northern carpet-baggers, the Southern scallawags, and the ignorant black ex-field-hands who now called themselves legislators. By

June 20, 1872, the first train puffed over the newly laid tracks, carrying the planters' goods and most of themselves, accompanied by their wives and children, into Vicksburg. But, of course, the lesson was lost upon the Reconstruction government. Any lesson which does not fit their preconceived notions is always lost upon a government composed of men.

But what truly escaped the attention of everybody concerned, except Paris Griffin, was the intricacy of the motives underlying their remarkable feat of railroad building. Or, more justly, rebuilding; for better than ninety per cent of the expense involved had been for labour. Most of the old rails had been usable once expert blacksmiths like Paris's own Samson had got to work reheating them and unwinding them from around the trees and telegraph poles where Wilson's raiders had twisted them in the first place. Rock for the roadbed cost them only the hauling; and the cypress logs for cross-ties they cut in the swamplands on their own places.

So, in the general aura of complacent self-congratulation, it was no wonder that the wry, antic humour of the real reason they had a railroad again escaped them all except Paris, who could not fail to see it, being, as he was, involved. Barry now, by calling his meeting, had acted for the public good; had unselfishly sacrificed time, effort, money, to push through a measure beneficial to all of them. For which, and rightly, he was highly praised. But, Paris could not help seeing, one of the most immediate results of their venture into railroading had been to make it possible for Barry to spend three evenings in Vicksburg, each and every week, squiring Ingra Holm about.

Again, good. Why not? Barry paid his fare, and the train was there to transport him on whatever errand he had in mind, including the delicate one of courtship. But—again that conjunction which was the determining factor in so much of human life—what about that courtship, itself? That courtship had been going on for the entire three years, from the summer of 1870, when Barry had met Ingra at Griffin's Way, until the summer of 1873 that it was now. Was Ingra blind? Couldn't she see that Barry was using her because calling on her gave him a chance to see and be near Candace without causing talk? No. Ingra simply wasn't that stupid. More than likely she was closing her eyes, swallowing her pride, hoping that one day Barry would turn to her in truth.

On the other hand, Paris was painfully aware that the rebuilt Junction & Vicksburg spur line had increased his own problems. He no longer had sufficient excuse to explain his reluctance to take Laurel into town. The wrecked railroad had been a splendid one, but now Barry's enterprise had removed that stumbling block. He fell back on the less sustainable explanation that his nerves still weren't up to the noise and bustle of Vicksburg. But the three years had worked wonders in him. He knew perfectly well that his nerves were up to noise, confusion, bustle, even battle—up to everything on earth except a chance encounter with Candace Trevor. And that, if he let Laurel crowd him into going to Vicksburg as frequently as the other planters now did, wouldn't remain a matter of chance very long. It would become inevitable.

He had got used to his semi-hermit's existence—even liked it, in a way. His life was confined to running the plantation, which he did very well indeed, reading the tons of books that he ordered by mail from New Orleans, Philadelphia, New York and Boston, and visiting his brother Hector's place, often accompanied by Barry.

Because now, despite the ancient bad blood between the Cadwalladers and the Griffins, a quarrel going back to their grandfathers' day, and whose origins—a boundary dispute, a horse race, a woman—had long since faded from human memory, leaving only the actuality of dislike, the propensity to violent outbreaks between the two clans even when the provocation was a slighter thing than Dion's half-concealed yen for Paris's wife; despite the extension of that ancient quarrel to include the Thurstons—an extension natural enough in a region where people took kinship seriously; and

114

the Thurstons and the Cadwalladers were, after all, first cousins; or, maybe even because—since that insane farce of a duel that had cost Hiliary Thurston his life at Paris's unwilling hand, or, more justly, at his own—the Thurston–Griffin feud had crowded the older semi-private war from the centre of the stage. Now, Hector had accepted Barry's friendship to an equal or greater degree than Paris already had. The occasion for Barry's visits to the Briars, as Hector was already beginning to call his plantation, as well as the slowly mounting brick mansion he was now building upon it, was Barry's and Paris's joint effort to prevent Hector from killing Hank Thurston, or vice versa.

Of course, Hector didn't know that. He was unaware that Paris and Barry both kept careful watch to see that Ernest Thurston didn't get within grabbing distance of either of Hector's pretty quadroon daughters. Because, to Ernest, with centuries of inherited lechery rioting in his eighteen-year-old veins, girls like Hector's daughters were fair game. That was what the renewed quarrel between Hank and Hector had been about in the first place, and not, as Paris had feared from old Josh's incoherent version of it, because Hector had found out that Hank had killed poor Ulysses.

Which was a point that troubled Paris, himself. By what right did he continue to let his brother's death go unpunished? In defence of his own sick nerves? Because of the impossibility after this great lapse of time to assemble the evidence necessary to convince a jury? Or because of his near certainty that any jury chosen from among his peers would acquit Hank Thurston hands down if for no better reason than to show those "nigger-loving" Griffins where they stood?

Or was it because—admit it, say the truth—the alternative had become for him unthinkable; that he was no longer morally prepared to kill? That, surely, if he had ever been —which was distinctly questionable. For his retreat out of life had been caused less by his very normal fear of dying than by his sense of guilt, his over-whelming repugnance at the thought of causing any man's death, even accidentally.

He had made a brave enough soldier, but it had gone against the grain. He had kept seeing Ulysses' face upon all the bodies of the slain; each time he had fired, he had murdered his younger brother anew, somewhere, somehow, in the darkness of his mind.

Now that was gone; but he had extended his revulsion at the idea of killing until it now included even a simian sub-human like Henry Thurston. And the only justice that could be taken for Ulysses' death would be for him to kill Hank, or to let Hector do it. And he couldn't. Not now. Not either way.

Better this uneasy peace, watching Hector use the kiln he had originally built to burn the brick for the Negro school that the absconding superintendent had terminated even before it was begun to fire those for his own house—that house which was sure to worsen Hector's already precarious situation in the community when the news of its imposing nature made the rounds. Paris had seen the plans, could now see their rising realization, was painfully aware that Hector was defiantly building the finest house in the history of Warren County as a home for his off-coloured yard children. But Hector was within his rights. That was unquestionable. But equally unquestionable was the fact that, when a man's rights and human prejudices clashed, human prejudices nearly always won. Hector was fairly courting disaster. And the sad part about it was that there was absolutely no way to stop him. Hector wasn't a Griffin for nothing; worse, he was the most stubborn of that mule-stubborn breed.

Paris smiled, one lip corner rising in that ingratiating expression of self-mockery that was almost a badge of the Griffins, so much so that they customarily reckoned the degree of the closeness of the kinship of any relative by whether he had or had not the Griffin smile. To hell with it, he thought. The only thing to do is to set up a sort of Underground Railroad to get Hector and his family out of the state when what he is purely asking for starts to happen. Barry'll help. We'll smuggle them out. Head south in the

116

direction nobody will expect us to take; and put them all on an upriver boat. . . .

He rode on out to the big gate. Opened his mailbox. There was nothing in it but *The Vicksburg Herald*. On the front page was another speech by Bruce Randolph. Paris read it slowly. For some reason or another, he just couldn't cotton to the Negro educator. He tried now to analyse that feeling. It had nothing whatsoever to do with overt racial prejudice, or even with that age-old, subsconscious emotional reaction of instinctive repugnance towards a people whose physical attributes are so vastly distinct from one's own which the most liberal individual on God's green earth has to watch and fight with, lifelong, to prevent its impairing the fairness of his judgment. What it was, Paris finally decided, was, in a way, disappointment. He had hoped that Randolph would be a better man than he was. He had wanted to be convinced that, despite all the overwhelming evidences to the contrary, the black race was capable of producing men of intellectual capacity and moral fibre equal to those of the best white men. About that intellectual capacity, there seemed little doubt: Bruce Randolph's published speeches and articles had style, polish, wit, even evidences of that indefinable extra something that one could legitimately call genius. But moral fibre?

Aye, that was the rub! The black paragon, as Paris had fallen into the habit of mockingly calling him—a reaction surely, to Barry's awed admiration and extravagant praise of Randolph—had leaped into politics like a rabbit into the briar patch. Within weeks after the former county superintendent of education had decamped, his carpet-bag stuffed with the school board's funds, Randolph had campaigned for that office and won it, largely by promising all things to all men. One day his goal was to produce neat, clean Negroes trained in domestic science, agriculture and the mechanic arts—which suited the Conservatives mighty fine. But the next, in a speech before the Radical Republicans, he had promised voting militants marching ahead into the new day: mutually contradictory promises. Which was, of course, merely politics. Only the Negroes couldn't afford leaders who were mere politicians; what they needed were statesmen—even saints, maybe. Too much to ask, of course——

But Paris's case against Ingra's, Candace's, and, by extension of natural sympathies, Barry's black friend didn't stop there. Randolph had held office for nearly three years now; and the public schools he had promised to make spring up like mushrooms were, as far as Paris could see, all sleeping underground. He had built one fine brick private school in Vicksburg, using the funds that the Presbyterian Board of Missions and the Lovegood people had sent him south with in the first place. Ingra was teaching in that one, now. But he had built an even finer brick house for himself in Vicksburg. Purchased a carriage for his wife. Hired servants. Enjoyed a scale of living that no county superintendent in history, nor any state superintendent for that matter, and possibly not any governor, had ever enjoyed before. So ostentatious flaunting of suddenly acquired wealth had called Randolph into question, of course. He had loftily replied that he had acquired his money by speculation in Wall Street, upon the basis of information supplied him by a Boston financier who was an old friend of his. He had made the gesture—all the more grand because he didn't have to do it, because by then utter corruption was so much taken for granted in the post-war America of the Tweed Ring, Crédit Mobilier, Jim Fisk, Jay Gould and the rest that nobody would have bothered, and, even if they had, he could have been sure of a collusive hiding of his felonies by men even more dishonest than he, lest the tide of reform endanger their own rake-off—of offering his books for examination by the Conservatives' own permanently out-of-office auditor at the auditor's own sweet leisure. And the auditor, grudgingly, had been forced to give him a clean bill of health.

Which, Paris thought, proves only that Randolph is clever, not that he's honest. Nothing worse than an educated crook. He'll probably make off with the dome of the Warren County courthouse before he's done. . . .

Paris turned his horse back towards the big house. He was

thinking about Candace as he rode. Poor thing, slaving endless hours in that miserable hospital in order to support that whining bastard! Dear Lord, isn't there any justice anywhere in this world?

When he got to the house, he went at once to his study, consciously trying to avoid Laurel, to escape her endless pleas to be taken into Vicksburg—pleas he was going to have to accede to any day now. He wasn't being fair to Laurie. Plantation life was a lonely, boring thing; and now that this harmless means of occasional escape existed——

He closed the door behind him. He had told himself that he had better have a look at the plantation's accounts; but, once he was seated at his desk, he found it impossible to concentrate. The figures on the ruled pages blurred into meaninglessness before his eyes.

Candace, he thought. Three years since I've seen her. Since the fall of '70. And yet I have the impression that, instead of shading off into time's merciless fading of all images, no matter how cherished, hers is sharper than ever. But perhaps even that sharpness——

"Paris!" Laurel's voice floated down to him from somewhere upstairs.

—is a distortion, my imagination's heightening of reality. "Think you there was, or might be such a woman. As this I dream'd of?" No apologies to the Bard for changing that line a little. Very likely not. I wasn't really well then—just well enough to keep from slipping back——

"Paris!" Laurel's voice was closer now.

And very likely Barry's eternal lauding her to the skies has sort of kept her image clear. Poor Barry. What a simple, decent soul he is. Sorry I spouted off to him about his black genius the last time I saw him. A man ought to be allowed to keep some illusions. Anyhow, what's it to me? Nothing, or less. Let the black crook steal. Long live larceny! Except the larceny Candace performed upon my life. She sure made off with a sizeable chunk of it when she left. Lord, how empty the world is without her! Wish it hadn't happened like that. I'd be satisfied just talking to her. The hell I would! How she could talk! Pin a fellow's ears back with the finest collections of polysyllabics anybody ever heard of. And I——

"Paris! Are you in there? Answer me! I know you are!"

And I love her. Fat lot of good that does me!

"Yes, Laurie, I'm in here," he said.

Laurel came into the study. Stood there facing him, both hands behind her back, like a child.

"Paris," she said; "will you take me into Vicksburg, today?"

"Vicksburg?" Paris said. "What do you want to go to Vicksburg for, Laurie?"

"Well," she said; "you know I haven't had a decent dress since before the War. And they've got some mighty nice watered silk and taffeta at Michell's. 'Sides, we can't go on bothering Hector to take me into town. He's got his own place to tend to just like you have, and you really aren't sick any more, and the railroad's running again, thanks to Barry, and——"

"What makes you think I can afford to buy you silk and taffeta?" Paris said.

"Well, you can. We're getting rich again. Being nigger-lovers like you and Hector has got its good side, I reckon. The darkies work for you two just fine. Only other place halfway on its feet is Walfen. And that's only because of Barry. Every time he gets his hands to feeling good and making a decent crop, that fool Di goes and spoils it. . . ."

Paris raised one eyebrow.

"Just how do you happen to know so much about the Cadwalladers' affairs?" he said.

"Oh, didn't you know?" Laurel said impishly. "Every time you ride away to oversee the hands, I sneak over there, and——"

He looked at her. The fact that she was willing to joke about it proved whatever had been was over now. Still, the effect was decidedly unpleasant. Perhaps he was, as he told himself, only living up to the conception of morality that Candace insisted upon; perhaps, as he told himself, Laurie was merely a habit. But, he admitted honestly, she'd been a habit mighty easy to form again, and certainly not hard to endure, even now. No—less than ever, now. He had the feeling that she was working at this business of being a wife. Giving it thought. For one thing, she was less—gauche. Her speech had improved. She was much more careful about her dress, for, though she'd always been clean, she'd been a trifle negligent about details. Now, even at home, she dressed as if she were always expecting visitors, kept her hair combed and out of her eyes. Moreover, she actually supervised the servants for a change; kept after fat, black Sarah, until her cooking became something less than disaster. The house was clean now; and the house Negroes looked at Laurie with dawning respect, and not a little fear. As far as her daytime relations with him were concerned—about the night-time ones, he had never had cause for complaint—she was, if anything, too anxious to please. She fussed and fretted over him continually, trying to get him to eat more, worrying about his occasional lapses of memory. And, wonder of wonders, she was beginning to read. He suspected she'd got her list of books from Candace, whom she admitted to having seen and spoken to on one or two occasions when Hector had taken her into Vicksburg in his stead. Certainly she hadn't dug those weighty tomes—on domestic science, etiquette, general culture—up for herself. It was hard going for her. She understood less than half of what she read, but she kept at it doggedly. With some success. It was possible to hold a reasonably adult conversation with her for as long as five minutes, now.

"Come on, Laurie; how do you know so much?" he said.

"From Samson," she said promptly. "He's sparking a wench on their place. Wench so light that I reckon old man Cadwallader must have changed his luck down at the quarters. You ought to see her! Real pretty. Samson brought her over here last Sunday morning, so I could see her. That was a sight. I'd loaned him my buggy, and given him one of your Pa's old suits. And a hat. Did he look fine! Wasn't so black, you'd have thought he was a—foreign dignitary. . . ."

"Say that again?" Paris said.

"Say what again? Oh—foreign dignitary. See how educated I'm getting to be?"

"Yes," Paris said; "I'm proud of you, Laurie. . . ."

"Then take me into town!" she said, and kissed him. On the mouth. Hard.

"If you really want to go to Vicksburg," Paris said, "you'd better quit *that.*"

She swung back against the circle of his arms, her blue eyes alight with mischief.

"Well, now," she teased; "maybe we can go to town, later. Better if you're all tuckered out, in case we run into— Candace. Or Ingra. Which one of 'em are you in love with now?"

"Both of them," Paris said. "I cut cards. See which one comes up: the Queen of Hearts or the Queen of Diamonds——"

"And which one does?" Laurie whispered.

"Neither one," Paris said; "it's always the Queen of Spades——"

He stopped, seeing her eyes. Something moved in them. Something like fear.

"Oh, Paris!" she said. "Is *that* what you call me?"

"Yes," he said; "what's wrong with it?"

"Do—do you want to get rid of me, Paris?" she quavered.

"Get rid of you? Lord God, Laurie, what an idea!"

"The Queen of Spades—means death, Paris," she said.

He pulled her close against him. He could feel her trembling. What a child she was! What a forlorn, lovely child!

"Come on, Baby," he said, "go get your bib and tucker——"

She pulled back, stared at him.

"My bib and—— Oh, Paris, you *are* going to take me to Vicksburg, aren't you?"

"Yes, Baby," Paris said.

But there was one matter he hadn't figured on—as if the chances of running into Candace weren't enough. When he left his team at the livery stable near the station, his gaze fell on a horse that the stable hands were rubbing down: a grey horse with the intelligent lift to his head, the brooding gaze, of an Arabian; but the tall, heavy build of a Morgan. A grey. One of the Cadwallader greys. Which meant that Barry or Dion was going to Vicksburg today. Barry likely. To see Ingra. Only this horse didn't look like Barry's favourite mount. Barry's grey was darker than this, with its mane and tail almost black, while this one, although dappled, tended more towards the white Arabian colouring. Its mane and tail were silvery instead of black. Then, looking closer, Paris recognized the gelding. Dion's. The one he usually rode. The showiest of all the Cadwallader greys.

Dear Lord, keep Di out of my way, Paris prayed, and, turning, strode towards the station where Laurel waited.

He had no idea what Vicksburg was like now. His three-year-long pampering of his mind, his nerves, had precluded his acquiring any very detailed knowledge of the world in which he now lived. He had heard, vaguely, that that world had been turned upside down; but hearing it was one thing, while seeing it was another.

For, as they were coming up Main Street in the buggy Paris had rented from a livery stable—combined with the advantages of the railroad was the disadvantage that, since one necessarily had to leave one's own team at home, transportation of some sort had to be hired in Vicksburg—a carriage swept past them: an imposing carriage drawn by two magnificent roans. In comparison to it, their hired buggy looked even shabbier than it actually was. The windows of the carriage were open, and from them dark laughter boomed, mingled with feminine giggles. The man was as black as night; while the woman——

He heard Laurel's low, throaty chuckle.

"Now we'll see how far that freedom and equality business you and Hec are always spouting goes! Don't like it, do you?"

123

"No," Paris admitted miserably; "I know it's irrational, but——"

"Hec and Roberta are one thing; but that there big buck nigger and that there pretty li'l white girl are another, right?"

"Right," Paris said.

"How come?" Laurel said. "The blacker the berry the sweeter the juice, I've always heard. Leasewise that's what you menfolk always say. So what's wrong with that filly's practising a little equality? Can't a girl 'change her luck' too, if she feels like it?"

"Jesus Christ, Laurie!" Paris said; "it *is* different! I don't know why, or how, but seeing that little blonde with——"

"That there great big brunette, charcoal brunette," Laurel said—she was, Paris could see, having herself a time—"just don't sit so well on your nice, advanced, liberal, little old stummick, now does it, Paris, dear?"

He saw she was trying to get him riled, so he threw a check rein on his temper.

"No, it doesn't," he said. "Reckon I'm not so damned liberal after all. . . ."

"Now you're telling the truth!" Laurel laughed. "So I'm going to reward you. That girl isn't white."

"The hell you say, Laurie! I've got eyes. That filly was blonde!"

"I know. You men have been bleaching them enough generations even for that. Her pa's a Swede named Svenson, and her ma's a quadroon. Old Svenson used to stand guard over her with a shot gun during the whole occupation. Scared she'd run off with a Yankee. . . ."

"That," Paris said, "would have made a hell of a lot more sense than this, for my money. . . ."

"Oh, I don't know," Laurel said, "maybe niggers are more fun. . . ."

"Goddammit, Laurie, I'm going to smack you in a minute!" Paris said.

"Why, Paris, you old brute, you!" Laurel said.

The carriage, flaunting its example of near miscegenation, swept on up Main Street, passing a smart landau coming from the opposite direction. This time there was no mistaking the racial identity of the dusky belle who sat in it. She was coppery brown and, Paris admitted without any effort at all, damned good-looking. Her clothes were, of course, extravagant; but against that glowing skin of hers they looked just fine. The landau was being driven by a liveried driver, a wizened little black who escaped being a dwarf by maybe an inch. The black drew the rig up, got down, and entered a store.

Gripped by curiosity, Paris stopped the sway-backed nag that even while doing his level best barely moved their rented buggy, and waited. Five minutes later, his curiosity was fully satisfied. The dwarf came out again, followed by a salesgirl. A white salesgirl. She had a bolt of watered silk in her arms. She was crying. She stood there crying while the dusky belle fingered the rich, watered silk. From the belle's gestures, she was clearly ordering several yards to be cut for her.

"Paris," Laurel said, "I hope you'll excuse my French— but I'll be goddammed!"

Revenge, Paris thought, is sweet, old saw that the saying is. . . . He took it.

"Why, Laurie?" he said. "That little lump of brown sugar sure Lord isn't hard on the eyes. And she's not behaving badly, or being rude, or offensive, or anything——"

"Ha!" Laurel snorted. "So now the shoe's on the other foot, eh, Paris? Brown sugar! I like that! She's not being offensive? Sending in there for a white clerk to come outside and wait on her! If that's not being offensive, will you tell me mighty kindly what is?"

"I," Paris said, "think she was afraid to go in. She probably knows they'd be as rude to her as they dared. And the clerk's a fool. What difference does the colour of that gorgeous creature's skin make, anyhow?"

"None, in the kitchen, where she belongs!"

"Well now," Paris drawled; "the kitchen wasn't exactly where I was thinking of putting her. . . ."

125

"Paris, I'm a going to smack you!" Laurel said.

He threw back his head and laughed aloud.

Laurel stared at him. Then, very slowly, the corners of her mouth started twitching. A chuckle escaped her. Grew into laughter.

"All right," she said; "we're even. I walked right into that one with my eyes wide open, didn't I?"

"You sure Lord did," Paris said. "Say, isn't that Michell's where you wanted to shop?"

"Yes," Laurel said; "but I won't go in right now. Wait 'til *she* leaves. And stop looking at her like that!"

"Sorry," Paris said; "didn't know my lechery was showing. . . ."

"Well, it is. Lord God, Paris; look at that poor kid crying!"

"I'm looking," Paris said; "and I still think she's a fool. She's done the same thing a thousand times, likely, for some of our overstuffed dowagers with more money than brains. Now things have been turned upside down. The coloured folks, some of them, anyhow, have money. How they got it is another matter. Why shouldn't they be accorded a perfectly normal courtesy?"

"You sure weren't even starting to accord that black buck any courtesies a little while ago," Laurel began; then: "Oh Lord, Paris, look!"

But Paris had already jumped down from the buggy and was crossing the street. Fast as he moved, he was too late. By then, Dion Cadwallader had sent the liveried little driver sprawling, torn the bolt of cloth from the clerk and hurled it into the gutter. Now he had the dusky belle by the arm and was dragging her out of the landau.

"All right, nigger wench," he said; "get down on your knees and beg this lady's pardon before I take that there buggy whip to you!"

The girl almost fell out of the buggy. Dion twisted her arm, forcing her to her knees.

"Now," he said, "start begging pardon real soft and sweet and humble, wench; or, by God, I'll——"

"You'll what, Di?" Paris said. Out of the corner of his eye, he could see the salesgirl. She had stopped crying. She was enjoying herself. For some reason Paris found that annoying. He turned to her, said: "Scat!" She did, pouring through that door in a rustle of skirts. By then, Dion's cart-horse of a mind had come up with what to say.

"Well, I'll be goddammed," he said, "if it ain't old loony, himself. Old nigger-loving loony. What's it to you, you crazy fool?"

"A lot," Paris said. "Turn her loose."

Dion grinned.

"This here is your fancy wench?" he said. "And you aim to defend her right in front of Laurie's face? Paris, boy, you don't know what a favour you're doing me!"

So you need favours, Paris thought. Thanks for the information, Di. He said.

"Don't reckon that's your business, Di, one way or the other. But I never did cotton to seeing women abused—not even coloured women. Turn her loose, Di."

"You aim to make me?" Dion said.

Paris smiled. This had gone on too long, now. He knew that Dion didn't want to fight, that all he needed to be given was an easy out.

"If necessary, yes," he said.

"Goddammit, Paris!" Dion said. "You saw what she was doing!"

"Yep," Paris said; "buying herself some watered silk. Hardly a crime. Now stop being unnecessarily stupid and turn her loose."

Dion released the girl. Stripped off his coat, threw it to the ground. Rolled up his sleeves. Fell into a boxer's stance.

Paris stood there grinning at him. At the histrionics. The manoeuvres.

"Oh, come off it, Di," he said; "every time we've had a fight, I've licked you. I can do it again, as you know damned well. So why make me prove it? We're both out of short pants now, boy. And among the childish things we ought to have put away by now is public brawling. . . ."

127

Then, without even waiting for an answer, he took the coloured girl by the arm, helped her to her feet.

"I hope you're all right," he said; "let me help you into your carriage, and——"

He saw Dion bend, pick up his coat, sling it over his shoulder. But the girl was speaking now, and both the timbre and the tone of her voice surprised him.

"Thank you," she said; "you—you're Mr Paris Griffin, aren't you? I've heard so much about you——"

Paris stared at her.

"You have?" he said. "From whom?"

"From a mutual friend: Mrs Trevor. She sure Lord dotes on you!"

"Now ain't we all nice and cosy!" Dion said. "Phew! Reckon I'll just mosey over there and say howdy to Laurie. Since you've got such a taste for dark meat, no reason for you to object, eh, Paris?"

Paris didn't answer him.

"You know Mrs Trevor?" he said. "She's a friend of yours?"

"Of course," the girl said. "I'm Eulalia Randolph, Mr Griffin."

"Bruce Randolph's wife?" Paris said. "I'm mighty glad to make you acquaintance Eu—Mrs Randolph. I've been wanting to meet your husband for the longest time. . . ."

"You'll meet him today," Eulalia said; "that is, if you're going to be in town for at least an hour. He'll come down here to thank you in person for what you've done—for both of the brave things you've done today. . . ."

"Both?" Paris said.

"Yes," she smiled; "coming to my aid, and not quite choking to death on that 'Mrs'. I thank you, too. And more for that than for the other. Defending me cost you less effort. Goodbye, Mr Griffin. All right, Tim—home!"

Paris stood there, watching her go.

"Well, I'll be goddammed!" he said.

He crossed the street to where Dion lounged against the buggy. Before he even got there, he heard Laurel say:

128

"Oh, for God's sake, will you quit pestering me, Di? Haven't you learned by now——"

"No," Paris said; "he hasn't learned by now, Laurie. He's a Southerner. A Mississippian, the quintescence of all Southerners. Which means he hasn't learned anything, or forgotten anything, in all his life. A pity. Maybe even a tragedy."

"Damned right I'm both," Dion said; "and mighty proud of it. That's not the question. The real question, Paris Griffin, is what the hell are you? Besides a nigger-loving scallawag, I mean?"

Paris looked at him. Then he sighed.

"A Southerner. And a Mississippian. In my case, an even greater tragedy," he said.

He put up his arms to Laurel.

"Come on, Baby," he said, "let's get that shopping over with. . . ."

But she didn't move.

"Why?" she said. "Why is it sadder in your case, Paris, love?"

She added that "love" to taunt Dion, Paris was wearily sure. But she did want to know the answer. So he told her, even though she wouldn't understand it.

"Because I, at least, have some idea of what it would be like to join the brotherhood, or maybe even, the race, of man," he said.

Laurel stared at him. Then she sniffed disdainfully.

"Riddles!" she said.

"Yes," Paris said, "riddles. Worse than that: riddles without answers that make any sense at all. Come on, Laurie. . . ."

He helped her down. Walked her across the street under Dion's baffled gaze. Pushed open the door of Michell's for her, thinking: How lonely I am. How goddamned lonely. . . .

"Aren't you coming in with me?" Laurel said.

"No. Shopping for frills and furbelows would bore me to tears. I'll be back for you in a couple of hours. That time enough?"

"Paris," she said, and he heard and recognized what was in her voice; "what—what are you going to do?"

"Me?" he said; "Oh, I'm going to have myself a couple of nice quiet snorts in that bar across the street. Celebrate Manassas. Or Appomattox—or something. . . ."

"Paris!" the thing in her voice was no longer anxiety. Now it was fear. Maybe even terror. "Don't! Please don't! I——"

He smiled at her.

"A couple of snorts. Alone. Not with Dion Cadwallader. But I damned sure don't mean to hunt another bar just because he's gone into that one. So gentle down. I don't even want to know where the body's buried, much less preside at the coroner's inquest. Life's been mighty peaceful, lately. Sort of like to keep it that way. . . ."

"Paris," she wailed; "I wish you'd talk so I could understand you, just once!"

"Now that would be a chore. 'Bye now, Baby," Paris said.

That phrase was getting monotonous. He had heard it all his life, but it seemed to him people said it more frequently now. Standing beside him at the bar, Dion repeated it once again.

"Damned if I can understand you, Paris!" he said.

"I know," Paris said; "so why bother?"

"It's your ideas!" Dion said. "Goddammit, boy, you wore the grey——"

"Butternut brown," Paris corrected him; "wasn't any grey to speak of below General's rank. And I damned sure wasn't a general. . . ."

"All right. But you did your part," Dion went on. "I know a couple of other fellows who rode with old Nat, and they both give you credit for being brave. Told me that even when you got your senses blasted loose, you was riding towards the enemy. So——"

"So?" Paris said.

"So how come you're acting like a traitor, now? You never even cottoned to Hector's ideas 'bout niggers before.

It's the duty of every able-bodied white man to keep the nigger in his place, I tell you!"

"Why?" Paris said.

"Why!" Dion exploded. "Lord God, Paris! We just can't let those black, liver-lipped, burr-headed sons of——"

Paris raised a weary hand.

"Let's change the subject, Di," he said. "The question of the coloured brother is tiresome. You can't imagine how blamed tiresome it really is. . . ."

Dion stood there, glaring at him.

"I'll be damned if I——"

"Can understand me. You said that before. Several times, in fact. Look, Di; to argue about this is a waste of time. Because it's not ideas or even logic that are involved, but feeling. And there are no arguments that have anything to do with the way a body feels about a thing. So let's just skip it, shall we?"

Dion tossed off his snort at a gulp. Banged the shot glass down on the bar. Motioned for the bar-tender to fill it up again.

"All right," he said; "but tell me one thing, Paris. Are you with us or against us?"

Paris looked away from him towards the swinging doors. Looked back again.

"Now that's a question I've often wondered about, myself," he said. "Am I with obscurantism, with unreasoning fear, with the brainless cruelty of children? With irrationality and against thought? Do I really believe I'm a superior being, made in the image of God? And, if I do, must I necessarily join a bunch of simians who haven't evolved yet to prove it? If a thing is so, does it even need proving? And how does a body tell the angels from the apes, anyhow? Complicated business, Di. Far from simple. When I spread out all of its ramifications before me, I'm not at all sure that I know the answer. . . ."

"Damned if Laurie isn't right," Dion growled. "You do talk in riddles, just like she said!"

Paris smiled.

"What else is life," he said, "but a riddle? That is, when it isn't something a hell of a lot worse. All right, I'll try to be clearer: I'd like to be against you knights of the dirty bedsheet. I don't cotton to your methods worth a damn. But, as far as really being against you is concerned, I'm not sure I am. . . ."

"That's a hell of an answer!" Dion said.

"I know. Truthful answers always are," Paris said.

He felt a hand tugging at his sleeve, looked down. The little Negro boy who had touched him carried a shoe-shine box.

"All right, boy," Paris said; "reckon I do need a shine at that. . . ."

"Nosir," the boy whispered; "didn't come in here to shine your shoes, mister. There a coloured gentleman outside who wants to talk to you. A rich coloured gentleman. Give me a whole quarter to come in here and tell you that. . . . You is Mr Paris Griffin, ain't you, cap'n? Mr Tim, the bar-tender, said you was. . . ."

"Yes," Paris said; "and here's another quarter from me for going and telling him I'll be out in a minute. Now you're a rich coloured gentleman, aren't you?"

"Yessir!" the boy said; "I ain't never had a whole half a dollar before in all my life!" Then he turned and scampered through the swinging doors, out into the street.

"What was you and that li'l' nigger whispering about?" Dion said.

Paris looked at Dion speculatively. To have the alleged head of the Warren County Ku Klux Klan witness his meeting with Bruce Randolph was indisputably the worst thing on earth he could do; but, perhaps because it was, it appealed to the sardonic bent of his mind. A catalyst to make things happen fast. A testing to see what an educated black was like; even to see what Dion was like, see if he had any hidden depths, which was a thing that Paris didn't believe.

He tossed a bill on the bar.

"Come on, Di," he said.

Dr Randolph was waiting outside on the sidewalk. Paris,

all his Southern instincts in momentarily complete control, wondered why a nigger—he didn't even correct the word into Negro as he ordinarily would have done—like this one was an offence in the nostrils of God. That is, if God were white, he added wryly. He'd seen dressed-up blacks before, but they'd always been sadly comic caricatures: black men trying to look white, if only in dress. They didn't look natural. A Negro only looked natural in overalls. But this one—Lord God!

I don't have a suit as good as that one, Paris thought; but it's not that. It's the way he wears it, like he's been accustomed to nothing but the best his whole life long. Standing there like he doesn't even know he's a nigger, and gives less than a damn about what I think, or what anybody thinks, this side of hell. . . .

The whole thing became suddenly, irresistibly funny. And it was characteristic of Paris that his wry, secret laughter included himself.

"Dr Randolph?" he said; and, watching Dion's face as he did so, put out his hand.

Bruce Randolph took it.

"I presume you're Mr Griffin?" he said. "And this other gentleman?"

"Mr. Cadwallader, a friend of mine," Paris said.

Randolph offered Dion his hand as well.

Dion stared at it for a good half a minute before he bothered to open his mouth.

"I don't shake hands with niggers," he said.

Randolph's expression didn't even change.

"As you like," he said calmly; "your manners or your lack of them are your own concern, sir. Mr Griffin, I must ask your indulgence for sending in after you that way; but I've had a few unpleasant experiences. . . ."

"And you don't want them repeated?" Paris said.

Bruce Randolph smiled.

"Say, rather, that I prefer to conserve my energies for more important struggles than quarrelling over the right to drink a glass of whisky in a common dram shop," he said.

"Isn't even that a part of the equality you're fighting for, Doctor?" Paris said.

Randolph's gaze became a little quizzical.

"When I find my equals, I'll take the necessary steps to associate with them," he said; "and, when I do, I don't think they'll object. . . ."

Paris threw back his head and laughed aloud.

"You're right," he said. "You know any place where we can sit and talk without starting a race riot?"

"Why, yes. As a matter of fact, I was going to suggest precisely that. But—your friend?"

"I'd like him to come along, if neither one of you objects," Paris said. "You see, I've been trying to reconstruct him all morning, and——"

"Count me out," Dion said. "The only time I want to be around niggers is when they're waiting on me. And when they know how to say yessir, mighty soft and humble!"

Bruce Randolph stared at him.

"A pity," he said. "You miss so much that way, Mr Cadwallader."

In spite of himself, Dion was intrigued, Paris saw.

"Just what the hell do I miss, Randolph?" he said.

"Variety, perhaps. The impact of different minds, other habits of thought. Even the opportunity to stop fighting with yourself, to give way to the sense of decency you must have hidden about you somewhere, and relax. Definitely a more pleasant way to live. . . ."

"Don't understand you," Dion said; "maybe I could if you'd talk like a natural nigger for a change."

Bruce Randolph smiled.

"Unfortunately," he said, "I know no other way of expressing myself, Mr Cadwallader. I was born in Boston. My father was sexton of Christ Church. I was taught to read and write at five years of age. I assure you my speech is perfectly normal for a man of my background and my education. But let that pass. I think I'd better explain that it is not my custom to force my presence upon anyone, male or female, black or white, who finds it in the slightest degree objectionable. Still less to waste my precious time upon people whom *I* find objectionable. Though that's a rule I waive upon occasions——"

"Why?" Paris said.

"When I think I can do some good; make a convert to the idea of simple human decency. The opportunities are not many, I can tell you. So, when one arises, I take it, despite my feeling. We need all the friends possible. . . ."

"So, in this case?" Paris said.

"What do *you* think, Mr Griffin?"

"Hopeless," Paris said. "Be seeing you, Di. . . ."

"Not if I see you first, Paris Griffin," Dion said.

10

BRUCE RANDOLPH looked at Paris. Picked up the double shot glass filled with raw whisky. Downed it at a gulp. Said:

"Just what do you mean, Mr Griffin?"

So, Paris thought, that skin is thin despite its colour. Now, let me see—what shall I hit you with next?

"I mean," he said, "that you, yourself, don't believe what you're saying; maybe not even in what you're fighting for. You're an intelligent man, even a brilliant one; I grant you that. But how do you know you aren't just an exception? The rare exception that proves the rule?"

"Or even," Bruce said, "how do I know that I'm really brilliant, or even intelligent? How much of my success has been due to concessions made me by idealists surprised at the dog walking on his hind legs? Not that he does it well, y'know; but——"

"That he does it at all," Paris said. "*That*, no. You'd stand out in any company, black or white. But are you sure you can find your like in reasonable numbers among your people? You'll need them, you know—leaders not merely *as* intelligent as the whites who oppose you, but actually superior to them in brains, character, will. Can you find them, Bruce Randolph?"

Randolph bowed his head. Looked up; called:

"Bring us another whisky, Peter. Hell, bring us the whole bottle!"

Why am I doing this? Paris thought. I don't dislike this man. Rather like him, in fact; certainly I admire him. Have I sunk to the Di Cadwallader-Henry Thurston level? Become one of the miserable bastards who wears his hide as a badge? Who, having nothing, knowing nothing, being capable of nothing, not even rational thought, must say: "Well, gawddammit, at least I'm white!" To which the answer is: "So is a billy goat, usually." Move over, Di! Get that stinking bedsheet ready. I join you in illogic: I am prepared to fight, to bend all my energies to the ridiculous proposition that a race of mindless sub-humans must be watched every minute, sat upon, struck down, to keep them from rising. If they are brainless, why bother? And, if they're not, who can stop them?

"I'm sorry," he said; "I'm afraid I've been baiting you——"

"Your question makes sense," Randolph said, thickly, the whisky clearly having its effect upon him, now. "And the answer is, no. I can't find them. Badly as we need the kind of men you described, it'll take a hundred years——"

"Or forever," Paris said.

"Or forever," Bruce Randolph whispered; "until the last dregs of the poison of bondage have been bred out of us; until what living in a white man's world, anywhere in a white man's world, including Boston, Massachusetts, has done to us, has been overcome, vanquished——"

"And what has it done?" Paris said.

"Made us doubt ourselves profoundly," Randolph said. "I tell you that no white man on earth believes half so firmly in our inferiority as we do ourselves. I think that belief is false, no matter who holds it; but——"

"But you hold it yourself, don't you?" Paris said.

Bruce Randolph looked away from him, out of the doors, to where the afternoon sunlight slanted along that street.

"I came down here with such high hopes," he said. "I was prepared to make allowances. I still am. I keep telling myself that prejudice creates a grotesque caricature of the thing it presupposes; but——"

"But what, Doctor?" Paris said.

"This mindless, gibbering horde of black monkeys! Dear God! Educate them? How? In the name of God, Mr Griffin, tell me how?"

"You might start by reducing your style of living a trifle," Paris said. "County superintendents don't ordinarily have two carriages, nor fine houses, nor servants, nor do they dress like you and Mrs Randolph do. Why don't you try building a few schools for a change?"

Bruce Randolph stared at him out of bleary eyes.

"You're accusing me of embezzlement?" he said.

"I'm not accusing you of anything," Paris said. "I'm merely pointing out to you that you're making excuses to yourself. How the devil do you know what your people can do, if you don't give them a chance? You said your father was a fugitive slave. Suppose he'd stayed down here? Ever thought about that, Bruce Randolph?"

"Yes. I should have been one of the mindless monkeys. Maybe I'd have been better off. Preferable, isn't it, to being——"

"Stop it," Paris said. "What you're doing is between you and the Good Lord. I don't want to know about it. What I really want to know is whose side *are* you on?"

"I don't know sometimes," Bruce Randolph muttered, "I don't know. We aren't a young race; but where are our monuments, our temples, our poetry? What have we ever done but made good slaves for other people? Who hasn't enslaved us? The Egyptians, the Greeks, the Romans, the Portuguese, the Spanish, *you*. . . . And, as I said, we made good slaves. Did you hear me? *Good* slaves! There is nothing more dishonourable. No wonder we're despised. You don't despise the Indian, do you? You hate him, you fear him; but you respect him. And why? Because he fights. Goddammit, how he fights!"

"Maybe because he's more savage," Paris said.

Bruce looked at him, dimly, sadly.

"In a savage world, savagery's an admirable quality," he said. "Docility's no attribute of greatness, Mr Griffin."

"Your turn will come," Paris said. "Maybe because you're not fighters. Maybe because of your patience, your good humour. I think you'll roll over us one day by sheer weight of numbers. The white races are outnumbered now; we're mighty few in comparison to the yellow, the brown, and the black peoples. And when you do——"

Bruce Randolph laughed bitterly.

"We'll put you on trial as criminals of war, like the Federals did Major Wirtz of Andersonville. If that time comes during my lifetime, I'd like to offer my services as attorney for the defence!"

"What plea would you offer?" Paris said.

"A new theory of the law: guilt of the victim. That sheep have no rights. That when they tempt the lion by being sheep, it is they, not he, who sin!"

"That's pretty far fetched," Paris said.

"Is it? I contend that people who don't know that any-thing—massacre, annihilation, death by fiendish torture, what you will—is preferable to slavery, have forfeited the world's compassion, and maybe even God's. All right, I can't absolutely absolve the slaver, I suppose. To enslave a human being is a sin, a crime. But to *let* one's self be enslaved, Mr Griffin? To accept the obscene depth of degradation that slavery involves, or the only slightly less degree of it under which we exist now? There is no word for that in any language on earth. No way to describe how contemptible it is. Because, in the final analysis, only one thing defines the stature of a man——"

"And that is?" Paris prompted.

"Knowing when, and how, to die," Bruce Randolph said.

Paris sat there, looking at him.

Funny thing, he thought, I've felt sorry for coloured folks before. But never quite this sorry. I suppose it's because this is—tragedy. Not even this mind, this first-class mind, can lift him out of the prison of his skin. Wish I could help him. Wish there was something I could do. . . .

Then he saw Candace coming through the door of the little Negro hash house and bar in which they sat: that place that no white woman should have even known existed, not to mention where it was.

He stood up, seeing her coming towards him in a great blaze, as though all the sunlight in the world had come in with her. The blaze was imaginary, he knew. It was the way he felt that pooled golden upon that dingy, ill-scrubbed floor, ran upward along the walls, flickered across the ceiling. It was his joy that flamed, leaped, stood tall. A yard from him, she stopped.

"Paris," she whispered, "Paris——"

He didn't move. He stood there, seeing with suddenly clearing eyes how painfully thin she was, the dark circles of fatigue beneath her eyes, the lines of suffering tugging at her mouth. But then, almost instantly, he saw it didn't matter, that the traceries of time, the marks of suffering were as nothing against her unique beauty; that it would take death itself to extinguish it, that she would be almost as breathtaking at sixty as she was now, precisely because that beauty was not of her flesh but of the soul he was, irrationally enough, quite willing to concede her, while denying such an illusory attribute to everybody else on earth, including, be it said, himself.

"Please forgive me," she said, her voice high, a little breathless; "I had to come. When Eulalia told me that you and Bruce were——"

"God bless Eulalia!" Paris said, and took both her hands in his.

Bruce Randolph got heavily to his feet. He swayed a little. "Please do sit down, Mrs Trevor," he said with drunken gravity.

"Oh, Bruce!" Candace said sadly; "you've been drinking again! And you promised Eulalia——"

"It was my fault," Paris said. "I've been plaguing him, I'm afraid. Rubbing him on some mighty sore spots. . . ."

"Pete!" Candace said with crisp authority; "make us some coffee. Strong, black; no cream or sugar. . . ."

"Yes'm, Miz Trevor," the bar-tender said. "It's already made. Bring it to y'all right away. . . ."

"You've been here before, then?" Paris said, as he held the chair for her to sit down.

"Quite often, with Eulalia and Bruce. That's why they know me here," Candace said.

"Please forgive me, Mrs Trevor," Bruce Randolph said; "but things get to be unbearable sometimes. . . ."

"I know," Candace said, "I know that only too well. Let's

make a pact, Bruce: I'll forgive you, if you'll forgive me."

"Forgive you? Good heavens, Mrs Trevor—for what?"

"For interrupting your chat with Paris. For coming here, where I have no right to be, to see a man who belongs to someone else. Only, I had to. I wasn't strong enough not to. At the risk of having both of you think I'm a brazen hussy, I came. . . ."

"If you only were," Paris groaned, "if you only were!"

"Perhaps I am," Candace said with a smile that shaded off into a grimace, "which is why I'm going to be safely home within the hour, long before either of us is tempted to try to find out. But I must say I'm disappointed in you, Paris. . . ."

"Are you?" Paris said. "Why?"

"You look so well! Rested. Filled out. Fairly purring with contentment. I'm human enough to admit that I'd hoped you were suffering, too. You look wonderful. While I need only a broomstick to join an ancestress of mine who was hanged, quite justifiably, I'll bet, a couple of hundred years back. A broomstick—or a ducking-stool. Preferably the ducking-stool——"

"Why the ducking-stool, Mrs Trevor?" Bruce Randolph said.

"There are," Candace laughed, "certain feverish states that cold water—helps. . . ."

The bar-tender, with accidental mercy, broke the appalled silence by appearing with the coffee. Candace wouldn't take any.

"I'm nervous enough now," she said. "Tell me, Paris, how is—Laurel?"

Paris looked at her.

"Are you being malicious, Candy?" he said. "Or do you really want to know?"

"Both," Candace said. "Being a woman, I can't help being malicious, but I really do want to know."

"Why?" Paris said.

"Because," Candace said, "the way you'll answer will tell me so many things. . . ."

"And if I don't answer at all?"

"That will tell me even more."

"Excuse me, please," Bruce Randolph said suddenly, putting down the cup he'd already emptied four times, hot as that coffee was, "but I'm afraid I'm getting sober. Perhaps I had better go home, or to my office, or to the devil, so that you two——"

"Can indulge in sinful verbal banter?" Candace said. "No, Bruce. Please don't go. Stay here and chaperon me. You'll be doing me a favour, I assure you. Time we changed this subject, anyhow. . . ."

"No," Paris said, "not until I've answered your question. Laurie is fine. She's reading all those books you told her to read. She has improved immensely in nearly every respect. She would make any man a lovely, charming wife. . . ."

Candace bowed her head. Brought it up again, smiled with lips gone whiter than her face. Said:

"Thanks, Paris. I deserved that. You can be—brutal, can't you?"

"Yes," Paris said, pain shaking his voice. "Now I'll ask you one: How is Henry?"

"Clinging to life," Candace said, "to the slender thread of life that's all he has left, now. He's been desperately sick a dozen times. Only he doesn't want to die. He can't face the prospect of leaving me behind—for you, or some other man, to enjoy. . . ."

"And you," Bruce Randolph said, "nurse him like an angel. Let's read that into the record, shall we? You've saved his life each of those dozen times to my certain knowledge. I find that awe-inspiring. When all you'd have to do would be to—neglect some small detail; fall asleep, say, for an hour, instead of watching, waiting, fighting for——"

"What I don't want," Candace said quietly, "for the life that is a burden to him as well as to me. Only, don't fit me with the halo of a saintly martyr, Bruce. I do it because I'm a coward."

"A coward!" Bruce snapped. "Nonsense, Candace!" He saw Paris's face tighten with shock. "Forgive me, Mr

Griffin," he said; "but Mrs Trevor and I are old friends. She doesn't insist upon the title——"

"In fact, it would be rather unnatural between good friends," Candace said. "Go on, Bruce. It's comforting to have someone laud my virtues—my quite nonexistent virtues. You were saying?"

"That to endure Henry Trevor is a martyrdom. I grant him his motives, but they don't excuse him. Other men in his position have learned not to complain. What you do, calls for courage, Can— Mrs Trevor."

"Oh, call her Candace if you like," Paris said, "reckon I've got to become civilized one of these days."

"Thank you. And, by saying that, you've taken the first step. Candace, Mrs Trevor, whatever we call her, is very brave. To do what she does——"

"No," Candace said; "I do it out of cowardice. To me, murder by omission remains—murder. Less worthy of respect or pardon even than the laying of violent hands upon one's victim, which at least calls for decision, nerve. And Paris knows what too much guilt can do to the human soul. I'm afraid of that. Afraid of despising myself more than I do now. So I accept my penance for my sins——"

"What sins?" Paris said.

She looked him in the face, and said it then:

"'As any man thinketh in his heart, so is he,' and, 'If any man looketh after a woman with lust after her in his heart, he hath——' and vice versa, Paris. Oh God, how I wish I could learn to lie a little! Or at least to keep my unbridled tongue in check. . . ."

"I don't," Paris said, "what I wish is that you'd pay a trifle closer attention to the rules of grammar."

She stared at him, wide-eyed. So did Bruce.

"I said, if I may quote myself, 'she would make any man,' and so forth. 'Would', third person, singular number, present conditional. Implying a reservation, or a doubt. Would make any man on earth a lovely, perfect wife; make him divinely happy, even. Any man—except me. . . ."

"Now I *know* it's time to change the subject!" Candace

said, "before we all become despondent and take to drink. Now, what shall we talk about?"

"A suggestion," Paris said; "I've got nearly two thousand dollars saved. They're yours, Bruce, to help build your school. My brother, Hector, has already deeded you a plot of land. Three years ago, to be exact. Or you can still use the Baptist Church——"

"I wish we didn't have to," Candace said, "either that land or the church. Not because they aren't perfect. But because I'm going to teach in that school, Paris. And that site is awfully close to Griffin's Way. . . ."

"And I," Bruce Randolph said, "have more than five thousand, out of the funds you accused me—with some justice—of misappropriating. The truth is that the cost of the Lovegood School was considerably less than they had anticipated, labour costs in the South being what they are. I should have returned the surplus, of course; but I justified my dishonesty on the grounds of altruism and expediency— to take care of Eulalia and the children—we have two, now you know, a boy and a girl—when the present political currents grow strong enough for the Klan to feel safe in assassinating me. But Eulalia won't mind. She'll be glad to make the sacrifice so she can stop feeling ashamed of the man she made the grave mistake of marrying. . . ."

"Good enough," Paris said. "Since everybody in the state today who has sufficient authority to be able to bring you to trial is at least twice as guilty as you are, you had to judge yourself. So now you've done it. You're restoring what you've stolen, and I don't need any words written in the dirt to keep my hands away from rocks. So now, let's forget it, and move on. Another point: Hector and I will supply you with free labour. Now, wait a minute! All I meant is that I'll ask my hands to volunteer. To build a school for their kids, I have no doubt they will."

"Thank you," Bruce Randolph said. "And I'm going to take a train for Boston, tomorrow!"

"Oh, Bruce, why?" Candace said.

"To raise more money. I don't want this school to be a

part of the county school system. It's got to be private, beyond the manipulation and thievery of politicians. And it should be built of brick——"

"Right—for the same reason Hector's building that imposing mansion of his of brick," Paris said; "more difficult to burn. Say—that's an idea! Hector has set up a first-class kiln on his place, and clay doesn't cost anything. . . ."

"Except labourers who dig, shape, and burn it," Bruce said.

"Again, in this case, volunteers," Paris said.

They sat there, all three of them, looking at each other.

"How long?" Candace whispered.

"A year——" Bruce Randolph said.

"Six months, or less," Paris said. "Candace——"

"Yes, Paris?" Saying his name, her voice transformed the words. To anyone with an ear for nuances, they came out: "Yes, my love?"

"It's got to be Hector's place. Or Griffin's Way, itself. Nobody else would sell or lease the land for this. Nobody else but us would dare. And Bruce needs your services. The kids do. . . ."

"All right," Candace said; "I'll fast and pray. Wear hairshirts. Practise the mortification of the flesh. . . ."

"I just don't believe that, Candace, dear," Laurel Griffin said.

They whirled then, all three of them. Paris had a wryly acute image of how ludicrous they must have looked.

"Laurel!" Candace said. "I——"

"Don't worry, Candace," Laurel said; "I'm not going to slap your face, or even make a scene. You've taught me how to be a lady, too well—with those books of yours and by example, too, I reckon. All I'm going to do is to ask you to lend me my husband back again, at least long enough to take me home. And I'm even going to wait until I'm out of here, before I start to —cc c cry—Oh, dammit, here I go!"

"Paris," Candace said; "go to her."

"Yes," Laurel said; "come to me, Paris—by her leave. She's being mighty generous; I know that. And lend me

145

your handkerchief, and a dime to give that little nigger shoe-shine boy who brought me here and——"

"Don't you think it's worth more than a dime, Laurie?" Paris said.

"Yep," Laurel said; "give him a dollar. Give him ten. You set the price on it, Paris—I don't know what it's worth. Just how do you figure out the value of a broken home? How much do you pay for a busted heart?"

Paris, stood up, slowly.

"Write me from Boston, Bruce," he said. "My humblest apologies, Candace. . . ."

"Why?" Candace said. "You didn't bring me here. I came on my own accord."

She got up, went to Laurel.

"Laurel," she said; "listen to me. I found out by accident your husband was meeting Dr Randolph here, and came a-flying. Yes—that makes me all the dirty things you're calling me in your mind. Only, I want you to know that Paris had nothing to do with it. It wouldn't be fair if I didn't tell you that. . . ."

"Candace, please!" Paris said.

"Do you believe me, Laurel?" Candace said.

Laurel looked at her a long time. While she looked, she went on crying.

"No," she said at last; "you're still a woman, Candace—and us women part company from the truth the minute that we're born. Maybe even before. Paris, will you come on?"

There are some situations, Paris thought, from which a man can never escape with either dignity or grace. . . .

"Sorry, friends," he said, and took Laurel's arm.

It was very late. Nearly two o'clock in the morning. With a grimace, Paris got up and put on his dressing-gown. Then he started down the hall towards the guest bedroom: that guest bedroom Laurel had locked herself into. But, halfway there, he stopped.

Would any woman, he thought, who was guilty of what I'm nearly three-quarters sure that little Laurie has done at least once, react like this? Then he answered his own question: Hell, yes! Women—with the possible exception of Candace—are *never* guilty in their own eyes. They were dragged into it, forced into it, tormented into it, anything on earth but a voluntary entrance into a state of sin because they damned well felt like sinning at the moment. Built-in rejection of the idea of personal responsibility. Let's face it: Laurie *is* shocked; she *is* outraged by my alleged faithlessness. And, even if she did once or twice stray down the primrose path, *that* has absolutely nothing in the world to do with *this*——

He went on down the hall. Knocked on the door of the guest bedroom. There was no answer. He hadn't really expected one. He knew just how stubborn Laurel could be. By pure reflex, he let his hand drop to the doorknob. Turned it. The door swung open with a noisy squeak.

But Laurel was no longer in the room. The bed was smooth, untouched. Her nightgown lay across the foot of it.

Paris turned. Went back to their own bedroom. Dressed with icy calm. Went downstairs to his study. Opened the drawer of his desk; took out his big Dance revolver, his cavalryman's sidearm that General Grant had generously allowed the defeated Confederates to keep; looked to its priming of copper percussion caps; stuck it back in its holster; belted it on. Then he went out to the stables and saddled his roan, noting as he did so that Prince was gone.

He rode off, thinking: When I catch them, I'm going to shoot—just like any other idiot would in my place. Conform to the norms of my upbringing, the customs of my world. My backward, benighted, savage world. Hurrah for us. Knights of Southern chivalry. Whip-wielders. Shack-burners. Nigger-lynchers. Men who equate murder with the loss of the exclusive possession of a woman's body. Defend my honour. The honour of a Southern gentleman—which honour can be defined by our actions, by the fact that, having been beaten fairly in a war that we did our best to win, we now descend to methods that would make a buzzard puke in order to negate the results of that contest. By our fruits ye shall know us, and our fruits are ignorance, barbarity and man's inhumanity to man. But I'm going to shoot, all the same; knowing all that, I'm still going to shoot. . . .

Half an hour later, he came out in a little clearing near the hunting lodge. Laurel was there, sitting on Prince, and staring into the double night, under the trees.

But she was alone.

Paris came up to her. Studied her pale, averted face.

"So he didn't come?" he said.

"Who didn't come, Paris?" she said tonelessly.

"Di Cadwallader," Paris said.

She jerked her face around towards him. He could see her features tightening with shock, with fear. Her gaze swept over him.

"You—you brought your gun," she whispered; "Oh, Paris, you brought your gun!"

"So?" he said.

Instead of answering, she reined Prince in beside him, leaned toward him until he had to put his arms around her to keep her from falling. She lay against him, shaking all over, soaking his shirt-front with her tears.

"Well, I'll be goddamned!" Paris said.

"Oh, Paris, honey!" she sobbed; "I'm so b b b blamed h h happy!"

"Why?" he said, his voice gentling now.

"Because y y y you c c cared! You cared enough to k k kill a m m m man over me!"

"Another man," Paris said.

"N n n no. Hil didn't count. You didn't kill him—you tried not to. But now——"

"Now what? Were you planning to give me grounds to shoot Di, Laurie? If you were, I'm damned sure going to take my riding crop to you when I get you home"'

She lifted her face. Smiled.

"It's worth a beating to know you love me," she said.

"Were you, Laurie?" Paris said.

"No. I just rode out because I felt so rotten I couldn't

148

sleep. Paris—did she tell the truth? I'll believe it, if you say so. You—you really didn't send for her to meet you there?"

"In a restaurant that doesn't even have upstairs back bedrooms to rent? Laurie, how silly can even you get to be?"

"When I think somebody's trying to take you from me," Laurel said, "silly's not the word. . . ."

"What is?" Paris said.

"Crazy. Plain stark raving crazy," Laurel said.

Riding back towards the house, Paris could see that Laurel was planning to cement their reconciliation in the usual fashion. But now the swift, unreasoning anger had drained out of him, leaving him nerveless and cold. He found, oddly, that he didn't want to. Worse, Candace's image rose unbidden so that, looking at Laurel, he realized that what he felt was more than reluctance, that it was something closer to actual revulsion—a faint sickness tugging at his middle.

He didn't say anything. He knew better than to pretend fatigue or a headache. Laurel's sure instincts would see through his pretence at once; and she would attribute his coldness, accurately enough, to how he felt about Candace. Better to go through with it. The sacrifice was small, and not entirely unpleasant, despite his mood.

But, when they came up the alley of oaks, they saw all the windows of the big house dancing with fire.

"Come on, Laurie!" Paris said, and clapped spurs to his roan. Laurel gave Prince his head, matching the roan stride for stride. They burst into the courtyard before the house, and saw, now that the angle of their view was changed, the windows untouched, lightless, black, no longer throwing back the reflections of the cross that flamed grotesquely in the yard.

"Paris," Laurel whispered, "that means the Kluxers, doesn't it?"

"Yes," Paris said, and swung down from his horse. He wondered if they were there still, in the shadows, watching.

But it made no difference if they were. The only thing that gave him pause was wondering exactly what to do. He had a soldier's contempt for heroics, for gestures. He knew that the bravest actions he'd ever seen had been done simply, woodenly, casually and without style. He'd led his share of cavalry charges, but he suspected that his troopers had always been more effective dismounted, lying on their bellies and shooting with care. His original impulse—to get an axe, and send that fiery cross crashing to earth—had that great fault. It was theatrical, showy. It didn't express the icy contempt he felt.

So, in the end, he went around the house to the pump. Came back with two oaken pails of water. Doused the fire with them. Stood there, watching it sizzle out. Laurel came towards him, had almost reached him when the ball ploughed into the earth a yard in front of him, throwing up clods of earth almost as high as his head; and he, through the flame-splattered whistling crack that came to him a measurable fraction of a second after the bullet had already dug dirt, said:

"Get back, Laurie!" And she:

"No, Paris! They kill you, they'll have to kill me, too!"

And Dion's voice, clearly:

"Come on, boys—let's get out of here. His woman's with him. We'll finish it another time. . . ."

Then the sound of horses, muffled, ghostly, moving out beneath the trees.

"Paris——" Laurel's voice was tentative; "Paris, you—you're all right?"

"Yes," he said, thinking as he said it: All right? Is anyone ever all right in this world?

She came to him in a blind rush. Clung to him, her body not trembling or quivering, but jerking, spasmodic, torn with convulsions that he couldn't bear watching, so he drew her to him, raised his hand, stroked her dark hair, said:

"Don't be frightened, Baby; they've gone. . . ."

"Paris——" she said; "Paris——" Then, because she was still in shock, and no other words would come, she said it

150

again, babbling like an idiot child: "Paris, Paris, Paris, Paris!"

"Come on, Laurie," he said; and led her towards the house, feeling her body subsiding into mere trembling now; and he, holding her against him, walking slowly, carefully, thought:

The lines are drawn now, and this is war. Looks like I've volunteered for the duration, or been conscripted. Yep— conscripted. By Candace, by a stupid impulse towards pity for a mental freak of a nigger cursed with a mind. Anyhow, I'm in this: a hayfoot pushed forward into the front ranks of a cause I don't even believe in, except maybe a little. But now partial commitments aren't even possible, and I can't salve my conscience by giving a few paltry dollars and a stretch of land toward the education of piccaninnies who can't be educated any more than a mule can, and maybe even less. So now I'm going to die, very likely, outnumbered and alone, to demonstrate that Sambo Cuffey has certain inalienable rights; that among these are life, liberty and——

He stopped. Threw back his head and laughed. Clearly, gaily.

"Paris!" Laurel said.

"He has," Paris said aloud; "by God, he has! Unless we can exclude him from the race of man, which we can't, because the main thing wrong with him now is that he's too damned human, we've got to grant him those things or see them lost to everybody in a hundred years of terror, with our blood, and our children's children's, soaking the ground, with the best of us and the worst converted into buzzard's food, without our qualities or the lack of them making a damned bit of difference to the buzzard. That's why——"

"Paris, honey, you feel all right?" Laurel said.

"—we can't surrender the South to the Klan, Laurie; why our impulses toward decency, however few and reluctant, must be maintained at any cost. Because it's not just Sambo. It's us—all of us—one nation indivisible under God, no matter what multicoloured hides compose it. That, and a few other things——"

"What things, Paris?" Laurel said, clearly trying to humour him, now, at least long enough to get him inside where she could make him lie down with maybe a cold compress on his forehead.

"Hard to tell you, Baby," Paris said; "without using words so big they sound specious and suspect. Long, solemn, two-dollar words that maybe mean something, after all: Freedom. Justice. Human dignity. Those, Baby, and all the inalienable rights of man: to laugh, to loaf, to go fishing on Sunday instead of to church, to chaw tobacco and spit on the sidewalk, to write a book or paint a picture without anybody's telling him what to put in, or take out; to love his neighbour, and maybe even his neighbour's wife, a little better than he does himself—Oh hell, Laurie, to be a man, and not a thing. That's what it all comes down to. And that's what I'm fighting for. . . ."

"Paris, you're *sure* you feel all right?" Laurel wept.

"Yes, Baby; now I feel just fine," Paris said.

PARIS looked at Laurel, sitting beside him in the rented buggy. These trips into town were getting to be a habit. It seemed to him that every time the weather was anything less than downright threatening, she found some excuse to drag him off to Vicksburg. Oh well, he thought; guess that's part of the penalty for committing matrimony.

"Michell's?" he said.

"Of course, honey," Laurel said; "where else could I buy white silk, and tulle for veiling?"

He turned the nag towards Main Street. Funny, he thought, but Laurie epitomizes the South. No use whatsoever for niggers in general; but nothing's too good for Samson. A real pet, that's what she's made of him. Any other buck on the place could damn well jump over a broomstick, and that would be ceremony enough. But not Samson. He's got to have a real wedding in the Baptist Church, white gowns for bride and bridesmaids, flowers, ushers, the works. Costing me a pretty penny; and, although we didn't suffer too much from the panic last year, I don't have money to throw around. Reckon those wenches are going to look like flies drowned in buttermilk in all that white—except the bride. Lord, that child is pretty! *Café au lait,* with a little more coffee than milk; but her ancestry certainly shows. Barry's going to give her away, just like a father, instead of her half-brother, which he probably is. Surely is—or why would Di have left a filly like that one grow up untouched? That's one taboo that's mighty strong. Only swamp-bottom folks break it to my knowledge. . . .

"Paris!" Laurel said; "they're mighty far off, but isn't that Barry driving that rig? Yes, it is! Out spooning with that big horse, Ingra, this early in the day!"

"Baby," Paris said; "Ingra may be big; but she sure has got her weight distributed in mighty fine fashion. Damned if her waist is very much bigger than yours. Actually, in proportion to the rest of her, it's even smaller. . . ."

"Corsets," Laurel sniffed. "Stays. Bet she's laced up so damn' tight——"

"No," Paris said, "she isn't. Nary a stay under that there dress. It's all Ingra; and mighty, mighty fine. . . ."

"Paris Griffin! Would you mind telling me how the devil you know *that*?"

"Well now, Laurie," Paris said; "it was like this: One night I was in town drinking with the boys——"

"Oh, foot!" Laurel said. "You're plaguing me again. You don't go to town, and you don't drink with the boys, for the very simple reason that you're an outcast. You and Barry both, because of that stupid nigger school you all are building. Never heard of anything so ridiculous in my life! Don't you realize that you've got about as much chance of teaching a nigger some book learning as you have teaching a mule to do sums?"

"I more than half agree with you," Paris said. "That's why I'm doing it."

"Paris Griffin, you don't make sense!"

"Who does in this world? Both Candace and Ingra, and occasionally even Barry, call me an old diehard. So now it's become a sporting proposition. We build that school. They teach even one little coon to read half as well as a white child the same age, I'll owe them all a big blow-out at the Planter's Hotel. They don't, you and I will be the guests of honour, and they, or at least Barry, will pick up the tab. Fair enough, isn't it?"

"No. They were silly to make a bet like that. You'll win, though that makes no sense either 'cause even a banquet can't pay you back for all the money you've spent on that school. Look, Paris; they coming this way. . . Don't go so fast! Let 'em catch up. . . . Anyhow, I don't believe that's the reason you did it: You don't ever tell me the real truth, mostly because you get so tired of having to explain things so I can understand them. But this time I wish you would. Why are you building that school, Paris?"

"Because," Paris said, "I may be wrong. Maybe they *can* learn. And, if they can, we've no right to deny them an education. . . ."

"Ha!" Laurel hooted. "Who ever heard of a nigger who could learn anything beyond how to plough a straight furrow and chop cotton—and that with a white man watching him every minute to make sure he does it right?"

"Samson," Paris said; "who's the finest blacksmith and worker in wrought iron I've ever seen. That's skill, Laurie. And Bruce Randolph, who's harder still to answer. Two black men who've learned a hell of a lot. . . ."

"Exceptions," Laurel said promptly. "Samson's the best nigger in the whole state and that there Bruce Randolph is purely a freak. Fair makes a body's head swim with all those big words. Now shut up, will you? Here they come! Why, howdy, Barry? Miss Holm, I must say you're looking mighty fine. . . ."

"Thank you, Mrs Griffin," Ingra said. Her voice sounded sad. Still getting nowhere with Barry, Paris thought.

"Maybe you can help me," Laurel went on in her best *ingénue's* tone.

Head for the woods, men, Paris groaned inside his mind, because hell is sure getting set to pop loose when my Laurie starts being *this* sweet!

"Howdy, folks?" Barry said.

Paris eyed him, thinking: Seems mighty calm. Wonder if he's convinced Ingra that fence-building prior to putting in a crop is absolutely necessary. Don't think so, but nobody, not even the Good Lord, has nullified human nature yet. . . .

"Help you how, Mrs Griffin?" Ingra said.

"To pick out the dress goods for Samson's wedding," Laurel said. "You know he's marrying a wen—a girl—off Barry's place and——"

"But I ought to pay for that part, myself," Barry said. "Lucinda's almost like family——"

Almost? Paris thought; but all he said was: "Forget it, Barry. This is Laurie's pet project. She's like a child with a new toy. . . ."

"Can't you spare me your sweetheart for a little while?" Laurel said, her voice so wistful, wheedling, like a little girl begging for a peppermint stick, that Paris had to smother his impulse to say, "Oh, Laurie, for God's sake!" aloud.

"Why, sure, Laurie," Barry said. "That is, if you don't mind, Ingra?"

"No, Barry," Ingra said; "I don't mind at all."

Translation, Paris's sardonic thought ran: "I mind like hell. I hate this simpering little southern bitchkitty's guts. But for you, Barry, darlin'—anything. Anything at all. Even —this. . . ."

Barry got down from the buggy, helped Ingra down in her turn. But, Paris saw, he wouldn't have to help Laurel. She had already jumped down with kittenish grace. Now, affectionately, she put her arm around Ingra's waist. Paris laughed then, clearly, and loud.

"Yes or no?" he said.

"No!" Laurel said. "And now I really want to know how you know!"

Ingra's face went very pale.

"Yes or no, what, Paris?" she said.

"Nothing, Honey," Paris said; "A little bet 'twixt Laurie and me. She's just mad because she lost."

"Since it seems that *I* was the subject of this bet," Ingra said; "don't you think it would be fairer to tell me what it's all about?"

"Well——" Paris hesitated; "it's nothing much, Ingra. Sort of thing that passes between husband and wife, so it shouldn't offend you. I was admiring your figure out loud as you and Barry drove up, so Laurie bet me you wore stays. . . ."

"And you bet her I didn't?" Ingra said.

"Yes," Paris said; "look, Ingra, Honey, I don't see the harm——"

"There isn't any in the bet, itself," Ingra said. "I'm a very modern woman, Paris. Candace even calls me 'advanced'. But now I'm going to ask you the same thing Mrs Griffin did. How did you—know?"

She was, Paris saw, looking not into his face, but into Barry's as she spoke; and her eyes were—appalled.

"I didn't," Paris said calmly. "It's just that I've been married a long time, and I was nobody's saint before that. A woman laced up to an inch of her life just doesn't move the way you do—so easily, so gracefully. Pardon me, Barry, boy. I'm merely indicating a few more of her good points, in case you haven't noticed. . . ."

Ingra's gaze swung away from Barry's face. She studied Paris.

"Yes," she said; "you're telling the truth. I—I was being over-sensitive. Will you forgive me, Barry?"

"Lord God, Ingra; for what?" Barry said. His voice, Paris noted, was utterly baffled.

"For what I thought, darling. Well, Mrs Griffin, shall we go?" Ingra said.

Paris and Barry waited in the saloon across the street while Ingra and Laurel shopped. Barry's face was troubled.

"Look, boy," he said; "about this school business; maybe we ought to just drop the whole thing. . . ."

"Why?" Paris said.

"Because there are too many things we can't lick against us——"

"The Klan," Paris said; "your brother, Di—what else?"

"The climate of the times. Some internal weaknesses on our own side. For instance—I don't even know how to start saying it, but I think you ought to know—that you were right, that Bruce——"

"Is no paragon of honesty? Allow me to be a poor sport, and say I told you so. It was you and Candy who nominated him as the eighth wonder of the world. I never entirely trusted him. Or, to be fair, I've a grown man's scepticism about the infinite perfectibility of human nature. Especially coloured nature, which is a little too human when it comes to the frailties. So he's relapsed. Backslid. Tell me, what's he done now?"

"Nothing that we can prove. It's just that Candace suspects that the new wing he's built on to his house, and that gorgeous new wardrobe Eulalia's sporting, came out of the building fund. Paris, what do you think we ought to do?"

Paris sipped his bourbon and branch water, slowly.

"Go on as planned," he said; "open our coloured school this September as planned. With Bruce heading it—also as planned. . . ."

"But, Lord God, Paris, he——"

"I know. But Randolph's an asset, sticky fingers and all. Of course, he'd be more of an asset if he were of the calibre of Hiram Revels, John Lynch, or Blanche Bruce. There you have three black men who are honours to their race, or any race, for that matter. Yet none of them is as downright brilliant as Randolph. Ever heard him speak? He's the damned best orator in the State of Mississippi, bar none. Time we put away all childish things, including the belief that a thing—or a man—has to be absolutely right to be useful. Learn to use the tools at hand, even if their edge is blunted——"

"Like Randolph?"

"Like Randolph. Only he damned sure isn't blunt. A sight too sharp, if you ask me. But I've got a great advantage there——"

"Advantage how?" Barry said.

"He got drunk in my presence once and unburdened himself. He happens to be ashamed of his own race, horrified at how damned backward the coloured people are. So he's lost his sense of mission, his dedication to a cause. Which is why sacrifice, any sacrifice, seems to him useless—especially giving up living in a style that damned few black men have been able to achieve, even by thievery. He's a sad case, poor devil. I pity him. But the funny part of it is that he respects me, cares what I think—damned if I know why——"

"I do," Barry said. "For the same reasons that I respect you."

"Let's skip the bouquet-tossing, Barry. In this case, the 'why's' don't matter. What's important is that I can control him. He thinks I'm contemptuous of him. He'll do damned near anything to prove to me I'm wrong——"

158

"Even taking his fingers out of the till?"

"Even that. Besides, all you starry-eyed idealists have to do is to produce one or two little cuffies who can actually learn. Reckon that would save him. Give him hope. Make him believe his folks are really climbing Jacob's Ladder like that song says——"

Barry looked at him.

"And you, Paris? Do you believe it?"

"No," Paris said; "but, like you said, I'm willing to be shown."

The morning of Samson's wedding to Lucinda—Samson Griffin and Lucinda Cadwallader, for, by common consent, both parties had been granted their former masters' names —the lawn in front of the Negro Baptist Church was covered with people. Among them were reporters from both the Vicksburg papers, *The Times* and *The Herald*. Paris knew why they were there, and he was a little sorry. To them, this wedding was the biggest joke in history. To-morrow, both newspapers would delight their readers with dialect stories, making exceedingly broad fun of the whole proceedings. But, since neither Samson nor Cindy would be able to read them, he supposed no real harm would be done.

What surprised him was the number of white people present. Laurie, he thought grimly, talks too damned much!

Because, as everybody concerned already knew, this tomfool wedding was going to be a source of embarrassment to the Griffins and the Cadwalladers both, what with Hector's openly acknowledged quadroon daughter, Rachel, serving as maid of honour, and Lucinda showing the Cadwallader strain in every look and gesture. He looked around for Barry; found him at last in earnest conversation with Hector; but when he beckoned to him, Hector came along, too.

Oh hell, Paris thought, no help for it, now. I'll just have to say it in front of Hec——

"Yes, Paris?" Barry said.

"Look, boy," Paris said; "you think there's going to be trouble?"

"Trouble?" Hector bristled. "From whom?"

"Will you kindly shut up, you hothead?" Paris said. "I'm talking to Barry. Do you, boy?"

"I—I don't know," Barry said. "You know what time it was when you and I got back from that school board meeting, last night. Damned late—and Di hadn't come home, even then. . . ."

But Laurie had, Paris thought; only she hadn't had time to get out of her riding-dress before I came. Same excuse: "I felt kind of nervous, so I took myself a ride———"

"You think the Klan———?" Hector said.

"Just like I said, Hec, I don't know," Barry said. "Ordinarily, I'd think they might. Play this up as socializing between black and white, in spite of the fact that good white people have always attended the weddings of favoured house servants and taken part in the ceremonies, too, for that matter. But this case is—different: not even Di is idiot enough to deny what any fool can plainly see—that Cindy's one of Pa's yard children and our half-sister. That kind of cuts the ground out from under him, appears to me. . . ."

"Just what are you all talking about now?" Laurel said. "A body would think that this was a funeral, 'stead of a wedding, from the way you three old fogies look. . . ."

"We were talking about Dion's bedsheet cronies," Paris said, "sort of wondering whether they'd make trouble."

"No," Laurel laughed, "they won't."

"You seem mighty sure of that, Laurie," Paris said.

"I am sure of it. Now, isn't this just too sweet! Look who's driven up with Ingra! Your lady friend, all decked out for the occasion. . . . Who invited her, Paris—you?"

"If you're referring to Mrs Trevor, Laurie," Barry said, "I did. And I don't see why you call her Paris's lady friend, anyhow. . . ."

"Only because she is, Barry, you sweet, innocent old thing, you," Laurel said; "they've been cheating on me for years, she and Paris. Haven't you all, Paris, love?"

"You want to believe that, Laurie," Paris said, "far be it from me to try to dissuade you. But what I'd like to know is why do you? To cover up for what?"

Laurel's laughter went brittle.

"I'm only teasing you, Paris," she said; "you just watch how nice I'm going to be to her. . . ." Then she sailed off towards Ingra's buggy.

Barry looked at Paris.

"She *wasn't* teasing," he said.

"No," Paris said; "she wasn't."

"Paris—it's none of my goddamned business, but——"

"You're right," Paris said; "it isn't; but I'll tell you. No. Laurie's wrong. There hasn't been anything between Candace and me. Now you tell me one: why should you care, one way or the other?"

"Because I'm in love with Candace," Barry said.

"Damned if this isn't shaping up into a joyful occasion, all round," Hector said. "Prospective visit from the Klan in the offing, and you two bickering over a woman neither one of you can have, seeing as how she's got a husband——"

"Who's going to die," Barry said.

"Whereupon you break poor Ingra's heart?" Paris said.

"I've done that already, I'm afraid," Barry sighed. "Anyhow, Hector, you're wrong. I'm not bickering. I wouldn't quarrel with Paris over this—nor over anything I can think of, offhand. He's the best friend I've got, and I want to keep it that way. . . ."

"Likewise," Paris said. "I think we'd better go rescue Candy from Laurel, now. My baby can be pure poison when she puts her mind to it. . . ."

"I wouldn't, if I were you," Hector said. "Candace is more than a match for Laurie, boy. Look, here comes Dr Randolph and his wife. Reckon I'll mosey over and have a word with them. Talking to them is a living pleasure. . . ."

"No, wait," Paris said; "Roberta's beckoning to you. There—at the front window. I suppose she's got the bride ready. . . ."

"She has," Hector said; "reckon we'd better start the proceedings, boys. . . ."

The wedding went off just fine. The people who had come to laugh found no occasion to. Samson's massive dignity seemed contagious. All the blacks behaved themselves as though they were consciously trying to defend their race from ridicule. The only sour note in the whole proceedings was caused by Paris's own stable-keeper and groom, Duke, who cleared his throat loudly, just as Lucinda said, "I do." But then, Duke had been sweet on Cindy, himself, Paris knew.

Rachel Griffin's looks caused near consternation among the white women, none of whom had ever seen her before. Ingra, Candace and Laurel cried. Women! Paris thought.

But, even so, the whole thing was spoiled at the end. For as the wedding party filed out of the little clapboard, white-washed church, the Klan was there.

Sitting on their horses in a semicircle before the door. Wearing their tall, conical hoods. Ropes and whips coiled around their saddle horns. Guns belted around their waists, outside their robes, where they'd show.

Lucinda shrank against Samson. She was shaking, Paris saw. But her bridesmaid, Rachel, his own quadroon niece, stood there, head up, defiantly. And that, Paris realized long afterwards, was the first time that Ernest Thurston had seen her since she had grown up, become the lovely, exciting woman that she now was.

But he didn't think about that, then. At the moment, he was remembering only that he had no gun. Nor did any other man of the wedding party. Men don't ordinarily wear sidearms in church. Not even in Mississippi.

Then, without a sound, at a gesture from their leader, the Klansmen turned their horses, and rode away from there, without having done anything at all.

As, Paris decided suddenly, Laurie had known they would. Which was another of the things she damned well was going to have to explain to him—and soon.

162

"ALL right," Laurel said; "I did meet Di that night—but only for a few minutes, Paris. I went to ask him not to spoil Samson's wedding. And he promised not to. Told me the Klan had to make a demonstration; but he'd see to it that there'd be no fighting, nobody hurt. And he kept his word. . . ."

"In return for what?" Paris said.

She glared at him.

"Anybody ever tell you you've got a dirty mind, Paris?" she said.

"Yes; I have, haven't I?" Paris said. "Maybe that's why I hit upon the truth so often. 'Bye now, Laurie. . . ."

"Paris! Where are you going?"

"To see Candace. I have to persuade her not to start a race riot," Paris said.

Laurel got up from her chair, ran to the doorway, stood in it with her arms spread out like a cross, blocking his way.

"Paris——" she said.

He saw that she was crying. But that weapon had lost its effectiveness. He stood there looking at her and his expression didn't change.

"Paris, listen to me!" Her voice rose, went ragged, shrill. "You're wrong about what you're thinking. I didn't! Paris, I—I love you. I never did love anybody else. I never will. Don't you believe me, Paris, Honey?"

He went on looking at her.

"No," he said.

She dropped her arms. Her small figure seemed to diminish, to shrink into itself. She stood aside.

"All right," she said tonelessly; "go to her."

"Don't worry; I will," Paris said.

He knew where to find Candace. She and Ingra had been

teaching in the completed wing of the new school since the middle of June, while the work went on in the other. This had been her own idea: she proposed to have several Negro children far enough along by opening day, September 15, 1874, that they could be called upon to perform at the inauguration ceremonies: read, write, do simple sums. Well, it was the end of August now, time enough to see how she was making out. A little over two weeks 'til opening day—if it ever opens, Paris thought. Everything is against it. The Democrats won the city election mighty handily on the Fourth. And, with this Grand Jury investigating Warren County's affairs, old Brucie boy is very likely to end up in jail. . . .

Time was running out for the Radical Republicans. The pendulum of history was making one of its massive backward swings. And he, just like Barry had said, a half-hearted warrior for a cause he didn't even really believe in, was in the way. So time was running out for him, too. He laughed then, softly, bitterly.

They're wrong, he thought, the things we're taught, the books we read, the lies of history, because the choice is never between Jesus and Barabbas, but between Judas and Peter; between the traitor who sold out the King who disappointed him by not being kingly enough as he understood that quality, and the coward who denied his Lord three times to save his hide. What do I have to choose between? On the one hand, thieves; on the other, assassins. So now I'm on the right side for the wrong reasons or maybe on the wrong side for the right reasons, I don't know. . . . All I do know is that I elect grudgingly to support black Bruce Randolph, a windy crook, against white men who cover their faces to do murder in the dark. I uphold the dubious proposition that it is desirable or even possible to educate black children, against the men who, throughout history, have educated nobody's children, not even their own. Dear Lord, why can't I be content with the lesser evil? When will I learn that there are no high and shining things left to die for, if there ever were. . . .

164

Only, a man ought to take some satisfaction out of his own dying; he oughtn't to be backed up into dingy corners useful only as places to die in rat fashion—defending his tawdry, tarnished hoard of things of little value: his stale crust, his mouldy scrap of cheese, his faithless woman, his own disintegrated integrity, the child-like, savage concept of honour he no longer believes in either, any more than he believes in the final judgment, the resurrection of the body and life everlasting, or even in You——

"So, Lord God I don't believe in, don't take away this cup, just transform it into a chalice, just make this sop of vinegar taste like wine. . . ."

Then he saw the school before him: red, raw and new-looking under the trees.

"I could leave here," Candace said. "Henry's Aunt Bess died on Christmas Day. I could go down to Natchez and run that hotel she left us, only——"

"Only you're a mule-stubborn Vermont Yankee who has to prove she's right," Paris said.

"No," Candace said. "You've always given me too much credit, Paris. I'm not doing it for that reason. I've lived in Mississippi since 1858, all of sixteen years—and, to tell the sober truth about it, I more than half agreed with you. I—I thought this was—futile. I didn't believe they could learn. I went into this not stubbornly, but rather humbly, out of respect for my father's opinions, Ingra's ideals—in deference to the example of Bruce Randolph. . . ."

"Exception," Paris said, "proves the rule."

"I thought so, too. But now, I'm not sure. You know Ingra and I opened these classes ahead of time to have a few children ready to show off on opening day. You see she isn't here. . . ."

"Yes," Paris said. "Why isn't she?"

"Because we've been overwhelmed. They—they want so desperately to learn, Paris! We've had to open night classes to take care of the grown-ups who came. Ingra's teaching nights, since I can't leave Henry——"

"I see. But wanting to is one thing. I'll even admit it's rightly kind of fine. But can they?' 'Paris said.

"Yes, Paris," Candace said. "Of course, coming from shacks that never had a book in them, and where newspaper is only used to paper the walls, they find it harder than whites——"

"Ha!" Paris said. "I knew you'd find excuses, Candy."

"Excuses?" Candace snapped. Then she turned, went to the door of her classroom. "Rod!" she called. "Come out here! And bring the Bible with you. . . ."

The slim black boy, about twelve years old, came out into the yard. He looked at Paris with eyes that seemed to have a fire behind them, so that light spilled through their darkness, illuminating his solemn face.

"Rod," Candace said, "this is Mr Griffin, one of our trustees. I want you to read for him. Give Mr Griffin the Bible, please. . . ."

"Yes'm," the boy said, and held it out.

Paris took the big book, looked at Candace inquiringly.

"You pick out the passage you want him to read," Candace said. "Any passage whatsoever."

"All right," Paris said; "I want him to read the Ninth Chapter of the Book of Genesis." Then he handed the book back to the boy, closed.

Rod took it, opened it, riffled through the pages.

"Here 'tis!" he said. Then slowly, haltingly, he began to read. He stumbled at first, had to repeat. But then the story of Noah's drunkenness caught hold of his imagination; his young voice came out clearly, reading without hesitation or mistake. But when he came to the twenty-fifth verse, his voice again faltered, dropped to a whisper, as he read:

" 'And he said, Cursed be Canaan; a servant of servants shall he be unto his brethren——' " He stopped, looked up at Candace, and Paris saw the hot tears in his eyes.

"Go on, Rod," Candace firmly, "read the next two verses——"

" 'And he said,' " Rod croaked, " 'Blessed be the Lord God of Shem; and Canaan shall be his servant.'

"'God shall enlarge Japheth, and he shall dwell in the tents of Shem; and Canaan shall be his servant.' Miss Candace, when it says Canaan, it means us, don't it?" Rod said.

"Yes, Rod," Candace said; "but now I want you to read something for me: the Twelfth Chapter of the Book of Numbers. . . ."

Rod found that one, too, read:

"'And Miriam and Aaron spake against Moses because of the Ethiopian woman whom he had married: for he had married an Ethiopian woman——'"

The boy looked up, wonderingly, then he plunged into the story, his voice trembling as he read of God's wrath against Miriam and Aaron; Miriam's leprosy; Aaron's asking pardon of Moses for their sin of prejudice; and Moses' intercession on their behalf before God.

"Now, Rod," Candace said; "in the Ninth Chapter of Genesis, that was Noah talking; and Noah, after all, was only a man; while in Twelfth Numbers, the rebuke and the punishment came directly from Almighty God. Shall we ask Mr Griffin which version he prefers?"

Paris looked at her, standing there chin up, her eyes alight with anger; and he knew again that there was nobody else like this woman, nowhere in the world.

"You win, Candace!" he laughed; and put out his hand to the boy. "Congratulations, Rod; you read just fine," he said.

Rod took his hand shyly.

"Thank you, sir," he said; then: "Miss Candace, can I go back inside, now?"

"Yes, Rod—only it's 'may I'," Candace said.

She stood there looking at Paris.

"You want to come in and hear the rest of them read?" she said. "Rod is the best; and some of the others are just about hopeless, but a goodly number are doing fine. You want to try them, too, Paris?"

"No, I'm willing to take your word for it, Candy," Paris said.

"Paris——" she said; "you—you're trying to make me stop loving you, aren't you? Mind telling me why?"

"Lord God, Candy! I——"

"You must be. Your tactics are superb. Abusing a child —not with blows, which he's probably even used to; but this way—this dirty way. Don't Paris. I ask you very humbly, don't."

"Don't what?" Paris said. "Abuse children or——?"

"Make me stop loving you. Both. I don't have to tell you why you shouldn't abuse children; but I don't think you understand the other. I—I need to love you, Paris. The way I feel towards you is the only good thing in my life; the only thing that keeps me going. I work here all day until I'm dog-tired; I go back to your brother's house—it was kind of him to take us in so I wouldn't have to take a train all the way to Vicksburg every night—I feed Henry, listen to him whining, crying, cursing me, calling me your whore——"

"Candy!" Paris said.

"And I don't even answer him, have not even any need to. I get him off to bed, sit there in my big chair, listening to him crying and cursing me some more until he falls asleep. Then, my hour comes. It's very quiet in the house by then, Hector's children are wonderfully well behaved, and I can think of you. I do—until all the misery in me, all the grief, the pain is gone. Then I go to bed, knowing I can sleep, knowing if I dream, the dreams themselves will be happy, filled with you. That's what you give me, Paris, without trying; maybe without even wanting to. . . ."

He could see she was crying, and the sight of it unmanned him. He knew he would never become invulnerable to these tears.

"So," she said; "don't take that away from me. Don't rob me of the only reason I have left to stay alive. . . ."

He forgot completely the black faces watching from the window, but, even if he hadn't, the fact of witnesses would have meant less than nothing to him, then. He stepped forward, took her in his arms, kissed her mouth with grave tenderness until its cold, salt-wet, hurt trembling became

168

another thing: still trembling, but no longer salt-wet, hurt, no longer cold. She tore her face away from his, buried it in the hollow of his throat, clung to him, crying again now, but for another reason; and he——

"Ahemmm!" the voice behind them said. Then all the world was afloat on throaty negroid laughter; and Candace jerked away from him, whirling, her gaze sweeping across the windows packed with grinning black children, until it fell upon Bruce Randolph's face.

"Oh!" she said. "Oh, Bruce, I'm so sorry!"

"Don't be," Bruce Randolph said; "I don't recall having been appointed custodian of public morals—in fact, my qualifications for the post are decidedly weak. And the children will forget it—I hope. Mr Griffin, I was looking for you. . . ."

"You were?" Paris said. "For what?"

"To give you this," Bruce said, and handed Paris a newspaper-wrapped package.

Paris stared at him.

"Go on, open it," Bruce Randolph said.

Paris tore open one end of the package. It was full of greenbacks: twenties, fifties, hundreds. He judged there must be several thousands there.

"It's for the building fund," Bruce said. "I've sold my house, the carriages, dismissed the servants. I let Eulalia keep her glad rags, though. Hadn't the heart to take 'em away from her——"

Paris lifted one eyebrow.

"Before the Grand Jury was ever thought of, much less formed," Bruce said quickly. "I've already appeared before them, voluntarily. My books were quite in order, Mr Griffin. Not, frankly, because they'd always been; but because I'd had time to put back what I'd taken. . . ."

"But the money you'd used for your house, and so forth," Paris said, "in effect, *this* money: what about that, Bruce?"

"Didn't come from Warren County—or rather it did, originally; only it represents the profit from some larger speculations in railroad bonds a Boston friend put me on to.

So, even after I'd put back every penny of the money I'd 'borrowed' to speculate with, this remained. All right, it's not completely honest; but, hell, what money is? The point is, it can't be traced, won't hurt anybody——"

"Except Eulalia and your children, who're out in the street," Candace said.

"And happy to be there, since now they can lift up their heads. An exaggeration, of course; I've been able to rent a neat little bungalow from a coloured politician who has decided that Northern air would be better for his health than the actual climate of Mississippi, now. There're ten thousand dollars in that bundle, Mr Griffin; enough to finish our school. Every penny I've got in this world above my salary, which, from now on, I mean to both earn and live within. Will you be so kind as to accept it, please?"

"Yes," Paris said; "I'll take it, mainly because I think I know why. Only, I want to hear *you* say it. So I'm asking you: Why, Bruce?"

Bruce Randolph looked at him. Said:

"Because I got tired of borrowing a white man's conscience, sick of your believing in me more than I did in myself, fed to the back eye-teeth of always being ashamed. The people helped—Candace's scholars. When I saw her take mumbling plough-hands, stinking worse than goats, their rags caked with dirt, and turn them in two short months into men, clean, neat, speaking out, unafraid, beginning to recognize their letters, taking between their work-worn hands——"

"He's talking about my grown-up classes, the ones Ingra's teaching now," Candace said.

"Such stuff as dreams are made on," Bruce exulted, "after centuries of being rounded by a sleep. I knew I couldn't betray that, Paris. It was too big, too big! I had to be what you thought I was, what I was maybe meant to be. . . ."

"What you *were* meant to be, Bruce. There's no doubt about that now," Paris said.

He was riding homeward again, back towards Griffin's

Way, thinking that the taste of vinegar had already improved and that he'd better have the grace to at least say thanks to the God that he, like all other men, was beginning to create in the image of his own helplessness, his loneliness, his despair; acknowledge that in this one coincidence, at least, the timing had been very good; be grateful for this crumb of comfort, accidental or not, this lessening still further of one of the evils he was confronted with; so he lifted his head and said:

"I thank You mighty kindly, Lord. . . ."

And it was then he saw the horse. He pulled his gelding up. Sat there staring through a break in the thick brush at the red glow of the dying sun on a horse's flank. A grey horse's flank. One of the Cadwallader greys.

He got down, let the bridle trail. His mount stood there. He moved off, quieter than an Indian or a ghost. He'd learned to walk like that during the War. Which was one of the reasons he was alive, now. He came up behind that screen of brush. Stood there, two yards away from the dappled grey.

Dion's voice came over to him, clearly.

"All right, Duke," Dion said. "You go right on keeping me posted. So that big buck Samson is head of the nigger Republicans in this district. When we get through with him, Cindy'll be a comely widow woman, and I'll see that you get her. Now you get along and take that note up to Mrs Laurel——"

"Yassuh, Mars Di, I sho' Lawd will," Duke said.

Paris looked down at the gun he already had in his hand. What was he preparing to kill Dion over? Laurie? His wounded pride? Over the fact that the common belief that cuckolds were ridiculous was entirely accurate? In one way or another, a man always earns his horns, he thought, and shoved the gun back into his pocket. He stood there. Heard the grey horse dance as Dion mounted. Listening to those hoofbeats drumming the earth, dimming, fading out of time.

Then he moved. His stride ate distance. He caught up with the groom not two hundred yards away.

"The note, Duke," he said.

"W w w what note, Marse Paris?" Duke stammered.

"The note, Duke!" Paris said.

Duke passed it over. His black face was grey. He was shaking.

Paris opened the note, read:

All right, Laurie, I'm going to give you one more chance. It's been more than a month now, and I'm getting mighty tired of being without you. I won't listen to no excuses like the last time. If you don't meet me down at Dutchman's Flats eleven o'clock tomorrow morning, I'm going to see friend hubby gets all them letters you writ me, including them what you writ *after* you married him. I hate to use force, but you're purely crowding me, Baby; what you got I ain't even fixing to do without, not now not never.

Your,
Dion.

Paris smiled.

Got hidden depth, haven't you, Di? he thought. Mighty fine note. Got style. I'll save this treacherous black bastard the trouble. Deliver your *billet doux*, myself. Want to see Laurie's face when she reads it.

"Marse Paris!" Duke wailed. "I never knowed there was nothing wrong——"

Which was a mistake. Paris had all but forgotten him. He swung his riding crop, hard. Duke jumped a yard high, came down howling.

"Marse Paris!" he moaned. "Lawd God, Marse Paris! Don' whup po' Duke! I ain't strong like Samson! Yo kill me in no time a—tall!"

"I aim to," Paris said, and swung again.

This time, when Duke's feet touched ground again, they were already in motion. Paris stood there, watching him go. Better like that. Duke would think twice before doing Dion Cadwallader's dirty jobs again.

172

Paris turned back to his horse.

Laurel was waiting for him when he came, her eyes red and swollen.

"So," she said, "you—you've come back? You didn't run off with her after all?"

"Evidently not," Paris said. "I had a few other things to do, first. Like delivering this note to you, for instance——"

Laurel took the folded piece of paper. Held it in her hands without opening it. Stared at him. Even her lips were white now.

"Go on, Laurie, open it," Paris said.

"Don't have to," she said; "I know who it's from. I even know what it's going to say. Reckon you've read it by now, haven't you?"

"Yes," Paris said.

"So what do you aim to do?" she said. "Beat me?"

He smiled.

"That would solve a lot of problems, wouldn't it? No, Laurie; I don't mean to beat you."

Her blue eyes were wood-smoke now, pale grey, searching his face.

"You—you mean to kill me, Paris?" she said.

"Now you're getting warm," Paris said.

"Oh—oh, Paris!" she said. "You—you're going to leave me! You're going away—with her!"

"So, there are fates worse than death, even by your reckoning, eh, Laurie?" Paris said.

"Yes," she said tonelessly; "*that* one sure Lord is. All right, what are you waiting for? Me to help you pack?"

"No," Paris said; "I'm waiting for you to read that note, and then to answer it, telling Di Cadwallader he can go to blazes, that he can send me those blackmail letters and be damned. . . ."

"And if I do that?" Laurel whispered.

"There's no if about it. You're going to," Paris said.

It was after midnight when he heard the pounding on the door of his study.

"Marse Paris! Marse Paris!" Sarah's voice wailed. "Oh Lawd, Marse Paris, is you in there?"

Paris went to the door. Opened it. The cook stood there, tears streaking her black face in the lamplight. She shook all over, all two hundred pounds of her quivering like a jelly.

"What the devil ails you, Sarah?" Paris said.

"It's Miz Laurel! I was coming through the hall when I thought I heard somebody moaning. I listened real good, then I heard it ag'in. So I flew up them stairs and—Oh Lawd, Marse Paris, if you don't come right now I'm scairt she's gonna be daid afore you gits there, suh!"

Paris pushed by her. Took those stairs three at a time. Opened the door. Laurel lay on the bed, clutching her stomach with both her hands. She was writhing, feebly.

Paris stood there, looking at her.

"All right," he said. "What did you take?"

"Rat poison," Laurel wept; "only I—I didn't know it was—going to hurt! Oh Lord, Oh God, Oh Baby Jesus! It hurts, Paris! It hurts!"

"How much did you take?" Paris said.

"A a all of it—the whole bottle—'nough to kill a team of horses—and it's going to—I—I want it to—but I didn't know it was going to—hurt!"

"Sarah," Paris said, "go put some water on. Get it good and hot. Then pour all the mustard you can find into it, and bring it here."

"Yassuh, Mister Paris!" Sarah said.

Paris crossed to the bed. Sat down beside Laurel.

"Open your mouth," he said.

"Why? I I I can't! Ooooh, Paris! It—it's getting dark! Oh, darlin', hold me!"

"Open your mouth, Laurie!" Paris said.

But she had her eyes shut now and her breathing had gone ragged. He felt her pulse. It was fluttery, uncertain, weak. It stopped altogether for second-long intervals.

He put his hand under her head, lifted it, clamped his big hand around her chin, forced her mouth open. Stuck his fingers down her throat as far as he could get them. She choked, retched, vomited; but not enough. He kept on trying until Sarah came pounding up the stairs with the mustard water, shaking the whole house as she came.

He held her while Sarah poured it into her. That did it. It all came up then. It smelt vile.

"Now go separate about a dozen eggs and bring me the whites," Paris said.

"Yessuh, Mister Paris!" Sarah said.

By morning they had won. Because rat poison is slow, because it burns like fire, doesn't even bring merciful unconsciousness; because, at bottom, a woman who had a fully loaded pocket pistol in her drawer and chose rat poison instead, didn't really want to die. But Laurel had come close to it. Closer than he liked to think about.

He sat by the bed in the pale light of dawning. Saw her eyes flutter open. He said:

"Why, Laurie?"

"What do I want to live for with you gone?" Laurel said.

At midday, she was stronger. He sat there watching Sarah feeding her the broth. And it was then that the housemaid, Ruby, brought those letters up the stairs.

Laurel gasped. Choked on the broth.

"Pound her on the back, Sarah," Paris said.

Sarah pounded, vigorously.

Laurel lost the broth, too. Turned over until she was face downwards on the bed. Lay there, crying.

Ruby and Sarah stared at each other.

"Get out of here, both of you," Paris said. "No, leave the door open. That way I'll know you'll have to go downstairs, and can't eavesdrop at the keyhole."

They went out with obvious reluctance. Paris went over to the bed, sat down on the edge of it.

"Laurie," he said.

"Oh, go 'way!" she said. "Why didn't you let me die,

175

Paris? How come you worked on me all night? So you could torment me like this?"

"Turn over, Laurie," Paris said.

"No!" she screamed, pounding the bed with both her fists. "Go on, read my letters, Paris! Find out what you're married to! What a no good, cheap li'l' whore! That's what you wanted, Paris? You've got it!"

"No, Laurie," Paris said, "that's not what I want."

Something in his voice got to her, then; its weary patience, perhaps; its pain. She whirled on the bed, looked at him like a trapped and tortured animal, her eyes colourless, hidden behind a wall of water, her cheeks whiter than the sheets on which she lay, her sullen mouth trembling, her hair a sooty smoke-cloud, tangled, wild.

He had the package of letters in his hand, the cords that bound them still unbroken. Quietly he crossed the room, and laid them, just as they were, in the fireplace. Knelt, struck a match. Saw the tongue of flame lick up around their edges. Stood back, watching them burn.

"Paris——" Laurel's voice was ashes, sand.

"That was all you ever needed to do, Baby," Paris said. "Just you tell Di to go to hell! Let him send me the letters so I could burn them. Simple, wasn't it? Or maybe, too damned complicated. Because it required knowing me. . . ."

"Paris!" Laurel wept. "Oh, Paris, Honey——"

He stirred at the smouldering fragments with the poker, until the last of them crisped, turned black. He hung the poker back in its place; said:

"Try to sleep now, Baby. . . ."

"Paris—where are you going?" she said.

"To pay a call on a friend of yours. I'll be back in a little while. Just you rest, Baby. . . ."

"Paris!" she said. "You—you're going to fight Di over this! Paris, don't! He can shoot too good! Oh, Paris, Honey, darlin'—you want me to die for real?"

He smiled.

"No, Laurie," he said; "I don't reduce a woman to a scrap

of meat to be fought over by savage dogs. 'Bye now, Baby——"

"Oh, Paris, Paris!" she wept.

He bent and kissed her, holding his breath against her sour smell. Then he straightened up, smiling a little sadly.

"Go to sleep, Laurie," he said.

Dion and Barry were in the south fields of Walfen, watching the Negroes chop cotton under the sun. It was very hot and the cotton was all the way up, the bolls bursting snowy-white under a yellow-blue sky. It was mere accident that Barry was there with his younger brother; ordinarily he would have been overseeing another section. But for a good long time now, Barry had been trying to get Dion to see the criminal folly of the Klan. The argument went on night and day, caused Barry to ride over frequently to where Dion was working to pursue it, which was why the two of them were together when Paris came.

Dion didn't even hesitate. As soon as Paris was close enough to make a hit reasonably possible, he reached, slapped leather, got two fast shots off before Barry slashed down across his arm with his riding crop, causing the third shot to plough dirt almost under Dion's own mount's feet. The grey reared, and Barry locked both his big hands around his brother's wrist, twisting. The two of them rolled off their horses together into the dirt. Dion kept his grip on the gun until Paris, without any haste at all, swung down from his roan, kicked it out of his hand, walked over to where it had spun, picked it up. He said:

"You can let him up, now, Barry. And thanks, boy. . . ."

"Don't thank me," Barry panted, "thank God! I just happened to be here! I just happened——"

Paris smiled.

"Things are always just happening, Barry," he said. "Reckon the laws of chance are all we live by. . . ."

"The next time I see you," Dion howled, "there ain't going to be any chance in it! I'm going to make mighty damn sure——"

"Of what?" Paris said; "of killing me? You might. But

then you might not. Even doing what a man sets out to do involves chance, Di. And if you think you can control the circumstances of living, you're a bigger jackass than I thought you were. Yesterday you tried to control Laurie and me. You failed both times——"

"Failed, hell!" Dion said. "You're here, ain't you? And that means——"

"What Di?" Paris said.

"That you read them letters! That you know Laurie's my woman! That——"

Barry looked at his brother. Spat.

"I've seen some puking polecat's puppies in my time," he drawled; "but you, Di——"

"No," Paris said. "There were a couple of things you didn't know. One: that I'd burned those letters in the grate without opening them. Two: that force and threats are the worst aphrodisiacs in the world——"

"I don't understand you," Dion said.

"You never do," Paris said. "Put it this way, then: the last thing on earth you ever figured was that before she'd come to you, before she'd have me find out what you'd forced her into, Laurie would prefer to die. Well, she did. She took poison last night."

He scarcely heard Barry's choked, hushed, "My God!" because he was too busy watching Dion crumpling behind his eyes. Under other circumstances the physical manifestations of the way Dion felt would have been merely ludicrous; but now that sagging jaw, that whitening face, that blank, stunned-ox expression and, even more, the quite visible sagging of knees—so that Paris thought with pure amazement: Why, he's going to faint! A big ox like him!—were sad. For the saddest thing in the world, maybe, is when Caliban truly suffers love.

But Dion didn't faint. He sank to his knees in a furrow, brought his big hands up so that they covered his face, knelt there shaking all over—his hoarse, animal sobbing sounding for all the world like the muted bellowing of a bull.

"Laurie!" he wept. "Laurie, Honey! I kilt you! And I —I loved you so!"

Barry put a hand on Paris's shoulder. His face was grey, taut with pain.

"Paris, boy," he said; "you just don't know——"

Paris held out Dion's gun, butt first.

"Give him this," he said; "but not now. Not until you tell him that Laurie isn't dead."

"My Laurie!" Dion moaned. "Oh, Jesus, she——"

"What?" Barry said.

"We saved her, Sarah and I," Paris said. "It was—rough. Wasn't until this morning I was sure she was going to make it. Tell him that, after I've gone. Let him suffer a while, first. May do him a mite of good. And, Barry——"

"Yes, Paris?" Barry said.

"He's *your* brother. So I can't kill him. That leaves the whole thing up to you. You understand me, boy?"

"Yep. If he even looks hard in Laurie's direction any more, I'll strip the hide clean off him," Barry said.

BOOK THREE

APOCALYPSE

★ 13 ★

PARIS stood by the window of his study, watching the pale winter sun struggling with the morning clouds. It looked as if the sun was going to win this time, and that worried him, because bad weather kept trouble from stirring abroad. Oh, damn Bruce anyhow! he thought. If he'd had sense enough to keep his big black mouth shut——

But there was no helping that, now. On inauguration day of the new school the ceremonies had gone off well. At least up to the point that Bruce had got up. He had been very slightly but noticeably drunk. And he had made a speech that had been a masterpiece of its kind: full of telling periods, rotund, florid rhetoric. A good speech.

Only it had been as inflammatory as old hell.

The wonder was, Paris thought, that they didn't lynch him that same night. Or burn the school with him in it. Why hadn't they? What did these three months of silence, of waiting, mean?

The weather maybe. It had been a rainy autumn, filled with torrential downpours. Enough to discourage even the Klan. Still——

Still, goddamn Bruce, however careless he may be of his own black hide, he had absolutely no right to endanger Candace like this!

"Paris—" Laurel said. "Why, you're not even dressed! And you promised to take me to church today. . . ."

Paris turned, seeing her in all her ribbons and flounces, a

bonnet perched upon her mass of jet-black hair. Lord, but she's thin! he thought; effect of what that rat poison did to her stomach, I suspect—she hardly eats a thing now. . . . He said:

"Sorry, Baby. I'd clean forgot it was Sunday. Hard to tell the days apart in December. But I'll be ready in a minute. . . ."

"That's true," Laurel sighed, "things do run together in the winter time. What day is it, anyhow, Paris? I mean, what date?"

"Let me see." Paris counted back. "The sixth, Laurie. Why?"

"No reason," she said. "You don't have to shave, do you?"

"No, I did this morning. Sit down and rest; I'll be back in a minute. . . ."

"All right, Paris," Laurel said.

This was a new thing, her churchgoing. Before her indifference to religion had been greater than his own in the peculiar sense that the unthinking believer is always actually less religious than the thoughtful agnostic; but now——

"*Primus in orbe deos fecit timor,*" Paris quoted from Petronius; and entered his room to dress. So now Laurie's become devout; and that devoutness, just as old Petronius said, is born of her fear. She's tried everything else, so now she's ready to take up God. I wish her joy of Him, and vice versa. Maybe He—or the idea of Him—will rid her of what's tormenting her. Because, by my lights, the only thing worse than sin is the belief in it and this sick craving to be punished for the little joy we steal in a generally joyless world. So now to church, the temple of unreason. But then, how much is reason worth? "Whom the gods would destroy they first——"

"And to hell with it!" Paris said.

The services at the Methodist Church at Junction Village —which, since the repairs to the railroad, had grown once more to respectable size—were easier to endure than Paris had anticipated. Reverend Brownley preached a thoughtful, searching sermon, using the text Matthew xxvi.52:

181

"Put up again thy sword into his place: for all they that take the sword shall perish with the sword."

As usual, Paris started off by not listening to it; but the urgency in the minister's voice broke through his daydreaming, and he sat upright, aware at last that the good man of God was trying to head off serious trouble. Only, in his anxiety not to offend the very men he was trying to reach, Reverend Brownley expressed himself by allegory and parable, in the very vaguest fashion. It wasn't until the service was over that Paris found out why the minister was so concerned. Barry Cadwallader, himself a regular churchgoer, told him.

"Crosby," Barry said; "Peter Crosby, sheriff *and* tax-collector of Warren County. Indisputably the biggest rogue in a collection of rogues unmatched in human history——"

"I grant you that," Paris said; "but what has old thieving Pete got to do with swords and bloodshed?"

"Plenty. You get your property-tax bill this year?"

"No," Paris said. "Come to think of it, that's funny. In fact it's damned strange. . . ."

"There's a reason for it," Barry said. "Crosby was due to collect one hundred sixty thousand dollars in taxes this month. But, on the second, four days ago, a meeting of tax-payers was held in Vicksburg. Didn't you get the notice to attend, either?"

"No, I—Laurie! You got that notice, didn't you?" Paris said.

"Yes," Laurel said, "and I hid it! I was scared, Paris. From what it said I figured there was going to be trouble, fighting and shooting maybe, so I hid it. And I'd do it again, Honey. Good as you've been to me, I sure don't want you dead. . . ."

"That was sweet of you, Laurie," Barry said, "and you were doggoned right. There was trouble. First the taxpayers voted not to pay one cent of taxes to Crosby; then five hundred armed men called on Sheriff, or, in this case, Tax-Collector Crosby, and forced him to resign. There, at least up until yesterday, the matter rested. . . ."

"And yesterday?" Paris said.

"Showed up again, like the bad penny he is, with a declaration that his resignation is null and void, since it was obtained by force, said declaration being signed by Governor Ames——"

"Legally," Paris said; "the governor's right——"

"I know," Barry said, "which doesn't help matters a goddamned bit—'scuse me, Laurie. Ames sent the adjutant-general back with Crosby to support his claims. And now they've called out the militia—which means, naturally enough, in this case, the Negro militia. Black men bearing arms in Mississippi! Lord, boy, you ever stop to think how strange that is?"

"No," Paris said, "by the logic of history, it isn't strange at all, Barry. We got licked. But, instead of lying down and licking our wounds as the vanquished usually do, we reared up on our hind-legs right from the first. Passed those 'Black Codes' of celebrated ill fame—worded clearly enough to convince friend Yankee that we were trying to cheat him of his victory, railroad Sambo Cuffey right back into slavery by the shortest available route. And, all our pious denials to the contrary, that was exactly what we were—maybe not even quite consciously—trying to do. So the results aren't strange. We asked for it, boy. We purely asked for it. Friend Yankee, who has no more love for the black man than we have, and maybe even less——"

"Surely less," Barry said, "we still haven't caught up with the number of coloured folks they killed in one night in New York City in the draft riots of 1863. And we've had ten years to catch up in——"

"Only because we've been watched mighty carefully," Paris said. "All I was going to say is that we—by shooting off our big mouths—more or less forced the Yankee to disenfranchise us; certainly forced him to give way to his more radical element, who were willing to use the Negro as the whip to beat us with. Result: a state government containing almost no white man who was not born north of the Mason and Dixon line and damned few who resided in Mississippi before the War. A state legislature filled out with guffawing black ex-field-hands the majority of whom cannot read or write their names. Under those circumstances, Barry, a black militia became an inevitability. Such a government, going, as it does, completely against the will of all responsible white men, can only be maintained in office by force of arms— which formerly meant the army. But the army has been down here long enough to learn to hate Sambo with a prejudice even more unreasoning than our own and to sympathize with the Southern point of view one hundred per cent. So, since the army's not reliable any more, that means the State Militia. And that part of the State Militia still made up of local white men can be trusted to defend our carpet-bagger, scallawag, Negro government even less than the army can. Ergo: militia companies made up of the only element the government can trust, the Negroes. Poor devils, they're going to get slaughtered."

"They are," Barry said; "and not only the ones in uniform. Those fools in the state Capitol must be pretty desperate. Because they've done one other thing. They've had all the coloured preachers tell the coloured folks to march on Vicksburg tomorrow—peacefully—to protest against our high-handed tactics in throwing out Crosby, now being billed as the Coloured Man's Friend. Old thieving Pete is the friend of just one man, himself, as far as I've ever been able to find out; but the poor damn'fool coloured folks don't know that. Also, they've sent riders throughout the county to pass the word among the darker brethren who maybe didn't go to church. So now, you know what's going to happen tomorrow?"

"Yes," Paris said. "We're going to catch up with Louisiana in one day, in the nigger-killing sweepstakes. Pile dead darkies up so high that the buzzards won't even have to come down to eat them. Which is exactly what those windy scoundrels in Vicksburg are counting on, what they're perfectly willing to sacrifice hundreds of Negroes to achieve. Another massacre, a few more bloody shirts to wave. Another excuse to force Washington to intervene, nail down their hold on us for at least ten more years by use of the army—who'll still obey orders in a case like that, boy, whether they like them or not. And nobody has the brains to see through it, or the patience to abstain even if they do see. Lord, what a thing!"

"Don't know about you," Barry said; "but tomorrow I'm going to play Old Master. Never did like the rôle but if I have to take a blacksnake whip to my people to keep 'em from getting their fool selves killed, I'll do it!"

"Likewise," Paris said. "Anyhow, there's one saving feature about the whole randy mess——"

"What's that?" Barry said.

"Time. We've got time. Nothing will happen before noon tomorrow. It'll take the niggers that long to get into town. . . ."

"We'll need it," Barry said. "I've to go into Vicksburg tonight to warn Ingra, while you——"

"While I've got even more to do. Because warning Candy to stay home now may not be enough——"

"Lord God!" Barry said. "Hector's place is only two miles from that school!"

"And will be next on their list. Adds up, doesn't it? Hector had to go and build that house in order to prove that not even the Klan could intimidate him. Compound the felony of miscegenation by raising it to a level of luxury that nobody's going to cotton to, not even the folks lazy, indifferent, or maybe even kindly enough to close their eyes to it on its usual plane of furtiveness and secrecy. No. Not my brother. Not Hector Griffin. He had to build The Briars, indisputably the finest manor house in Warren County, as a home for his coloured concubine and his yard children. And, even more, after he—with you and I more or less encouraging him to do it, let's admit that, Barry—had put his neck in the lyncher's noose by giving that land for the school building, he had to go—again with my approval—and forge one more link in the iron chain of man's fate by taking Henry and Candace in. So she can teach nights, along with Ingra, because those delicate Yankee schoolmarms the Lovegood people sent down here wouldn't do it——"

185

"As much out of fear of being raped by the big black bucks, like your Samson, for instance, who flock to the night classes, as from any anxiety over the Klan," Barry said.

Paris smiled.

"I've always sensed that particular fear contained the germ of hope," he said.

"Why, Paris Griffin!" Laurel said.

"Anyhow, Barry," Paris said, "you're right. Something could be made of it, just as you said; but it would take Euripides to do it justice, because this is damned sure going to be bloodier than his *Medea*. Beyond the fact that Candace has moved into the zone of acute danger both in time and in place, she has also extended that zone to include him, Roberta and their brood by accepting Hector's idiotic offer —and, what is maybe worse, even if she escapes this time, even if Hector's monument to racial equality survives the Klan, she has at least prolonged her slavery——"

"I'm afraid I don't follow you," Barry said.

"I mean that Roberta and the girls have made a new man out of Henry. He has gained twelve pounds eating Roberta's cooking. And you ought to see the way 'Berta and those two kids Rachel and Matty fuss over him! Even the boys, Billy and Hubert, take turns pushing him around in his wheel chair. Funny, those kids have known nothing but kindness so naturally they're kind. And how old Henry loves it, the miserable whining—strike that one from the record, boy. That was rotten of me. Pot and kettle, I reckon. He whines, but I ran—clean out of life, damned near back to babyhood. But I guess we've jawed enough—even twenty-four hours is not *that* much time. . . ."

"Right," Barry said. "So long, folks——"

When they reached the alley of oaks leading to Griffin's Way, Paris didn't turn into it, but went on down the road they were on in the direction of Hector's place.

"Oh," Laurel said; "Candace. You—you're going to warn her just like you said——"

186

"Yes—not to hold her classes tomorrow night nor any other night for the next two weeks; to go back to Vicksburg with Henry, where, riot or not, she'll be safe in that quiet neighbourhood where she lives. Beyond that, I'm going to try to make Hector hide out somewhere with his brood, damn that house and his tomfool pride! Though I'll just be wasting breath talking to him, I know. Anyhow, before you start in on me, Baby, I want you to pay attention to the fact that I could have dropped you off at home and have taken myself a little ride. I'm warning Candace just like I'd warn Ingra if I didn't know Barry is going to do that; just like I'm going to send a note to those two dried-up, vinegary Yankee spinsters who haven't the nerve to teach nights, and to those two New England maiden aunts in trousers who, up to now, at least have; giving Candy and Ingra the protection of their damned dubious masculinity. Is that clear?"

Laurel wrapped both her tiny arms about his one big arm, snuggled up against him; said:

"Thanks, darling. . . ."

"Lord God, Laurie," Paris said; "for what?"

"For taking me with you. For knowing I'd suffer something awful if you hadn't. For always being ever so much nicer to me than I deserve. . . ."

"Hell, Baby, any man who could be mean to you ought to be shot with slops and arrested for stinking. Besides, you deserve the best there is in this world. . . ."

"No, Paris; no I don't," Laurel said.

"Where're the boys?" Paris said to Rachel.

"Out riding somewhere. Why, Uncle Paris?" Rachel said.

"And your Pa?"

"Inside, taking a nap," Mathilda giggled. Matty always giggled, whether a thing was funny or not. Paris wondered if it weren't a nervous tic.

"Go wake him up, Matty," he said; "tell him to send somebody to find Billy and Hubert. Lock 'em up, if need be, until I find out whether or not this is going to blow over. If

187

not, I'll arrange to get you all out of the state. Then you tell Mrs Trevor to come down here. . . ."

"Yessir, Uncle Paris!" Matty said, and scampered away.

"Uncle Paris," Rachel whispered, her blue eyes widening, "you mean there's going to be *more* trouble?"

"I mean there's going to be trouble. 'Twas you who hung that *more* onto it, Rachie. So now I'm going to ask you: why?"

Rachel looked at Laurel a little uncertainly.

"Mrs Griffin," she said: "why don't you and Uncle Paris come in a while? You've never seen our new house. . . ." None of Hector's children ever called Laurel, "Aunt Laurel". They knew better, Paris realized.

"I'd be glad to, Rachel," Laurel said; "but——"

"But we just haven't got the time, today," Paris said. "When I leave here, I've got to find Samson, send a note to those Yankee schoolteachers, and—— Doggone it, Rachie; don't sidetrack me! Why'd you say *more* trouble?"

"Daddy had words with Mr Hank Thurston day before yesterday," Rachel said slowly, "because of the way Ernest is always picking at me. I—I haven't been able to go anywhere for weeks, Uncle Paris! I don't even dare take a ride on our own place 'less Daddy's with me. Mamma won't let Hubert or Billy go with me, for fear that——"

"I see," Paris said, "and what was the result of your Pa's talking to the original hairy ape?"

"It was awful," Rachel whispered. "He said—Oh, Uncle Paris!"

"Go on, Rachie," Paris said. "You'd better tell me. Could get to be too much for your pa to handle alone——"

"He said I was lucky. That Ernest was doing me a favour. That a yellow nigger wench like me should be highly honoured that a white boy was paying me attention. That I should just—just——"

"Just what, Rachel?" Laurel said.

"Just lie down and let him!" Rachel wailed.

"Don't you worry your pretty little head, Rachie," Paris said. "Reckon your Pa and I are up to handling those two

188

throwbacks. But you stay home and keep the boys home, too; because——"

Then he felt Laurel's convulsive grip on his arm, and looked up in time to see the last of the joy fading from Candace's eyes.

Riding back home, Paris tried to keep the sick worry he felt from showing on his face. Maybe he was successful; he didn't know. At least Laurel didn't say anything.

Women! he thought. Oh, damn Candy, anyhow! Maybe taking Laurie along was the mistake. Should have known she'd refuse with Laurie there. Pride! No, more than that. Sense of duty, too. Says she has no way of notifying the niggers not to come; and when I told her they'd know better, she still insisted that she had to be there in case—Oh Lord, I——

He pulled the buggy up before Griffin's Way. When Duke came to take the reins, he said:

"Saddle Big Red for me, Duke; I'll be right back down soon as I get some riding pants on——"

Laurel looked at him.

"You—you're going back to try to make her change her mind, without me in the way," she said.

"No, Baby. When Candace makes her mind up, nothing short of killing her can make her change it," Paris said. "What I've got to do now is find that fool Samson. I only hope he hasn't taken Cindy into town. . . ."

"Oh, Paris, honey, please do!" Laurel said. "I couldn't stand having something happen to poor Samson. . . ."

"I'll do my best, Laurie," Paris said.

But, again, his best wasn't good enough, no more than it had been with his brother Hector or with Candace.

"Mister Paris, sir, it's like this," Samson said; "I got to join that march on Vicksburg tomorrow. I'm a leader of the people and I just can't let 'em down. That's one thing——"

"And another?" Paris said.

"Hard to explain with talk. Put it this way, sir: you could

189

of got out of going to the War, now couldn't you? You was more than covered by the twenty-nigger law. But you went anyhow, didn't you?"

"Yes, Samson; I went," Paris said.

"'Cause you'd of knowed you wasn't no man you hadn't went," Samson said; "and you'd of had to live all the rest of your life a-knowing that. Mighty hard thing to stummick, sir. Reckon that's the second thing——"

"Go on, Samson," Paris said.

"Well, one of these nights, them Kluxers is gonna come after me, anyhows. I ain't humble enough to suit them, and I damn sure don't mean to start now. Last week I took Cindy into town to buy some dress goods, and we run into Mr Hank Thurston. He was with Mr Di Cadwallader, Mr Reeves Jurgens, the brother of that there Phil Jurgens folks thought Mr Di kilt that time, and Mr Foster Whitfield and some more white menfolks I don't even know——"

"And?" Paris said.

"Mr Hank was drunk and powerful evil. Started in to pick at Cindy right in front of my face. I stood it long as I could with them blocking our way and standing there a-laughing. But when Mr Hank reached out and put his hand down inside the front of Cindy's frock——"

"You hit him?" Paris said.

"I'm still alive, ain't I, Mr Paris? No, I didn't hit that there monkey-looking white man; but only 'cause Mr Di beat me to it. Reckon blood's thicker than water, sir, even when part of it is mixed. . . ."

"So Di defended Lucinda?" Paris said. "Proves that there's good even where a body least expects to find it. Then what happened?"

"Nothing, sir. While the rest of 'em was separating Mr Di and Mr Hank, I got Cindy out of there. But you have to admit, Mr Paris, that's one hell of a way to have to live. Man say one half of the things that there half-human critter said to Cindy to Miz Laurel, and they wouldn't even need no undertaker to bury him 'cause you wouldn't of left a piece of him big enough to say a prayer over. . . ."

"Damned right, I wouldn't," Paris said, "only——"

"Only," Samson said, "I'm black, and a black boy ain't never s'posed to get to be a man. Got to stay a boy 'til he's forty, and after that he's Uncle. White folks plain don't realize how them little things rile a body. It's always nigger this and nigger that; and come here you burr-headed black bastid, afore I tan your hide! Always calling our wimmen-folks by their first names when they's young, and A'nty when they's old. Other day my ma asked Mr Foster Whitfield when he called her that: 'Whose sister is I? Your ma's or your pa's?'"

Man does not live by bread alone, Paris thought. There are other necessities: like dignity, like pride. He said: "Maybe you're right, Samson; and maybe I even agree with you, at least part of the way. But what the hell good is that going to do Lucinda after you've got your foolself killed?"

"Well, now," Samson said, "ever since I didn't hit Mr Hank last week, I done caught Cindy looking at me mighty funny like, more than once. I know a mighty heap of coloured menfolks beat their wives to keep 'em in line. But I don't mean to never lay a finger on Cindy. I aim to treat her just like you treats Miz Laurel, sir. Anyhow, there's the whole trouble right there: a gal wants to be proud of her man, wants him to *be* a man, sir. And the first time a black boy starts thinking 'bout being a man in Mississippi, he winds up dead. So there's the choices I got, Mr Paris: winding up dead or having my Cindy git so she plain despises me. Don't reckon I even need to tell you I'd druther her remember me proudlike after I'm gone, than have her look-ing at me like I was something that crawled out from under a rock, whilst I'm living. So I'm going to Vicksburg, tomorrow, sir. Maybe, like you said, I'll get my foolself killed, and maybe I won't. But one thing is sure: I won't never feel free, down deep on the inside, 'less I go. And a man's just got to feel free, Mr Paris. . . ."

And that was almost, but not quite, that. Not quite. For

when Laurel Griffin awoke at dawn that Monday morning, December 7 1874, she found her husband gone.

It was of course, slaughter. Afterwards the Conservative newspapers listed two white "and more than a score" of Negroes dead. What they didn't say was how much more than a score that count was.

Because, Paris thought, the transition from slavery to the martial spirit needs at least a century, maybe more. Because there weren't many Samsons among the blacks. Because the few there were had to face white men born to arms; veterans, most of them, of the bloodiest conflict in modern history.

So there were more than a score of black men dead. Among them, Duke, Paris's own groom. Paris was sure of that, because he saw his groom die. In a way, he killed Duke himself.

For—after the initial scuffle between white men trying to stop the Negroes from marching into Vicksburg to maintain in office a windy thief, not knowing, of course, that he was a thief, or not caring if they did know; being in their untaught loyalty, content with the belief, false, as such beliefs usually are, that Sheriff Crosby was "for" them; after the inevitable "person or persons unknown" that the Southern reporter always mentions in his story, even when he was standing by the person's or persons' side, and maybe even had had dinner with them the night before, had started to shoot—most of the Negroes ran like sheep, and like sheep were slaughtered. But a few, notably Samson, held out, shooting back bravely and with care.

In fact, Paris saw, Samson had chosen his terrain so well that there was absolutely no chance of the whites getting him or the men under his evident command until their ammunition ran out. And they seemed to have plenty of ammunition.

Paris stood there watching it and swearing in that way in which profanity becomes almost a prayer, when he saw

Samson pitch forward headlong like an oak, saw simultaneously, without really changing the position of his eyes, Duke lowering that ancient Enfield some twenty yards behind Samson, and he, Paris, either thinking, or saying aloud, "You treacherous bastard!" because afterwards he would never know whether he said it or merely thought it, which made no difference anyhow for he had not terminated either the spoken syllables or the unspoken ideas before the big Dance bucked and bellowed in his hand and Duke spun out from the protection of the tree he'd been hiding behind, dropped the Enfield, executed a grotesque dance step something like a buck-and-wing for a full second or maybe even two before half-a-hundred rifles, pistols and shotguns held on him and crashed—and he hanging there, his mouth gaping open with a ludicrous expression of surprise but absolutely no hint of either shock or pain because surely he was dead before he felt either——

And Paris, hearing Reeves Jurgen's high tenor piping, "Did you see that, Di? Was Paris who shot that nigger!" and Dion's rumble, "Hell, Reeves, you can never figure Paris, loony as he is. . . ." running out, crouched over low, towards the place where Samson's squad was, or rather had been, because without the big Negro there to sustain them they broke—ran—attained, most of them, five or six yards before the bullets ploughed into their backs—got there, knelt beside Samson, saw instantly that he lived, that he was merely out from the hammerblow impact of Duke's Minié ball, which had only furrowed his head, opening the black skin and red flesh down to the white bone, but leaving that uncracked——

And Paris, thinking faster than he'd ever thought before, tore off his own coat and covered Samson's torn and bloody head with it, stood up and walked back to where Dion and the others were already beginning to thin out to take up the chase that was going to last all night, and said:

"Samson belonged to my pa, Di, hope you fellows won't try to stop me from taking him home and giving him Christian burial. . . ."

"Hell, take your black carrion," Dion said, and ran after the others, shooting as he went.

Paris brought Samson home in a farm wagon that he found in the square and appropriated from among all the hundreds of buggies, wagons, surreys, saddle-horses and even mules that were tied up there with nobody watching them because their owners were either watching the slaughter or engaging in it. Long before they got there, Samson had regained consciousness; but Paris wouldn't let him sit up, made him, in fact, lie there with his head still under the coat until they were inside the plantation's own grounds. When Lucinda saw that bloody, terrible head, she fainted. Samson bent and picked her up in spite of the considerable pain he must have been in by then. He looked at Paris like a great stunned ox, sheepish and afraid, too; waiting to be told what to do next.

"You see, you damned fool!" Paris said. "What she wants is a live husband, not a dead would-be hero. I'm going to send Sarah down here to attend to you; but, come dark, I want you packed and ready."

"Packed?" Samson mumbled. "Ready?"

"Yes," Paris said; "you're a fair-to-middling carpenter and a first-class blacksmith, so you'll be able to eat and take care of Cindy even up North. . . ."

"Up North?" Samson said. He was a little in shock; but Paris was too driven by then to even notice it.

"Where I'm going to send you," he said; "where you'll stay. There's a downstream boat to New Orleans at nine o'clock tonight. Yes, I said downstream; because, even if they find out you're not dead, they'll never figure on your heading south. Soon as you get to New Orleans, you buy yourself and Cindy tickets on the train to Boston. I'll have Bruce Randolph write or wire——"

Then he saw how grey Samson's face was.

"Oh hell, get into the house and lie down! I'll send Sarah right away," he said.

That night he waited with Samson and Lucinda beside the huge bonfire that planters always built when they wanted to signal a steamboat to put into their private landings. Naturally, as it always does in times of stress, at least one thing went wrong; the steamboat was one whole hour late. Paris had to wait that hour, trying to tear the night and the distance between him and the school apart with his eyes. He didn't dare leave them for fear some of the riders scouring the whole of Warren County that night—practising that simultaneous addition and subtraction by which fifty-odd black corpses could add up to fifty dead black men that night and still be reduced to "a score" by the time the papers appeared in the morning—might be attracted by the fire he didn't dare put out either, because, in that case, the downstream boat would pass them by, and also because he had to be there to make sure the captain would take a wounded giant of a nigger and a girl who looked too damned white in the firelight aboard after having stopped at Vicksburg and learned all that had gone on there.

But, in that, they were lucky; the boat, for reasons known only to Almighty God, had had neither passengers nor freight for Vicksburg on this trip. And Paris was able to explain the turban of a bandage Sarah had wrapped around Samson's head with a remarkably truthful lie:

"Hit a no-account white man who was picking at his yellow gal, Captain. So I'm sending them down to New Orleans 'til the whole thing blows over. He's a valuable hand, and a good boy most of the time. Just couldn't stand that fellow's picking at his woman. Besides they've beat him up enough, now. I don't aim to have my lead-hand strung up over a redneck's bloody nose. . . ."

"Wasn't real smart to let your buck marry a wench this light," the Captain said: "but I reckon that's your business, Mister. Anyhow, with your guaranteeing 'em, it's not my worry. I'll drop 'em off at Nawleens for you, all right. . . ."

"All right," Paris said; "up with you both. You can write, can't you, Lucinda?"

"Yessir," Lucinda said; "and so can Samson, now. . . ."

"Well, send me a telegram when you got to the end of the line. . . ."

"Yessir," Lucinda said; "And, Mr Paris, sir——"

"Yes, Lucinda?"

"I reckon you's just about the best white man born," she said.

"Amen to that," Samson said.

An hour late. A whole hour late. Sixty minutes that could never be made up, not only no more than any period of time in a man's life even can be, but more terribly, since that was maybe the one space of bloodrace gut-twist breath-labour which, more than any other up to that moment, he could least afford to lose. He knew that at once because while he was still two miles away he could see the flames from the burning school building turning the sky above the trees a dirty yellow; and his roan already blown, exhausted, done, no more to be gotten out of him, so that he, Paris, had to sit there through an agony of plodding slow clipclopping through a nightmare of time turned fluid, viscous, thick, until he came to the edge of the clearing just as the fire reached the two hogshead of black gunpowder that Dion had left in the middle of the auditorium before he and the others soaked the floors and the walls with coal oil and, leaving, threw in the torch. . . .

It was, Paris realized in an odd, ice-cold suspension of the rage that tore him, a majestic sight—as destruction is always more awe-inspiring than the slow fitting together of bits and pieces, the patient, plodding labour that creation is. There was a rumble, spreading, deepening, becoming a roar, flame-shot; a lifting, a separation, a division again into the bits and pieces of creation, but whirlwind borne, blast torn, solid showering downward, whistling shrapnel-like through the trees, earth thudding, before the fireball, the smoke billow, the awful, earth splitting, night shattering, ear deafening, eye blinding, gut stabbing, wild torrent of sound had become mere echoes dying out of time.

The black children, huddled with their teachers two

hundred yards away, guarded there by four or five Klansmen, made to watch it, were screaming soundlessly, their
voices lost against that wall of sound. In the same unearthly
glare that had already let him see that there weren't any of
the usual group of adult students there, Paris saw Candace
and Ingra, and, beyond them, the measure of Dion's confi-
dence, his contempt for even the remote possibility of help
coming to them, because now he turned back to what he had
already been doing before the fire had reached the gunpowder: snaking that mule-skinner's whip out, swinging it
so that, even through the dark thundering echoes of the
explosion rolling back from the four corners of the sky, it
sounded pistol-crack loud as it but into Bruce Randolph's
black flesh.

Bruce was brave enough. But he was human. He couldn't
hold his pain throatlocked any more. His head arched back,
back. His mouth came open. He screamed.

And Candace, who might have, up to that moment,
escaped anything more than they'd already done to her, that
is cropped her honey-blonde hair down to a golden fuzz on
her head, crossed the fireglow in one long smooth rush, her
fingers curved into claws raking for Dion's eyes and he, the
blood showing black in the furrows she'd ripped into his
face, turned, dropped the whip, and slapped her, hard across
the mouth. Again, his hand a blur, moving, a volley of
musket-fire exploding against her face, right and left slapping, and she, her knees buckling under her, going down
very slowly, crumpling to earth; and he, Dion turning——
to meet Paris Griffin, his blue eyes gone black, moving
in, his fists hammering like the very wrath of God. Dion
went down. Paris bent, jerked him to his feet, stood there
holding him by the stuff of his robes with his left hand while
his right made ground meat of Dion's features, wet-smash-
ing, blood-splattering, louder even than the screams of the
children, until inevitably he, Paris, felt that mule-sick
impact jar his middle and turned Di loose, letting him slide
downwards to the earth, hearing, the tiniest measurable
fraction of a second later, the crack, whanging, already-

terminated whistle because sound is always slower than sight, and he, hanging there waiting for the pain that hadn't even come yet, saw on the other edge of his field of vision Candace getting up from the ground, racing toward him, and said:

"Get back, Candy!" And she:

"No, Paris! I won't let——"

And somebody saying, "Goddammit, Hank, didn't I tell you there wasn't to be no shooting against white men?"

Then:

"Paris——" Candace's voice rose, edged; "Paris—are you all right?"

"Yes," he said, and clamped his jaw against the sudden searing, the hot wet pumping jetting against his clothing, the warm flooding, the hollow weakness spreading out from his middle in ever-widening waves, and Candace whispering, her voice gone hoarse with horror, because she was in front of him, now, close enough to see:

"No. No, you're not all right, Paris; you're——"

Then all the night bent itself into a funnel, tornado whirling, through which he heard dimly Candace starting to scream. He lay at the bottom of the funnel at the vortex of the whirlwind in the deepest heart of night, hearing, before sound faded out of existence, too, Reeves Jurgen's voice saying:

"Well, I'll be goddamned! Hank didn't miss!"

And Candace, not screaming any more, kneeling beside him ripping at his clothing, and they the tall hooded shadows picking Dion up, carrying him away; then the sound of horses moving off, and the night air on his belly so that he seemed to be drawing it in through his middle; and Candace was saying very, very softly: "Oh, my God!" Then her voice, scream-shrill, rising: "Ingra! Come here! Oh dear Christ!"

Then nothing. Absolutely nothing at all.

And, afterwards, the things he couldn't know: They, the two women, alone—because the two Yankee male school·

teachers had defined the limits of their courage by not even showing up that night—aided only by the black children, lifted him, big and heavy as he was, into Ingra's buggy, and afterwards cut down Bruce Randolph, unconscious, too, and hanging from the tree he'd been tied to like a trussed and gutted hog, and got him up on to Paris's horse; swinging head down across the saddle; then, with Candace driving the buggy, and Ingra walking behind her leading Paris's roan and looking back every minute to see that Bruce didn't fall off, the two of them, surrounded by the black children no longer crying either, started off, not for Hector's place which was close at hand, because they were afraid it would be next on the Klan's list, but for Griffin's Way.

And getting there finally, and the Negroes bringing Paris in and laying him on the sofa, and Laurel coming down the stairs and seeing him like that, kneeling beside him wordlessly and bending with some acutely awful impulse to kiss his mouth, and his head lolling lifelessly away from her, leaving a long smear of blood on her face as his lips trailed across her cheek; and she, Laurel, whispering:

"Paris, Paris——" then hideously achingly terribly starting to scream, falling across him, clutching him with demented fury, insane grief, until Candace had to tear her away from him, and she said:

"For you. Like a dog. Like a gun-shot dog. If he dies, if he dies, I'll——"

"You'll what?" Candace said, not because she cared or wanted to know, but to distract Laurel, quiet her——

"I'll kill you, Candace Trevor," Laurel said.

14

"ALL of you get out," Dr Harley Benson said, "except Nurse Trevor and Sarah. I need some elbow room. . . ."

"Please, Doc," Laurel whispered, "can't I stay, too?"

"No, Laurie," the Doctor said, "what I've got to do, you'd likely faint seeing. . . ."

"But—but——" Laurel said, "I'm his wife! He needs me! And——"

"He will need you later on. But not now. Now he needs a doctor and a trained nurse and this fat nigger wench to fetch and carry for them both. I only hope she's got a strong stomach. With all due respect to your natural feelings, Laurie, will you please get out of here and stop wasting the time that Paris sure Lord hasn't got?"

"Oh!" Laurel said; then she fled, trailing a *glissando* of sobs behind her like a banner.

Harley Benson bent to his task.

"Gut shot," he murmured, "high. Missed the big gut. Looks like it hit the stomach, though it's a mite high for even that. I sure Lord hope it didn't—You've done a good job, as usual, Nurse. . . ."

"Doctor——?" Candace said.

"Can't tell. Have to go in there and see." He raised his eyes to Paris's face. "Dear Lord!" he said.

"Doctor!" Candace's voice tightened out of sound.

"The oesophagus—almost at the intersection where it joins the stomach. Look, Nurse—blood coming out of his mouth. . . ."

"That bad, Doctor?" Sarah said.

"Could be. Depends upon the amount of damage. A heavy calibre ball could have torn that tube all to hell. Good thing I thought to bring some ether. Don't need much. He's in shock. There, that does it. Now we'll just wait five minutes. . . ."

The five minutes ticked away, prolonging themselves along the plane of Candace's anguish, endlessly.

The Doctor said: "All right, Nurse Trevor, here we go: scalpel!"

Candace slapped it into his palm.

He worked with intense concentration, silently.

"Forceps!" he barked. Candace handed them over.

Doctor Benson pushed the forceps into the incision he had made. Their jaws opened, closed, came out holding the ball.

"Doctor!" Candace's voice was imploring.

"Don't know," he said. "He's got a chance. Nurse. A mighty slim chance; but still a chance. Ball didn't flatten. Tube's not collapsed. Hole in it, that's all. So now I'm going to suture it and——"

"And what?" Candace whispered.

"And pray," Dr Harley Benson said.

Laurel was waiting when he came out. Her eyes were the only things left alive in her face. Dr Benson looked at her, wearily.

"Have Ruby fix me up a room, Laurie," he said. "Send somebody over to old Doc Miller's. Tell him to take care of all my patients for the next three or four days. I get Paris that far along, he'll make it—maybe. I'm not promising anything. If the wound's healed enough by the time the hot weather sets in so that he doesn't get gangrene; or if it doesn't rain too much the rest of the month and give him pneumonia; or if we can get enough soup and other liquid foods into him to keep him from starving, or if any of ten thousand other goddamned things don't happen, he'll live. Mighty heap of ifs. As I told Nurse Trevor, prayer is indicated. It's in the hands of the Lord. Who did it? Have to make a report, you know. Gunshot case. That's the law."

"I—I don't know," Laurel whispered. "Ask Candace. She was there. Her and Ingra Holm brought him home. . . ."

"Nurse!" Harley Benson called.

Candace came to the door.

"You know who shot Paris?" the Doctor said.

"Yes. Hank Thurston. I didn't see him do it, or rather I can't swear he fired the shot, because they all had their hoods on except Di——"

"The Klan, eh? That ties it. Hardly worth the trouble to report the case to Crosby. Hell! I can't report to him; he's skipped. . . ."

"I heard them say, 'Hank, I told you not to shoot,' or words to that effect," Candace said, "so it must have been——"

"Heck, Nurse, that would never stand up in court. There're at least three fellows named Henry who belong to the Klan. Anyhow, it's not important now. First things first. And number one on my list right now is saving Paris. You got any drinking whisky, Laurie?"

"Yes, Doc," Laurel said.

"Send somebody to fetch me up a snort. I sure Lord need it," the Doctor said.

The next four days and nights, Candace snatched minutes of sleep in her chair beside Paris's bed. Laurel walked the halls, a wan and ineffectual ghost; but she didn't interfere. Candace blessed her for that. Hector stormed in and out, gaunt and shaking. His two sons had had to use force at first to keep him from going single-handed after the entire Klan.

The fourth night, Paris Griffin woke up raving.

"Candy!" he wept! "Candy my angel, my good angel I can't have. Henry crippled, Henry in the way, always in the way and Laurie, poor little Laurie, I can't, I can't——"

Candace put her hand on his forehead. It was like touching a stovelid. She looked around for Sarah, but Sarah wasn't there, nobody was there but Laurel, standing in the doorway with her lips only distinguishable by reason of the fact that they were at that moment actually whiter than the rest of her face, and the light in her blue eyes splintering like slivers of glass into the planes and angles of grief.

"Go get the doctor, Laurel," Candace said.

"All right," Laurel said, her voice flat, nasal twanging; "but, before I go, I reckon you realize I heard that—what Paris said, I mean. So when he comes back to his senses you tell him——"

"What?" Candace said.

"That I've gone. That I won't be in the way no more. Not in his way nor yours. Not in nobody's Tell him that——"

"Oh, don't be a fool, Laurel!" Candace said. "Just you call the doctor for me, right now!"

After she'd waked Dr Benson, Laurel didn't come back to the sick room. Instead she went to her own room, walked over to her dresser and stared at her face in the mirror. She wasn't even crying, yet. She sank down in a chair before the dresser, picked up her brush and began to stroke her long black hair. Brushing her hair had always soothed her before, but tonight it didn't. She had the feeling that nothing would ever soothe her again. A million, million invisible ants crawled over the surface of her skin under her clothes.

I'm just too nervous and upset, she thought, and—

She put the brush down and her gaze fell on the tray full of notes that had been arriving all day from Paris's friends. Two days ago Dr Benson had been forced to put a notice in *The Herald* begging them not to call, due to the gravity of Paris's condition. So they didn't come any more to drive her further out of her mind than she already was: they just sent notes asking after Paris and extending her their sympathy. What a lot of friends Paris had!

What a lot of friends, and I have none, she thought. I've been trying to live like a decent woman, going to church and all. Reading and improving myself so he'd really forgive me and love me again, and instead of that he—— It's not fair! Just because I was a silly little warm-hearted fool who never did know how to keep her knees together—no matter what I do now he'll never forget what I did with Di or believe I was forced into it! I won't stand it! I won't!

Her eyes swept over those notes again. They were all addressed to her. But suddenly the bold script of the note that lay on top of all the rest leaped up and fairly slapped her in the face. She put out a trembling hand towards it. Jerked her hand away as though from fire. Put it out again. Took up that note. Tore it open. Read it. Sat there a long time holding it. Said:

"Why not? Paris doesn't want me, even out of his head it's her he calls on not me, so I'm all alone now, so why not, so what have I got to lose?"

She turned, raced for the closet, drew out her riding-habit, tore off the housedress she was wearing, began feverishly to dress again.

"You came," Dion said, "Lord God, Laurie, you came!"

"Yep," she said; "just what do you aim to do about it, Dion?"

"This!" he said, and dragged her into his arms. He ground his mouth against hers, hurting her.

"No!" she said. No. Dion! You got me wrong, I didn't come for that, you don't understan——"

But his arms tightened around her in ferocious jerks, so that it felt as if her ribs were being bent in, maybe even broken, and she couldn't breathe any more, so she pushed her head back, opening her mouth even to gulp in air, seeing that it was a cloudy night without even any stars; feeling on her face the fine misting that was more like a heavy fog than actual rain; but he put his big fingers into her hair and forced her head down and his mouth was on hers and his big body pushed her to the ground there almost under the horses' hooves. She saw, as his mouth came away from hers, the insane glitter of his eyes.

She didn't say anything, knowing that talk was a waste of breath. She fought him until fighting him became another waste of breath and of time; then she didn't fight him any more but moved outwards beyond herself and stood at some point of extreme emotional detachment just beyond the rim of life maybe and watched what was going on almost beneath the horse's hooves, there on the muddy ground. It was a wet, cold night in December, and with all her strength she resisted being dragged into the ugliness she was watching, into that duel to death in the mud, in the singularly appropriate mud, between two frenzied wrestlers who had already stopped being entirely human and who maybe had never really achieved humanity if that quality includes the attribute of tenderness and the possession of a mind; but in the end she was dragged into it, left her point of detachment and entered into that female body twisting on the ground.

"Dion," she said; then her voice rising rising rising: "Oh, Dion—Dion—Di!"

Dion looked at her, and if she could have seen his eyes she would have recognized the hurt in them. But it was too dark. She had the feeling that it was always going to be too dark for her now, that she would move forever through a landscape without figures, by the waters of desolation, over which no sun would ever rise. She was a very primitive woman but she was also very complicated, for primitives are as complicated as civilized people, the only effect of civilization being to increase people's awareness of their complications, but not necessarily to make them suffer more. She was suffering now. She didn't need to know precisely why she was suffering to spin arabesques of argument and counter-argument over the degree of her guilt. No, she suffered as a dumb beast suffers: on one level, in her bruised, hurt, torn. violated body; and on another, in a peculiarly feminine way, she was contemplating a series of concrete images, partially because she was arriving at total honesty, and partially because it is woman, not man, who is realistic. Those images were contrasts, comparisons: the horses' hooves; the icy drizzle falling into her face; her bedraggled, mud-plastered clothing; the mud even in her hair; the world of mud—and their antitheses: the soft yellow glow of the firelight in her bedroom; the warm, faintly perfumed crispness of sheets; the rain misting the window-panes; the good, clean, well scrubbed, fine soap and shaving lotion smell, of Paris with, rarely, a lingering hint of cigar smoke sometimes added; and also a good many things she didn't even know how to put into words, but which she summed up in one long interior wail: He never hurts me, never, just makes me feel so good I think I'm going to purely die from how good I feel instead of—of dirtying me like this! Oh, Lord, I——"

"What I want to know," Dion said, his voice thick with the hurt she was too absorbed with self to notice; and certainly not cultured enough to recognize its tragic depth, because to pity the inarticulate sufferings of Caliban one had to know who Caliban was, "is why the hell you came if you didn't know what you was letting yourself in for?"

"I didn't know," she said. "No, that's a lie. I did. I was just mean mad and hurt because Paris was raving and he called for Candace, not for me. Only I've been a fool. Again. And maybe I'll go on being a fool all the rest of my life. But one thing I ain't never going to be again——"

"What's that, Laurie?" Dion said.

"This particular kind of a fool. All right, he doesn't love me and maybe he never has. But I love him. And when you love a person who doesn't love you back no matter how you try to hurt him, you can't, because to be hurt, a body's got to care. That's one thing. . . ."

"That's goddamned well enough for my money," Dion said.

"No," she said, "it's not enough. The other thing I found out tonight is that I love him enough to put up with his not loving me. That love purely hasn't got any pride. If I was fair, I'd give him up, let him run off with Candace, only he won't do that 'cause he's too honourable, the damn fool; and she won't either because maybe she's too honourable, too, though it's awful hard to believe that any woman even knows what being honourable means. . . ."

"But me," Dion said; "what about me, Baby?"

Laurel stood up, then. Put out her hand to him.

"Goodbye, Dion," she said.

She was almost back to Griffin's Way when she heard the sound of hoofbeats, recognized that moving segment of deeper darkness as horse and rider. She pulled Prince up and waited, aching all over, inside and out; but the interior ache was terror, because a horseman coming from Griffin's Way at this time of night meant, had to mean——

"Laurie!" Barry Cadwallader called. "Is that you?"

"Yes!" she called back, her voice a rusty blade cutting the darkness dully, painfully.

Barry cantered toward the sound of her voice. Even then she was woman enough to bless the darkness that kept him from seeing what a mess she was.

"You—you better get along home, Honey," Barry said; and she heard, astonished, the tears drowning his voice.

"Why," she whispered; "why, Barry, you're crying!"

"Yes, goddammit!" he said. "I am. Who wouldn't? He was the best friend a fellow ever had. Hell, he was more than my friend; he was the brother that Di never had either the gumption or the decency to be. A man. A little lower than the angels, but not much. So I'm crying. I'm going to go on crying on the inside forever, Laurie. I'm never going to quit. . . ."

"Barry——" her voice was a breath-rustle, less and more, than sound; "Barry, you don't mean——"

"Not yet. Only Doc Benson's given up. Told Candace to send somebody for the preacher—Laurie!"

He leaped down from his mount. But she hadn't fainted. She was lying face down in the mud, pounding the earth with her fists, so that with each blow she made a splashing, and screaming like a demented woman, which, maybe, at that moment, she was:

"You can't! You can't; do you hear me? He's good! Paris is all good, it's me who's bad, who went out in the night in the rain to wallow in the mud with a man and left him dying! You can't, it's not fair. It's me You've got to take and burn in hell forever! Not him! Not him! I won't let You! You take Paris, good like he is, You aren't fit for folks to pray to! You're mean, do You hear me; mean!"

"Laurie!" Barry said.

"I'm sorry! I shouldn't have said that! You're not mean.

207

You're kind. And, because You're kind, take me. Let me die in the dirt like a dog like the she-dog I am, let me die in the worst way You can figure out for a person to die, covered with sores like Lazarus and screaming all the way to hell. Please, God, do that for me. Do anything to me, but don't take him. . . ."

Barry touched her shoulder.

"Leave me alone!" she shrilled. "Leave me here in the mud where I belong, to die!"

Wearily, tenderly, Barry picked her up.

"No, Laurie; your place is with Paris, now," he said.

Candace and the doctor stood there looking at that still figure on the bed. Then Paris's lips moved. He said, his voice the rustle of dead leaves on a bitter day:

"Non fui, non sum, non curo. . . ."

"Oh, my God!" Candace said.

"Why?" Harley Benson said. "What did he say?"

"'I was not, I am not, I care not,'" Candace translated.

"You see? That mean's he's given up. You'd better send for that preacher like I told you. . . ."

"No! I don't want preachers or anybody else in the way! I'm going to save him, you hear me, Doctor? I'm going to——"

She stopped, staring at that apparition in the door, at that tiny trembling figure who looked for all the world like a little girl who had been playing at making mud-pies, with a good bit too much enthusiasm.

"Yes," the apparition said, "you are. And I'm going to help you. Between us, we'll do it. Between the two who love him the best of all the world."

Candace stood there, staring at her, hearing like an echo the utter self-negating sincerity of her tone.

"All right, Laurel!" she said, "go wash and change your clothes, then come back here."

Then she turned back to the bed. She did not leave it for the twenty-seven days and nights he lingered on, his life hanging by a spider's thread. She forced liquids down his

208

throat, drop by drop. She fought the fever down night after night, did all of the thousand and one dirty, disagreeable tasks necessary to keep him alive. Laurel worked at her side, doing all her total ignorance of nursing permitted her to do, relieving Candace at the intervals when fatigue overcame her, or when she absolutely had to leave the room. But, even in this, Laurel was not lucky, for it was Candace who was there with him on the morning of the twenty-eighth day.

She slept in her chair. Her eyes were blue-ringed, sunk in their sockets. She had lost twenty pounds. Even in her sleep she trembled.

On his bed, Paris Griffin opened his eyes. Even that motion cost him effort. He closed them again. Lay there like that, feeling the weakness unto death, but, under it, through it, the first faint stir of returning life. He lay there, puzzling it all out in his mind, until he had it clear.

Somebody shot me. Not Dion. He was already down. But I—I didn't die. I—am not going to die—because Candace saved me. I'll just lie here until my strength comes back —I——

He slept.

When he woke again, he felt stronger. Opening his eyes cost him far less effort now. The room came slowly into focus. Griffin's Way, he thought. Home. Who brought me —home?

He turned his head. Saw the woman sleeping in the chair.

"Candy," he whispered, "Candy. . . ."

But he could not make her hear. Her sleep was too profound, his voice too weak.

He tried to lift his arm to touch her. It fell back under its own weight. He tried again. Gave it up. He couldn't. He just wasn't strong enough yet. He lay there very peacefully, waiting for her to awaken, until Sarah came into the room and saw his opened eyes.

"Mister Paris!" she breathed.

"Howdy, Sarah?" he said.

"Praise Jesus!" Sarah thundered. "Praise the good, kind Lord!"

"Sarah," Candace said, without opening her eyes, "you mustn't! He——"

Then she came bolt upright in that chair, staring at him, her face ghost-white, her pale lips trembling.

"Candy——" he said, clearly, "I——"

She was out of the chair in one wild rush. She fell to her knees beside the bed, her head pillowed on his bony chest, her arms clutching him with convulsive strength, her whole body racked with the torrential outpouring of her grief turned joy.

"Candy," he said, "don't cry. Please, Candy, please don't cry. . . ."

"Let her, Mister Paris," Sarah said, her black face streaked now, too. "Let her cry it out. 'Cause them there is purely healin' tears!"

15

THE girl Rachel Griffin came out of the house. She looked out towards the fields where her father Hector and her brothers Hubert and William were. Then she came down the stairs of the house her father had built. It was a very beautiful house, bigger than Griffin's Way. It was of white-washed brick, with fluted columns supporting the roof. It was the biggest house in Warren County. And the finest.

It was the gauge that Hector Griffin had flung into the face of the world.

Rachel lifted her slim, white hands and stared at them. She always did that. She was trying to see if she had blue half-moons at the base of her fingernails. People said that when a person had coloured blood—however remote, however little—it showed that way. She hadn't any half-moons, and it didn't show in any way at all. She was several shades whiter than nearly any white person she knew except perhaps Laurel. She was an exquisitely lovely girl with proud, patrician features. The only thing wrong with her was that she had been born at the wrong time, in the wrong place and among the wrong people. Which was enough. More than enough.

She drew her riding-gloves up over her hands. Then she went around the house to the stables.

"Caesar," she said to the groom, "saddle Nancy for me."

"Yes'm," Caesar said sullenly; and she could feel his hatred rise up between them like a wall.

That was bad. That was, perhaps, the worst of all. On other plantations, the Negroes loved their masters. On every place where they were treated with anything remotely resembling kindness, they responded with a boundless measure of devotion. But not at The Briars, as Hector had proudly started calling his place after the house was built.

At The Briars, the blacks were treated very well indeed. Yet, to every kindness, every indulgence granted them, they returned this silent, sullen hate. She knew what they called their masters. She had heard them. All too often, and with deliberate malice, they raised their voices when she was near.

"Uppity yaller niggers," they snarled; "playactin' like they's white!"

We, she thought again, are caught between the upper and the nether millstones. We are being ground slowly out of life. . . .

She waited without protest, while Caesar took five times longer to saddle her mare than that simple task required. Then she mounted and rode away from there.

She hadn't anywhere to go. When she tired of the company of her mother Roberta and her sister Mathilda, all she could do was to lock herself in her room with a book. Because of Ernest Thurston, she hadn't even been able to indulge in her second favourite pastime, her solitary rides through the woods, for more than six months. But she was sure he must have given up by now; he was too stupid to keep anything on his mind that long. She had no friends she could visit. There were no people of her race with anything comparable to her wealth, her culture, within hundreds of miles. My race? She thought bitterly; what race am I? Where do I belong? And to whom?

She tired very easily of Roberta's and Matty's company. The conditions of her life had made her a person of painful sensitivity. Her mother's untutored dialect distressed her as did her sister's scatterbrained carelessness. Worst of all, now, was the presence of that awful, crippled white man in their house. Who was crippled in more ways than one, because self-pity, her father had taught her, was a crueller wound than the one that had wasted his legs away to mere stilts. So now when Candace came home from nursing Uncle Paris, Rachel made it her business to go out in the yard. She didn't want to listen to Henry Trevor screaming at Candace, calling her whore, sometimes even throwing things at the woman who had saved Uncle Paris's life: at the pallid, tired woman who was angel and saint, and the only true friend that she, Rachel, had. So she would take her book, go out to the garden house and sit there reading. Her father indulged her whims, spoiled and petted her. As a result, there were more books at The Briars than anybody could have gathered in all the rest of the state of Mississippi. And Rachel Griffin had read them all, had got from them the materials for dreaming; had further walled herself away from what had to be her world.

Today, she had made her mind up to visit her Uncle Paris. That called for a great deal of courage, because she knew that Laurel hated worse than the very dickens for any of them to come up there. Rachel was sure that Laurel would send her away, or tell her to come in the back door, if she dared. Only, she didn't dare. She would just sit there looking at Rachel as though she had committed a crime when she came in the front door. And Rachel wouldn't go around to the back. She'd quite literally die first. But, anyhow, she was going up to Griffin's Way. Dr Benson said Uncle Paris needed to get out of doors, now that the weather was getting warm, that riding would do him a sight of good. So she'd take him riding with her. Poor Uncle Paris! He was still so grey, so pale. . . .

She was thinking about all that as she cantered through the woods in the dusk of evening. She was always thinking about things like that—which was why, perhaps, she didn't see Ernest Thurston in time.

At twenty, Ernest was a duplicate of his father, except that he was bigger. In fact, he was grossly, obscenely fat. The reason she'd always outdistanced him before was that even the powerful bay he rode was hopelessly handicapped with Ernest atop him. That, and the fact she had always been lucky enough to encounter him out in the open where her superb horsewomanship told.

But she wasn't out in the open, now. Worse, she was too preoccupied with her thoughts to take any of the usual precautions that bitter experience had taught her she had to take in a world of white men. Or, for that matter, in a world of black men. Girls in the middle, like she was, were considered fair game by both.

She rode on, thinking: I wonder what Oberlin will be like? Daddy says I'm not to come back even after I finish college. He's right. The South's no place for me. But, Oh, I'll miss him so! Him and Uncle Paris and Candace——

Then she felt Nancy jerk. She looked down. Saw that hairy fist clamped over her mare's bridle. Raised her eyes inch by inch to the leering proof of Darwin's theories that served Ernest Thurston for a face.

"You gonna git down, Rachie?" he said. "Or do I hafta drag you off of there?"

Rachel sat there looking at him. Her slim hand closed over her riding-crop. She lifted it, swung it sideways with all her force. Caught Ernest full in the face. Brought blood.

He howled, and dropped the bridle. Rachel clapped spur to her mount. Got out of there. But Ernest Thurston didn't make the mistake of mounting and riding after her. Instead, he sent his big hand clawing backwards under the split tail of his coat until his fingers closed around the butt of the Navy Colt he had in his hip pocket. He jerked it out, sighted on the mare. Touched the trigger.

And poor Nancy somersaulted, throwing Rachel over her head.

Ernest came up to where Rachel lay. She was unconscious. She also had three fractured ribs. But Ernest didn't know that. Not that he would have given a damn had he known.

Hell, he thought; sure hope she ain't dead. Be a shame to kill off a fine piece like that. . . .

He bent down, saw her breathe. Straightened up, grinning.

"Oh boy!" he said aloud. "This here is sure Lord my lucky day—'cause now, she can't even fight. . . ."

Then, catching her by her ankles, he dragged her into the underbush.

Life is forever pitiless. Rachel did not stay unconscious. She came back into awareness, both too soon and too late. A few minutes sooner, with her Griffin's heart, she might have escaped him still. Some minutes later, since the lusts of the obese are quickly appeased, she might have escaped the knowledge of it. Awaking when she did, she escaped neither.

She fought like a cornered wildcat, despite the agony in her. Left not an inch of his face unbloodied by her nails. Sank her teeth into that sweaty hollow of his throat. Hung on until he spread his powerful fingers wide and pushed against her face with all his force. Even then she went on fighting with silent ferocity until he lifted his great mallet of a fist, brought it whistling down. And red fire and utter dark exploded once more inside her head.

When she came back again, he was gone. Had been gone for hours. The trees were ghost shapes, black upon blackness. Stars stood high above them, glittering. Like mocking eyes. Like the cold fires of evil.

She rolled over. Her body was one long bruise in the places where it wasn't broken, torn. She lay there. Put down her hands to push herself up. She couldn't. She tried again, two dozen times, before she gave it up. Sank back. Lay there clawing the earth and crying.

Until her father found her.

Hector bent down and lifted his daughter up. Walked back to where he had left his horse. Slung Rachel over one shoulder so he could mount. The jagged edges of her ribs bit into her flesh. She screamed.

But not even then did Hector speak. Not until she lay once more on her bed, with Mathilda and Roberta sobbing as they attended her. Then he said one word, that one quietly:

"Ernest?"

"Yes!" Rachel wept. "Oh, Daddy, I——"

But he was gone. He stopped only long enough to lock Hubert and Billy in their room. Then he mounted. Rode away.

To Hank Thurston's place.

He sat there on his horse, facing Henry Thurston.

"Tell that boy of yours to come out, Hank," he said.

"Now you look ahere, Hec," Hank Thurston said; "Ernest ain't here. Dunno where the hell he——"

"Tell him to come out," Hector said.

"I told you he ain't here!" Hank said. "Sides——"

"I'll come in after him," Hector said.

"Lord God, Hec, I——"

"And drag him out from under the bed, or out of the clothes closet, or where ever else he's hiding. Ain't one full set of guts amongst all you hairy apes; but whatever part of a gut he's got, he's going to need. Go get him, Hank. Or else I will."

"You won't have to, you nigger-loving bastid!" Ernest said from the doorway. "'Cause you're getting yours right now!"

The roar of the Navy Colt in his hand cut off his own words. Hector felt the mule kick of that ball as it smashed into his hip, breaking the bone. He gave with the impact, came up again. Drew. Fired. Taking deliberate aim, as though he were shooting a snake.

Ernest swayed there. Then he loosened. Slumped, his thick legs suddenly boneless. Bent forward, gathering speed. The crash he made striking the veranda shook the whole house.

Hank Thurston stood there, staring at his son.

"You killed him!" he said. "You killed my boy!"

"Naturally," Hector said; "what else did you expect me to do?"

But the ugly, ape-like man bent, clawing for that pistol on the floor. Came up with it. Sighting, Hector shot him, in the belly, where it would hurt.

Then he turned and rode away, knowing that he, too, was done. That when he got down from his horse, he wasn't even going to be able to walk, much less remount. That he would have to sit by the window, gun in hand, and wait for the Kluxers. But first, he had a thing to do.

"Look, 'Berta," he said, as she was bandaging his broken hip; "you take the kids and strike out for Griffin's Way. Right now. Don't argue; just get going!"

"And leave you, Honey?" Roberta sobbed. "I can't. I purely can't. And Rachie ain't in no state to be hauled around. Then there's Mr Trevor, crippled up like he is——"

"He's in no danger. Put him in the stable. He'll be perfectly safe there and you can't be burdened with him now! You've got to move fast! You hear me, 'Berta? Get the kids out of here. Especially the boys. What the blackguards would do to them——"

"Not—Griffin's Way, Daddy," Rachel whispered. "Uncle Paris can hardly hold himself up, much less a gun. And they'd come there, too; soon as they found out we weren't here. Why must Uncle Paris die, too? And for a thing that's not his fault?"

"Then head for Walfen! Tell Barry Cadwallader I sent you! Dion won't be there. because he's as sure as hell out rounding up the Kluxers by now. Barry'll get you to Vicksburg, put you on a train——"

"Pa," Hubert said, "I'm staying. You can't make me go. All right. I may get killed. Dying's nothing much, Pa. It's living that's rough. 'Specially the way we have to live——"

Hector stared at his son. He thought: And the brand I put on him doesn't even show. Doesn't show, doesn't count, doesn't even matter—except to fools: except to the blind and murderous fools we live among. He said:

"I'm sorry, son."

Hubert smiled. He had the Griffin's smile, that crooked twist of lip that mocked all the world, but most of all himself.

"Don't be, Pa," he said. "It's not your fault. You didn't make the world—or put evil in it. Chalk that one up against God. All you did was to buck it. Which wasn't smart. But then, being decent never is."

"Hubert, listen to me!" Hector said, urgency shaking his voice. "You're young! You've got all of life before you. Get out, boy! Go North. Looking like you do, nobody'll——"

"Know?" Hubert said. "I will, Pa. I—and God, if there is a God, which I doubt. You're asking a sight too much, old man. Asking me, your son, to do what you never did:

bow my head; accept evil; bed down nightly with a lie. No, Pa. I'm sorry; but, no."

"Hubert, for Jesus' sake——"

"Don't call on him, Pa. He didn't run. He died. I'm a Griffin, ain't I?"

"Yes, Hubert," Hector whispered; "you sure Lord are."

He turned to his younger son.

"Billy?" he said.

Billy was crying.

"Pa, I—I'm scared!" he wept. "I'm so damned scared that——"

"Go, son," Hector said, "go—with my blessing. . . ."

"Hue," he said, "we could get Pa into that trap! Big as he is, we could! Maybe we'd have to put Rachie on top of him, but——"

"No, son," Hector said; "that little rig was made for ladies, not hauling shot-up carcasses big as mine. Even if you could get me into it, one horse could barely move us all; and one horse is all you can hitch up to a trap."

"I'll walk!" Billy said. "That rig's too small for more than Ma and the girls, even using that nigger jump-seat in the back——"

"You see," Hector said, "you've proved my point——"

"Oh, damn them!" Billy said. "Pa, why'd you have to be so damned generous and warn the niggers anyhow?"

"Didn't want them killed, too," Hector said; "only——"

"Only you didn't know they'd take the mules and all the light wagons to get away in, except the trap. And the only reason they didn't take it, too, was because they realized it wouldn't hold one filthy mattress and the pots and pans they were bent on saving like the pack rats they are. And they took the feed wagon, the only one big enough to hold us all. And you goddamned sure can't ride a horse, now. In other words, Pa; you just didn't expect them to act like—niggers," Hubert said.

"No," Hector said tiredly, "say I didn't expect them to act like slaves. That I thought I'd taught them how to be free. I failed. So now I've got to pay for that failure and a

218

couple of others—like thinking I could buck the whole world. But *you* don't have to; not either one of you."

"Pa, you and I have settled that argument," Hubert said; "so let's skip it. It's up to Billy, now. . . ."

Billy stared at his brother.

"Hue," he said, "I'm not brave like you. I wish to God I was, but——"

"It's all right, boy," Hubert said. "Somebody's got to take care of Ma and the girls."

They put Rachel in the little trap—which was a smart, topless little vehicle made of rattan woven basket-fashion, with one broad seat upholstered in topgrain calf-skin wide enough to hold three people if they squeezed in tight, and behind that, and slightly above it a jump-seat where a servant usually rode when smart ladies went for a drive. Billy drove, with Roberta sitting beside him, holding Rachel in her arms and crying. Because there was no more room inside the body of the trap, Matty had to ride in the high, small jump or "nigger" seat above and behind them.

Billy flapped the reins over the back of the horse. Moved off. Got, perhaps, five hundred yards from the house. Then Roberta said:

"Stop this buggy, son."

"Ma!" Billy said. "There's no time! They'll be coming and——"

"Stop this here buggy, Billy!" Roberta said.

Billy drew back on the reins. Saw his mother stand up, climb down.

"Ma!" he said. "Ma, where're you going?"

"Home," Roberta said, "where I should have stayed. Done lived all these years with your Pa, boy. Reckon I can die with him, too. . . ."

"Ma!" Billy cried. Then he felt Rachel's hand on his arm. Turned to face his sister.

"Turn the trap around, Billy," Rachel said. "We're going back—all of us."

"Rachie, Lord God!"

"Listen to me, Billy. We're done—this family is finished. All finished, boy——"

"But, Rachie——!"

"They'll catch us, Billy. Tie you to a post, pour coal oil over you, set you afire—if they're feeling kind. If not, they'll chain you down to a green log wet with water so it'll take a long time to burn and they can hear you screaming for an hour, maybe two. Then you know what they'll do to me and Matty? Maybe even to Ma, who's still young-looking? Dying, as long as you can choose the way you do it, is not so hard, just as Hue said. But *that* is. Too hard, Billy boy; believe me, I know. People die—some young, some old. Makes no difference. All you can do is put it off—maybe. Say you got away. Say you did put it off a while——"

"Rachie——" Billy's voice was calmer now.

"Say," Rachel went on tiredly, "you lived fifty more years. Fifty years of remembering what you'd have to remember: that you left Daddy and Hubert to die, and ran like a rat to save your skin. The skin you can't save anyhow, since we start dying the day we're born. D'you think you can stand that, Billy?"

"No," Billy said. "No, Rachie, I couldn't."

Then he tugged at the reins, turning the little trap around.

Mathilda stood up then. Leaped to the ground.

"Fools!" she screamed at them. "Crazy damn yellow-nigger fools!"

Then she whirled, dived into the underbrush, running hard. She kept on running until she came out on the road. But, by then, the horsemen were there. And little Mathilda Griffin, flighty Matty Griffin, ran straight into them.

Which was what delayed them long enough for the trap to reach the house.

From The Briars to Griffin's Way was roughly twelve miles. Too far for the sound of gunfire to carry. And the flames from the burning mansion needed time to leap high enough to catch the eye over that distance.

"They've won, now," Bruce Randolph said. He sat on the veranda of Griffin's Way with his wife Eulalia, Paris and Laurel, Barry Cadwallader and Ingra Holm. And Candace Trevor. He knew Laurel Griffin didn't like his being there; at least, she hadn't at first; but, now, her intense curiosity had overcome her objections. "They've won; and every bad thing we've done will be remembered, will be enshrined, along with all the exaggerations and inventions they will add, in history; and every good thing destroyed, forgotten. . . ."

"Maybe," Barry said, "maybe it's God's will, Bruce."

"God," Paris whispered, because speaking aloud cost him too much effort still. "Don't drag Him into this, Barry! You think He cares what happens to mankind? You believe He's even there?"

"What good thing?" Laurel snapped suddenly, "What good thing have carpet-baggers and scallawags, and you nig—coloured folks, done?"

Bruce smiled.

"Thanks for changing in midflight, Mrs Griffin," he said. "We've done a lot. In fact, we've done more than you Southerners ever did, even granting that the stealing and corruption is greater today. Do you realize, Mrs Griffin, that white children are going to free public schools in the South, their teachers' salaries paid, for the first time in your history—thanks to us? That in state after state, the most enlightened constitutions you've ever had have been written —by us? That public works have been started, institutional care provided for your insane, public hospitals for your sick poor, roads built, sanitation improved—by us? Of course these things cost money. Of course some of that money gets stolen by the thieves who spring up out of the moral decline that follows *every* war. But most of it has been used with fair wisdom to give the people of the South, all the people of the South, a few of the things that your Conservatives have robbed them of, throughout your history——"

"Well, I like that!" Laurel began; but she never finished, or even remembered, what she was going to say after that moment. For Dion Cadwallader, like nearly every man who invents a successful technique, saw no reason to change it: that black gunpowder was most effective against walls of brick, which mere fire took too long to bring down, he already knew from his experience with the school.

They saw the sullen, awful whitening of the night. Heard, a considerable time afterwards, for twelve miles was a long distance for sound to travel, the deep, slow rumble rolling in upon them from every direction, the echoes having caught up with the original thunder.

Paris was already on his feet.

"Laurie," he croaked, "send Ruby out to the stables. Tell her to tell Josh I want Big Red saddled, right now, at once!"

"Paris!" Candace said sharply. "You can't! You're in no shape to——"

Paris looked at her.

"That was my brother's place, Candy," he said.

"And *your* husband was in it, in case you've forgotten, Candace, dear," Laurel said. "All right, Paris, I'll send Ruby right now. . . ."

"Ingra," Barry said, "you womenfolks get inside the house, and don't come out 'til me and Paris get back. . . ."

"And I," Bruce Randolph said.

"No, Bruce," Barry said; "if it comes to a fight, the worst they'll do to Paris and me would be to shoot us. But they wouldn't just shoot you, boy. They wouldn't do you that much of a favour. . . ."

"I insist!" Bruce began; but Paris cut him off.

"Here," he said, handing Bruce the pocket pistol he always carried now, because it was smaller and less burdensome than his big Dance and because he figured the Klan certainly wasn't ever going to give him time to go in the house and dig his cavalry sidearm out of the drawer; "take this and guard your wife—and mine with it. Miss Holm and Candance as well. That's job enough. Calls for all the guts you want to display. I've *got* to see what happened; but it's ten to one they're already on their way here. You'll be doing me a mighty big service, boy. . . ."

222

"That's true," Bruce said and took the pistol. "Where do you keep your ammunition, Paris?"

"In my study. Right hand top desk drawer. Will you bring me my other gun out here, Bruce? Now all you girls get inside!"

"No," Candace said; "I'm going with you, Paris."

"Candy, for God's sake——"

"As you said before, I don't see what He's got to do with this, except, maybe, by default, neglect. And, though I had to be reminded of that fact, my husband *is* there. That's one thing. Another is, female or not, I'm far stronger physically than you are, right now. In fact, *you* ought to stay home and let me go in your place. They'll hardly shoot a woman; and Barry's Di's brother, and——"

"Candy," Paris whispered, "I've been tempted to smack you many times; but tonight, so help me, I'll do it!"

Candace smiled.

"Smack away," she said; "I won't even hit you back. I, at least, don't take advantage of the weak. . . ."

"Oh, hell, Candy!" Paris said. But Bruce came out of the house with the big Dance in its holster, and the gunbelt. And, as Paris strapped it on, the groom came around the house with the horses.

Paris and Barry sat there on their mounts, looking at it. At that pile of charred rubble. At the trees seared black for nearly twenty yards all around it. At the stables which were farther away even than that, more than a hundred yards, in fact, but which still burned stubbornly all the same. They didn't say anything. They sat there, looking at it. And then they heard the hoofbeats. They whirled, reaching, drawing their revolvers in an absolute unison of motion; but then they holstered them again; for it was Candace Trevor who rode out from under the trees.

"Candy, goddammit!" Paris said. "I told you——"

"Paris," she said; "you suppose that they——"

"Are under that?" Paris said. "Yes, Candy—I think they are. At any rate, I mean to see——"

He climbed down, stiffly. He wasn't over his wound. It had healed all right. He was getting better, Candace knew, but so very slowly. Now, almost a year after he'd been shot, he was still terribly weak. Too weak to do what he had to, now; to see what he had to see.

"Stand back, Paris," Barry said; "you aren't up to it; let me——"

"Barry," Candace said, "this isn't smart. We aren't very far from your place, are we? So why don't you go home and bring back a gang of Negroes? Paris and I are in no danger, now. The Klan won't come back. While you're gone, we'll look around to see if anybody—escaped. . . ."

"Fat chance!" Barry said. "But what you said makes sense, Candace. One man could dig all night in that and still not find them. Paris, you'd better sit down. You don't look so good to me. . . ."

"I'm all right, Barry," Paris said; "just go and get your hands, boy——"

Barry rode off. They heard, in the deepened silence after he had gone, the shrill, frenzied neighing of a horse.

"Paris!" Candace said. "There's horses still alive in the stable! And it's burning! Oh, darling, we can't——"

"I know. Come on, Candy!" Paris said.

They stopped long enough to get a crowbar and an axe from the tool-shed near the quarters. He looked around, but there wasn't a single Negro to be seen. Then they went to the back of the stable, because the front, where the doors were, was one mass of flames. They tore down a plank, another. Candace worked harder, and with greater strength, than Paris could. But his grip was iron suddenly as he hurled her back, just as Hector's bay stallion burst through the opening they had started, sending the planks flying, and raced away, his mane and tail aflame. The other horses followed him, those of them that could.

"You suppose there're any left in there?" Candace said.

"If so, they're dead," Paris said; "anyhow, we can have a look. This end isn't even burning good, yet. . . ."

He stepped through the opening. Stopped. Said, his voice sand-dry:

"Get back, Candy."

"Why? I'm a nurse, remember. I've seen———"

She stepped in beside him.

"———worse things than a dead horse, and——— Oh!" Her voice dropped down, down below the surface of sound.

He caught her to him. She rested her face against his chest, crying very quietly.

"I prayed," she whispered. "I asked God for the strength to never wish—his death, Paris. No matter what he said to me, however much he tormented me, knowing that he was tormented, too. Yet I have wished it, many times, in my mind. Being human, I—I couldn't help that. Only, Paris, I never wanted him to die like this! Never so terribly. Nothing he's ever done could be equated with—with having to sit there helpless and alone—having no one to call to, being unable even to run—seeing the fire getting closer until—they burst their stalls and———"

"Trampled him to death," Paris said. "An easier way of dying than—fire, Candy. Think about it that way, and don't———"

Then they heard Barry calling them.

"Now what the devil?" Paris said. "He sure Lord hasn't had time to go to Walfen, much less come back! I wonder———"

"Here we are, Barry!" Candace called.

Barry rode out to the stable. He said:

"Paris, reckon you'd better come with me. No, Candace, not you. What I got to show Paris just isn't a fitting sight for a woman's eyes."

"Get down, Barry," Candace said. "Get down—and look in there. Then you tell me if what you've got to show Paris is worse than—that———"

Barry got down. Went inside the still burning stable. Came out again. Said:

"Yes, Candace. A sight worse even than that. Come on, Paris. Reckon we'd better get poor Henry out of there, first.

Even though he can't feel it now, 'twouldn't do to let him burn. . . ."

They brought the crippled man's body out and laid it on the grass. Covered it with a horse-blanket they found in that part of the stable that hadn't burned.

"Please let me come, Barry," Candace said; "I—I don't want to stay here. . . ."

"All right," Barry said, "you're a grown woman and a nurse. Come on. But I'm warning you right now, it's the worst goddamned thing you've ever seen. . . ."

It was. They hadn't killed Matty Griffin on purpose. She had merely died of what they had done to her. All of them, so many that their numbers couldn't even be guessed at, now.

"She was small," Candace said in that flat-toned, counterfeit calm of utter hysteria, "obviously virgin—So—so she haemorrhaged; and they—— Oh, Paris; why do we fight so to go on living? Who wants to live after this?"

"Paris," Barry said, "promise me one thing: when we run into Di and his crew of buzzards, the first shot's mine. You hear me? Brother or not, the first shot's mine!"

Paris didn't answer him. He couldn't.

Candace stared at him.

"Paris——" she said; then: "Paris! Paris! Oh, my God!"

She caught at his arms, shaking him furiously, crying: "Paris, you can't! Not now! Not after so long, not when I was sure I'd got you cured—— Oh, Paris, please!"

His eyes were the eyes of a man awakening painfully from sleep.

"I—I'm all right, Candy," he said.

"Are—you, Paris?" she said. "Yes—yes you are. You've got past this. Even this. And that means——"

Slowly Barry took off his coat and covered Matty with it. Then he knelt down beside that little bundle on the ground.

" 'Our Father, which art in heaven'," he began; but Paris cut him off.

"Shut up, Barry," he said. "I asked you before if He

226

were there. Now I ask you another thing: even if He is, what good is He?"

"Paris!" Barry said.

"What good at all?" Paris raged. "If He can't protect the innocent, He is useless. If He won't, He——"

"That's quite enough, Paris," Candace said.

"Yes," Paris said, "it is, isn't it? More than enough. I'm sorry, Barry. Pray if you like. Maybe it'll make *you* feel better."

Barry came back with a gang of Negroes. The blacks made short work of what still had to be done.

They were unrecognizable. It was difficult even to distinguish between the sexes. Barry looked up into Paris's face.

"They didn't suffer, boy," he said.

"Didn't suffer?" Paris said. "Barry, for God's love!"

"No, Paris," Barry said. "They've each got—a ball through the head. Reckon Hector——"

"Paris, hold me," Candace said. "No, don't. Hit me. Slap me across the face. Hard."

Paris stared at her. Her teeth were chattering. Her lips were white.

"Please, Paris," she said, "or else I'm going to throw up. Or faint. Or something equally as stupid. Hit me, Paris."

He did. Hard. She came to him, whimpering a little.

"Now hold me. I can cry now. Now I can," she said.

They buried Henry Trevor in the Griffin family's graveyard under an inscription which read: "Blessed be the Stranger Who Sojourns within Our Gates." But Hector and the others they laid together in a common grave. Their headstone bore simply the words: "Hector Griffin and Family," and nothing else, not even the dates.

Coming back from the funerals, Candace saw that her troubles had not ended. She had already lived past her major fear, that this, piled atop all he had already suffered, would drive Paris Griffin—a man who had already once before lost his grip on the realities, the certainties, or on what we assume to be both real and certain with enormous and childish conceit—finally and irrevocably insane. Then it came to her that this would never break Paris, precisely because, try as he would, he could not assume the responsibility for it. The only way he could react to it was with anger. And just anger was a pure and cleansing thing, diametrically opposed to the slow poison of guilt that had almost destroyed him before.

Now the danger was that he would find his death, fall riddled before the guns of the Klan. She knew Paris very well, now. And one of the things she knew about him was that he wouldn't even consider the odds against him. That, alone, or with Barry helping him, he'd ride out against the men who had done this thing, no matter how many they were. So he had to be stopped. But how, how?

"Candace," Laurel said; "reckon you'll be leaving us pretty soon now?"

And won't you be ever delighted! Candace thought. She said: "Yes. I'm thinking of going to Natchez to see what can be done with that hotel Henry's Aunt Bess left us. . . ."

"Oh," Laurel said, "so you won't be going back up North?"

You're right, Candace thought; Mississippi isn't big enough for you, me and Paris, now that I'm a widow, is it, dear? But then, is the whole United States? Or even the entire world?

"Perhaps," she said; "I don't know. That depends upon so many things, Laurel. In any event, if you'll be so kind as to help me pack, I'll leave *here* day after tomorrow."

Paris spoke then, for the first time.

"No, you don't, Candace," he said; "don't let Laurie chase you off any faster than you want to go. She's in one of her stupid jealous moods again. And her moods are no damned justification for anything. Stay as long as you like. . . ."

"I shall," Candace said; "but as long as I like is until day after tomorrow, Paris. In fact, it's longer. If I didn't have to pack all the things I had stored at the lodge, which saved them from getting burned, I'd leave today. . . ."

Paris looked at her. His eyes were lifeless, dull.

"All right, Candy—since you want it that way," he said.

Candace didn't undress that night. Instead, she had old Josh, restored in actual fact now to the post of groom as a result of Duke's death, saddle a fast horse for her on the pretext of taking an evening ride. She tethered the horse in a clump of woods a few yards from the house, where she could see the door.

Just before midnight, Paris came out. He wore a gunbelt. He went around the house in the direction of the stables.

Candace ran to where she had left her horse. Mounted. Sat there, waiting. When she heard the sharp staccato of hoofbeats coming on fast, she kicked her mount in the ribs, rode him out upon the road.

Paris almost crashed into her. He yanked back on the bridle so hard his roan reared.

"Candy! What the devil are you doing out here?" he said.

"Waiting for you. Isn't that obvious?" Candace said.

Paris stared at her face, clear in the moonlight.

"Why?" he said.

"Haven't you guessed? To hurl myself at your head. Induce you to leave Laurel; run off with me, and——"

"Stop it!" Paris said. "The truth, Candy."

"All right," she said; "I—I'm trying to stop you from doing what you're planning to——"

His face tightened.

"Get out of my way, Candy," he said.

"No. You'll have to ride me down, Paris. Listen to me, darling. You can't kill them all. Say you get one or two. What have you proved?"

"That no dirty, stinking, murdering rat bastards can——"

"No, Paris. That doesn't need proving. Vengeance ultimately belongs to God. Whether you believe in Him or not, it still does. All you'll prove is that you can also shoot, stab or even choke a man to death. Great trick, isn't it? The science—or is it the art—of murder. That's what I meant by trying to save you: not your life, for, in the final analysis, life can't be saved. All I can do in that regard I've already done: postponed your death as long as I could, given you a few more days under the sun——"

"Days I don't even want," Paris said, "and I reckon you know why. . . ."

"Yes, I know. Time doesn't count, either for you or for me, now. No, Paris; it's *you* I'm trying to save."

"Me?" Paris said. "I'm afraid I don't follow you, Candy. . . ."

"It's hard. I could be sententious and say your immortal soul; but we're too advanced for that kind of talk, aren't we, Paris? At least we think we are. Let me see—this is like blind man's bluff; and I told you once I don't like children's games. Put it this way: I'd like to go on believing that the man I raked up hell to bring back into life is somebody—special; that there is nobody quite like him, anywhere in the world. I want to hang on to that belief—or, more likely, that illusion—because no one, not even you, could really live up to it, I suppose. And, even if it is awfully cold comfort, Paris, allow me to keep that much. In fact, I'm going to. I'll fight, spit, scratch and claw, before I'd let my concept of you be diminished, spoiled. Even by you. Especially by you. You see, what other people do, including what those featherless buzzards did, doesn't matter——"

"Doesn't matter!" Paris said. "Killing Hector, murdering all his family, didn't——"

"Matter? Only to their murderers. The one thing they had to do was to die and they did that well. With courage, with dignity. But those others have to live with that on their consciences — if they have consciences, which I doubt. Because essentially a man can't be damaged by what's done to him. All that counts is how he takes it, whether he responds like a man or like a beast. It's what *he* does that twists his soul into the ugly image of sin, Paris. So you're not going to do this. I won't let you. There's been blood enough, and the stink of it never gets off a man's hands. You can scrub and scrub, but——"

"Goddammit, Candy." Paris said.

She smiled; but her smile was the saddest thing in all the world, Paris saw.

"If I am ever yours, Paris, if you are ever mine, I shouldn't like you touching me with hands that smell of death. That's one thing——"

"And another?" Paris said.

"That it has to stop somewhere, love. There must be an end to this obscene business of man-killing. We can't go on piling corpses up to the sky, muddying all the earth with blood. Somebody has to call a halt. Somebody has to be big enough to. Big enough, even, to leave Hector unavenged and, if need be, play the coward in their eyes, give the only answer there is to the question of evil, the one you men never see——"

"And that is?" Paris said.

"To refuse to participate in it. To refuse at any cost. What Hector did was easy. As big and terrible as it was, it was still easy. What he should have done was harder, called for more courage than he had—or at least a different kind. I suppose that was too much to ask—too much even to expect, that a man, seeing his daughter hurt, bruised, torn—shamed in the way that hairy brute had shamed Rachel, would be able to say: 'Father, forgive them, for they know not what they do——' "

"My God!" Paris said.

"But you can. At least the image I bear of you in my heart is capable of that. Don't prove me wrong, Paris. Don't make all these years I've devoted to your worship a waste and a cheat. I've asked nothing of you in return, except your presence, except the joy of knowing you're alive and in the same world with me. But now I ask you this hard, this awful thing: that you live up to my concepts of manhood, and not the world's; that you realize once and for all that nothing in history has ever truly been, or ever truly can be, settled with a gun. Will you, Paris? For me?"

Paris sat there, looking at her. Slowly, crookedly, he grinned.

"I haven't my dress sword with me, General," he said; "but in its default——"

He drew his revolver, and held it out to her, butt first.

She sat there, the corners of her mouth twitching; but crying a little, too.

"Paris, will you put that thing away!" she said.

He did. Then he stretched out his arms to her.

She came to him. Kissed his mouth with tenderness. With a frank passion that startled him. Then, very gently, she pushed his arms away.

"We had better stop *that*, my boy!" she said. "Now a few more orders. The General hereby commands that you go home and go to bed. You look very tired, Paris. . . ."

"I am," he sighed; "but I can't go home. You see, Barry's waiting for me down by the hunting lodge to help me with the manhunt you just called off——"

"I'll go meet Barry," Candace said; "I'm not at all tired; and, even if I were to go to bed now, I'm quite sure I couldn't sleep. . . ."

Paris sat there, frowning.

"All right," he said grudgingly; "don't reckon there's any danger now. . . ."

"Of course not," Candace said; "the worst they can do would be to cut my hair off again. . . ."

"Lord, you looked cute like that!" Paris said, and tried to take her in his arms again. But she danced her mount away.

"That's just what I mean," she said. "That's *why* I can't sleep, now. You want me to lie awake, tormented by sinful thought for a whole week? And now, darling, I'll go calm Barry down. . . ."

He sat there watching her go. Long after he couldn't even hear the hoofbeats where she rode, he didn't move. Then he turned the big roan's head, and put more distance between them still; more darkness, more silence, and more night.

232

16

WITH Barry, it was both less difficult, and more.

He came out of the hunting lodge and stood there, looking at her.

"Where's Paris?" he said.

"I sent him home," Candace said; "he's a good bit too sick to ride out in the night air, and especially not up to indulging in your favourite Southern pastime of murder."

"Murder?" Barry said. "I don't call it murder to——"

"I know you don't," she cut him off; "but *I* do. Help me down, Barry. You and I, to use another of your Southern expressions, have a crow to pick. . . ."

He put his arms up, helped her down. But he did it very slowly, holding her a long, long moment with her feet just off the ground; and, unmistakably, she could feel him tremble.

Oh Lord, she thought, what have I let myself in for, now?

But once her feet touched earth, he released her, stood back.

"Listen to me, Barry," she said. Then she stopped. His eyes stopped her.

"I'm listening, Candace," he said.

"I convinced Paris," Candace said, "that there was nothing to be gained by more bloodshed. I'd like to convince you of the same thing. Only I—I don't know how to go about it. . . ."

"Try," Barry said. "Don't reckon there's anything you couldn't convince me of, Candace, if you really wanted to. Just hearing you say a thing makes it sound right, merely because it's you who's saying it."

Oh, no! she thought. This is wrong, wrong. . . . She said:

"Very well, Barry; but not because I'm saying it. Because

233

it *is* right. You can't do this thing, any more than Paris can. Because, first of all, you would have to kill your own brother, or stand by and let Paris kill him. Amounts to the same thing really. And, knowing you, I'm betting you couldn't support it, that you couldn't live under the burden of so much guilt. . . ."

Barry looked at her. Said, at long last:

"You're right. This war is over——" Then he reached out and took her hand.

"Sit down, Candace," he said. "There's a thing I've been meaning to talk to you about. I was going to put it off for six months, or a year—out of respect for the dead. But I don't have to, now. In fact, I'd better not. You didn't love Henry, did you?"

"No," Candace said; "that would have been an awful lot to ask of me, the way he got to be before the end. . . ."

"I agree. But, Paris. You're in love with him, right?"

"Right," Candace said.

"Natural enough. Only you can't have him. He's got a wife. Of course, he could petition the State Legislature for a bill of divorcement. But upon what grounds? All right, say that there *are* grounds. I still don't need to point out to you that Paris is not the kind of a man to wash his dirty linen in public. He'd either shoot—or forgive. And, knowing him, I'd bet on his forgiving. So, that's out. One more thing: before you start, I'd just as soon you skipped all the noble arguments women use to make a poor devil of a rejected suitor feel better. I'm not a poor devil, and I don't mean to be rejected if I can help it. I know you don't love me; that, from your point of view, it would be unfair of you to marry me without love. But, Candace, Honey, I've got love enough in my heart for both of us and to spare. You wouldn't be cheating me, because I'm not asking you to pretend a blamed thing you don't feel. I know you like me, even have a certain amount of respect for me and, to begin with, I'll settle for that. Because I think the love would come with the years. I'd take you away from here, up North or out West, 'cause I sure Lord don't mean to stay on the same place with my

234

polecat of a brother and run the risk of having to kill him, after all. That way you wouldn't see Paris daily; that way, in time, you'd forget——"

Wildly, Candace shook her head.

"No, Barry," she said. "You see, I shall never forget Paris, not even on the day I die. And you're right, it wouldn't be fair to you, *because* I like and respect you. Not so much my marrying you lovelessly; that, as you said, wouldn't be dishonest because you know I don't. What would be criminal would be to enter upon a life together upon the basis of a non-existent hope: that I'd forget Paris; that I'd come in time to love you. I wouldn't, Barry. I'm an antique among women—in fact I'm as extinct as the Dodo bird—the kind that when she really falls in love, never falters until she dies. You say I can't have Paris. But I do have him, as the exact centre of my life. And he fills it completely to the exclusion of everyone else, even you. A pity. Because you *are* my kind of man; and I could have loved you, had it not been for him——"

"I see——" Barry said. "You're not offended that——"

"You asked me? No, Barry. I'm sorry that you made me hurt you, as I see I have. But I'm not offended. Proud, rather. Most awfully proud. You don't know what you've done for me: I'll walk like a somnambulist for a week, alternating between that pride, and sorrow——"

"Sorrow over what? Refusing me? Don't be sorry, Candace. It's all right, and——"

"Over being a backward fool who can't arrange her wayward heart, even for such a man as you. And it's not all right. I know I shall regret it. . . ."

"But not enough. Look, Candace, I'll see you back to Griffin's Way now. . . ."

"No, don't. Please don't. I'd rather go alone," Candace said.

But after she had gone, sleep would not come to him. So Barry Cadwallader mounted his grey and rode the woods nightlong until the sun was up. Turned his mount around at last, and rode homeward in the morning light, head down, shoulders sagging, until——

Very slowly he pulled back on the bridle; before, in fact, the polished yellow spoke of the buggy's wheels became recognizable to him as such; before his mind let go of this sight enough for him to raise his eyes, to see the smart little rig deliberately blocking his path, see——

That too-white face, kept valiantly under control; the shell-pink lips whose quiver was all but imperceptible; the blue eyes but faintly misty; the high-piled white-blonde hair——

"Ingra!" he said. "Lord God! What on earth——"

"Am I doing here?" she said. "Blocking your path, Barry. That's quite evident, isn't it?"

"Yes," he said; "but why are you, Ingra?"

"Get down," she said; "get into the buggy. Tie your horse behind, first. Come on, Barry; do as I say!"

He stared at her. This time he didn't really know her voice. She sounded—furious. He had seen her sad, before—but angry, never. She had all the slow placidity of her race. Lord, she's pretty! he thought. I wonder——

He got down, tied his mount behind the buggy, climbed up beside her.

She flapped the reins. The horse moved off. Away from Walfen. She didn't say anything. Not anything at all.

"Ingra, honey," Barry began.

"Don't call me honey!" Ingra said. "That's hardly becoming of you now, Barry. Let me be the first to congratulate you. When will the wedding take place? Six months from now? Or is she making you wait a whole year? She has a lot of respect for public opinion, your Candace. . . ."

"Not *my* Candace," Barry said. "Guess again, Ingra."

She didn't turn to face him. She went on driving.

"She—she refused you then?" Her voice was very low.

"Flatly," Barry said. "She has—well—other interests——"

"Paris. Who's not a bad person, really; but—weak. He'll keep her dangling her whole life long, and then——"

"Now look, Ingra," Barry said; "Paris has his defects but

being weak sure Lord isn't one of them. Besides, who hasn't got faults in this world?"

"You haven't," she whispered, still not looking at him, "not even a tiny one, as far as I'm concerned, Barry. . . ."

"Ingra——" he said.

"Wait!" she said. "I don't know what you're about to say. But I do know that I don't want you to say it. That I'd probably be terribly hurt if you said it— now, under the present circumstances, Barry——"

"But later, I can?" he said.

"I don't know. I doubt it. Those circumstances apparently aren't going to change."

"I see," he said. "Then what did you come out here for, Ingra?"

She faced him then, at last.

"To say—goodbye," she said.

"Goodbye!" he exploded. "Lord God, Ingra!"

"Yes, Barry. Goodbye. The only thing that's left to be said between us. I have about three hours to catch the train that makes connections for St Paul. Which is why I headed this way. I left my valises in Junction Village. So now you can stand in the station and wave goodbye to me. Less—lonely, that way. Having someone to wave goodbye. Or—is it? Isn't it, maybe, more?"

"Ingra, Baby," he groaned, "why'd you just up and decide to leave this way?"

She looked away from him; sat there without answering.

"I see," he said. "You figured that the minute Henry Trevor passed on, I'd be after Candace so damned fast—— And you were right. Only neither you nor I realized there'd be—other obstacles. So—you didn't want to be here to see it, because you——"

"Barry," she said; "would—would you strip a woman naked in a public place?"

"Lord, Ingra! What a question! Of course not! I don't see——"

"That's what you're doing now," she whispered. "Our— modesty requires more protection than mere clothing, Barry.

237

You've always been kind. So I am asking you not to take away the only thing I've got left now. Please—don't take away—my pride."

There wasn't, Barry realized, anything to be said to that. He rode beside her, a tiny new ache beginning to form in one dark corner of his heart. It grew and grew until it threatened to choke him. How many nights had he ridden beside Ingra like this? The answer his mind gave to that surprised him: never. Never quite like this. Because all the other times he hadn't really seen her; dreaming of Candace, he had not marked the serene perfection of Ingra's beauty. Besides, he'd never been partial to blondes as pale as Ingra was, considering them somehow cold.

But Ingra wasn't cold. Proud, yes. Reserved. Modest. But cold—no. Not ever cold. And he had been so busy running around in circles like a snakebit coonhound baying the unreachable moon, that he hadn't even seen this flesh-and-blood, honest-to-God woman at his side. This woman who could have been his before, to have, to hold, to—love. Before. But not now. Because he'd hurt her too much now, put himself into a position where anything he said or did must be wrong. All he could say now to this proud, lovely, too controlled creature would be, in effect: "All right, you're second choice. You're catching me on the rebound. Be content with that, Ingra. It's better than nothing, isn't it?"

Only he suspected that it was not better than nothing. That Ingra preferred to take nothing than to accept him on that basis. That pride he ought to have known before now she had would never permit her to accept his shoddy offer. Not now. Not—ever.

Good Lord! he thought. What a fool I've been! What a long-eared, braying son of a jackass!

They came to the station. Dumbly he retrieved Ingra's bags. They stood there waiting for the train.

"Barry," she said; "I'm making you a present of my horse and buggy. I've no way to take them with me. And I know you'll be good to Gustave Adolphus——"

"Well, I'll be! Is that what you call your nag, Ingra?"

"Yes. He's a noble beast. So I named him for a very noble king. You'll take care of him, won't you, Barry?"

"Of course," Barry said. He felt as if someone were strangling him.

"Well," Ingra sighed; "here comes the train."

The train snorted up to the platform. A Negro porter shuffled up to them, touched his cap.

"Put your and your lady's bags on, suh?" he said.

"Yes," Barry said. "Ingra——"

"Yes, Barry?"

"Mind—if I—if I—kiss you goodbye?"

"No, Barry," she whispered.

He took her in his arms. Touched her lips as though they were made of tiny, fragile crystals. Stood back. Saw the tears flooding her face. Hung there, woodenly, as she whirled, fled up the steps, into the coach.

The train groaned, snorted, puffed. The bell jangled. He looked up and saw her face, white against the black rectangle of the window. She was not looking at him. She had her face buried in her handkerchief. He could see her shoulders shaking.

It was not to be borne. But he didn't know what to do about it. His brain was numbed.

The train crept off in a slow crescendo of steam-hiss, smoke-pant, bell-jangle. One yard, two. She looked up, turned. He could see her lips forming, soundlessly, his name.

"Barry!" she cried. And now he heard her, her voice clear above that din: "Oh, Barry, I love you so!"

And then he was released, freed, his brain marvellously clear, his long legs pumping like pistons as he ran, leaped, caught the handles, swung himself aboard, pounded up the aisle to her seat. She sat there staring at him as he jerked the window open with a crash that almost broke it, tore her valises down from the rack, hurled them one by one through the open window. He turned, caught her wrists, pulled her from her seat, yanked her down the aisle, saying:

"Run, dammit! We'll be going too fast to jump in a minute!"

They almost were. He hurled himself down, stretched out his arms to her. She hesitated, then jumped, striking him with such force that they both went down, rolled.

He helped her up, his face white.

"You aren't hurt, are you?" he said. "You're all right, aren't you, Ingra, Baby? Tell me you're all right!"

She swayed there, dizzily. She had a sharp pain in her left ankle, but she didn't tell him that.

"I'm fine, Barry," she said; "I—I've never felt finer in my whole life!"

He drew her into his arms, stood there holding her. In front of the porter. In front of all the village idlers who always gathered to meet the trains.

"Oh, Barry!" she wailed. "My clothes!"

He turned and saw them, blowing down the track behind the train. One of the valises had burst. Naturally it was the one that held her underthings.

"You wait right here, Honey!" Barry said, and started up the track. The idlers followed him, grinning. For a few minutes it looked like a cotton-picking time. Barry stuffed all those caste, intimate garments into the bag. He was blushing furiously. He came back, put the valises into the buggy, aided by the grinning idlers. He turned to Ingra.

"Come on," he said; "the justice's offices are right down the street. We don't need the buggy."

"I—I'm afraid we do, Barry," she said; "I twisted my ankle when I jumped. It hurts quite a lot, love. . . ."

"Lord God," he said; "I'll take you to the doctor right now! I'll——"

She smiled at him with tender mischief.

"No, Barry. The justice's office, first—before you change your mind," she said.

240

17

"WE'VE won the War, boy," Barry said. "Took us eleven more years after the shooting stopped to do it, but we've won."

"Looks that way, doesn't it?" Paris said.

"We have. Lock, stock, and barrel. Gained all our objectives. Re-established slavery——"

"Now, wait a minute, Barry," Paris said; "aren't you laying it on a mite thick?"

"You name it, then. I say that when a man works all year to make a crop, then ends up not being able to leave a place because he still owes the boss money—having to accept the boss's figures, naturally—no matter how damned many bales he makes, that man's a slave. All right, call it peonage. That sound any prettier?"

"No," Paris said.

"So we've won. And by methods that would make a buzzard puke. You see this, boy?" He took a sheaf of newspaper clippings thick enough to choke a horse out of his pocket.

"I see them, all right; but what are they?"

"Clippings. Bruce loaned them to me. He's been cutting these ever since '66. Every time there's a race riot, by which we mean a mass slaughter of Negroes, he cuts the report out of the papers and saves it. You know how many there've been now, Paris?"

"No," Paris said; "how many, Barry?"

"Sixteen. And only the major ones get printed. The little piddling affairs, with only five or six blacks shot, stabbed, beaten to death and sometimes even burned, don't make the papers. But sixteen major massacres—I'm calling them by their right name—in ten years. I know them by heart. I can name the names, sound our roll call of dishonour; Norfolk, Virginia; Memphis, Tennessee; Camilla, Georgia; Eutaw and Eufaula, Alabama; Laurens, Hamburg, and Ellenton, South Carolina; but award the palm to Louisiana, boy— the South's undisputed champion at the art of human butchery, with the biggest pile of slaughtered nigger carcasses; at New Orleans, Bossier, St Landry, St Bernard and Colfax, she heaped up five hundred and thirty-three dead——"

"Good God!" Paris said.

"Amen. But we're no pikers in Mississippi, boy. I give us second place. Meridian and Vicksburg and Yazoo City and Friars Point are our contributions to civilization, Southern style. You know what the grand total is for all the South up through this year of Our Lord, 1876?"

"I've no idea," Paris said.

"Eight hundred and twelve. Which is an underestimate. As I said, the small affairs don't get counted. And nobody can tally up the lynchings. Bruce's educated guess is that there have been more than a thousand, maybe more than two. And let's not forget the specialized nigger-killers, those boys who provoke a black into a show of fight, then gun him down. I know, personally, three—with eight, eleven, and thirteen notches respectively, on their gun-butts—who're walking around as free as you or I. Throw in your 'peace' officers, who've built a new meaning into the term 'resisting arrest'. Right now it means the nigger frowned, maybe; or didn't rip that 'Yassuh, Cap'n!' out fast enough. Add to them our chain-gang guards and prison wardens, specially selected for their skill at 'adjusting the Negro's sense of reality'. Yep, I'm quoting again. That sterling phrase comes from the local sheet——"

"Barry," Paris said, "ever since your charming cousin perforated me, I've had a delicate stomach. And you aren't doing it any good right now, boy."

"Sorry," Barry said. "Paris, before we ride any closer to my place, reckon I'd better tell you something——"

"Go on, tell me," Paris said.

"Candace is visiting us. She has been for about a week."

Paris looked at him.

"And you didn't let me know before now!" he said.

"You know how it is. She wouldn't let me. Doesn't want to cause trouble 'twixt you and Laurie, boy."

"She couldn't do that," Paris said; "reckon pity's the strongest emotion I've got left, and Laurie has my pity—all of it. . . ."

"What's the matter with her?" Barry said. "She sure Lord doesn't look good these days. You had Doc Benson in, boy?"

"Repeatedly. He says it's all in her mind—that whatever damage that rat poison did her stomach that time has long since healed. Yet, she's lost eighteen pounds since then, and Laurie never had eighteen pounds to lose. She's always in tears, over nothing. Every two or three days she's begging me to forgive her, though for precisely what isn't clear. Maybe for that episode with Dion she claims she was forced into——"

"Claims? She was!" Barry said.

"I know. In a way she was. I burned those letters without opening them; and forgave her, freely. Which was my mistake. I should have beaten her. She would have understood that. She's such a child, Barry, such an idiot child. . . ."

"Yes, Laurie is mighty childish, all right," Barry said. He thought: Time to change the subject, before you find out that what's eating Laurie is not what she did before, because of those letters, but afterwards, while you lay there a-dying. You call her idiot, but she's not. She'd be better off if she were. She's a stupid little backwoods filly, but an idiot she's not, nor a moron either. She's got just brains enough to suffer remorse, and not enough to forget, so—He said:

"Reason I told you that Candace was back from Natchez was so you could turn back if you want to. . . ."

"Turn back?" Paris said. "Not your life, Barry. I want to see her. I need to. But why did she come back?"

"Ingra wrote her about our expecting a baby. She came the same day she got the letter. Her excuse was she wanted to pay us back the money we loaned her——"

"Money *you* loaned her?" Paris said. "She came to you, not to me. . . ."

"Of course. You know how delicate she is. Couldn't expect her to borrow money off a fellow she admits to being in love with. Anyhow, we loaned her two thousand dollars. With that, she not only made a go of that white elephant of a hotel Henry's auntie left them; but, from what I've heard, she's turned it into one of the showplaces of Natchez. Wanted to pay me interest, but naturally, I wouldn't hear of that. . . ."

"And she—how is she, Barry?" Paris said.

"Just great. Prettier than ever. Rested, filled out, calm. Anyhow, you'll see in a little while. We're almost home."

They trotted into the gates of Walfen. Candace stood at their approach. Something—the last ray of the sunset, or maybe even joy—poured illumination into her face.

"Paris!" she said. "You've saved me a trip. I was going to have to come looking for you. Didn't quite know how to manage it. I shouldn't want Laurel to think——"

Barry bent and kissed his wife. Ingra's pregnancy showed by now.

"What didn't you want Laurie to think?" he said. "That you're a housewrecker, Candace?"

"Exactly," Candace said. "Actually, Barry, I meant to look for you, as well."

"Well, I like that!" Ingra said.

"Don't worry, Lamb," Candace said, "this is business." Her voice slowed, became worried, said. "Rather serious business. It—it's Bruce. He's been invited to make a speech before the coloured Republicans. And you know what the situation is, now. Ever since Lamar, George, Walthall and Stone organized their revolt last year, maybe even ever since the Vicksburg riot, the Negroes haven't a chance. . . ."

"And certainly not if Hayes gets in," Barry said.

"Bruce knows it," Candace said; "and he'd planned to make a conciliatory speech, urging the coloured people to more or less lie low. Only, a band of men—led by your brother Di, Barry; he wasn't even hooded—burned a fiery cross before Bruce's door, and threatened him with death if he makes that speech. So now——"

"Now," Paris said, "he considers it a point of honour to make it."

"Yes. Poor Eulalia's almost out of her mind. And rightly. Seems to me he ought to think of her and the children first. Don't you agree, Paris?"

"Yes. Barry, I reckon we'd better ride down to Junction right now and take a train for Vicksburg. Try to talk some sense into Bruce's kinky head. Damn my soul, I don't want to see that boy killed!"

"Why, sure," Barry said. "Ingra, honey, you'll be all right, won't you?"

"No!" Ingra said. "How do you expect me to be all right, when you ride off and let the Kluxers kill you? I want my baby to have a father! And some brothers and sisters! And——"

"Aw, Ingra, honey——"

"Stay with her, boy," Paris said; "I'll go alone."

"No, you won't!" Candace said; "I'm coming with you!"

Paris stood there, staring at her.

"All right," he said; "come along."

They rode in perfect silence. Paris could feel that brooding quiet. It had thickness, texture, weight.

"Candy——" he said.

"Yes, Paris?"

"Tell me—forget the circumstances and say the truth— do you still love me?"

She looked him straight in the face and said it.

"Yes, Paris."

"And I love you. For all the good it does. Which would be, maybe, an insult. Only I don't mean to do anything about it. I—just wanted to know."

"Thank you, Paris," she said. "I'm glad you told me. But now that we both know that nothing has changed, let's not talk about it any more, shall we?"

They rode on in silence until they came to Junction Village. Even on the train they talked but little, knowing that talk was useless, that time and hope were running out. When they got off the train in Vicksburg they decided against taking a hack, because the driver would surely talk about the queer business of two white people going to a Negro's house. And all the livery stables were closed by then. So they walked the considerable distance to Bruce's rented bungalow. Again in silence, both separated, and united, by their thoughts.

Eulalia was in a state of near-hysterics. She couldn't stop crying.

"Look, Bruce," Paris said; "bravery, by itself doesn't mean anything. Not a goddamned thing. It's got to stand for something. For instance, during the War, that bastard Reeves Jurgen, a Klansman now, was one of the bravest men I've ever seen——"

"And so were you," Candace said.

"No, I wasn't. Insanity and bravery are two different things. But I did fight, Bruce—and in defence of the dirty proposition that your people should be kept in slavery."

"But what I'm fighting for now, is right," Bruce said. He was afraid. Paris could see that. But he wasn't going to knuckle under to that fear.

"Doesn't matter. There are rights and rights. You think you can win now, boy?"

"No," Bruce said.

"Then what you're planning to do is false heroics. And cheating."

"Cheating?"

"Yes. Dying's easy, Bruce. Sometimes it's easier than living."

"Like now," Bruce said.

"And worthless. Even cowardly. Goddammit, Bruce, every General worth his salt knows when to beat a strategic retreat! Even Lee did, at Gettysburg. 'He who fights and runs away, will live to fight another day.' Fight and win, maybe. That's why I say you're cheating. Your people have damned few leaders. And, for my money, none of your calibre. They're going to need you, boy. The next few years are going to be rough. You want to rob them of that leadership to grant yourself the selfish luxury of martyrdom?"

246

"I—I never thought about it like that, Paris, my friend," Bruce said.

"Yes, your friend. Just like you're mine. I've got two, Bruce, whom I don't think I could do without, now: Barry Cadwallader—and you."

Eulalia came up out of her chair. She stood there staring at Paris.

"You mean that, don't you?" she said. "God bless you! Please make him see——"

"I aim to," Paris said. "Eulalia, go get your kids. I want to see them. I want Bruce to see them."

"You're not fighting fair, now, Paris," Bruce said.

"To hell with that! Go get them, Eulalia."

She went and got the children. They were very pretty. Dark chocolate. Fat. Mahogany cherubs with close curling hair. The oldest was a boy.

Paris took the boy from her. Candace reached for the girl. Paris liked what was in her eyes, then. A hunger. A good, deep hunger. The best.

"Look at him, Bruce," Paris said; "look at your son. Jesus, how I envy you! I've never had a son. Your son— your hostage to fortune. A future leader for his people. Go on, Bruce Randolph, make your stupid speech! Leave him to grow up in want, to become a bootblack or a stableboy. Still the voice he has likely got from you. Deprive your people not only of your services, but of his!"

Bruce smiled, slowly.

"You've often said I was a better dialectician than you," he said; "but I'm not. You win, Paris. I won't make that speech. . . ."

"Oh, Bruce!" Eulalia said, and kissed him. Then she turned to Paris. "Mr Griffin," she said, "how I wish I could kiss you, too!"

"You go right ahead, Honey," Paris laughed; "a kiss from you sure Lord won't make me mad."

Shyly she kissed his cheek.

Paris stood up.

"I guess I'd better take you home now, Candy," he said.

"Come, Eulie," Bruce said; "we'll walk with our friends part of the way—at least until they are out of this ghetto——"

"I'd better put the kids back to bed, first," Eulalia said. "I won't be but a minute. . . ."

They waited. Then all four of them strolled out into the street. Walked down it for about a hundred yards.

"I don't know how I can ever thank you, Mr Grif——" Eulalia began; but the flash, the glare, the nerve-shattering roar, drowned her voice. The white-hot blast flattened them to the ground, singed their clothing, even that far away.

Paris was the first up. By the time Candace got to her knees, he was already running, towards that pile of flaming rubble that had been Bruce Randolph's home.

She raced after him. Then all four of them were clawing in the burning wreckage with bare hands, searing them raw, without noticing it, tearing at that pile.

Paris found the boy. Two beams, falling, had propped each other up, a foot above his bed. The boy hadn't been touched. Paris lifted him out. He let out a lusty cry.

"Papa!" he cried. "Mama, I——"

"Glory be!" Paris said, and handed the boy to Eulalia. Then he went back to his digging. Bruce found the girl. She was dead. There wasn't a mark on her, but she was dead. Candace leaned against Paris, crying.

Bruce turned, holding the boy out to Paris. Paris took the child. Bruce was in time to catch Eulalia as she fell, ease her down upon the hard-packed earth. Candace dropped to her knees beside her, chafing her hands, slapping her cheeks lightly to bring her around.

Paris put his arm around Bruce's shoulder.

"Boy," he said, "if you can even stand listening to a white man, now, I'd like to say——"

Bruce turned to him, his black face streaked with tears.

"No. Not all," he whispered. "Not you—nor Barry—nor Candace—nor a dozen more, I know. There must be hundreds of others—only I——"

Eulalia opened her eyes. She didn't scream. She just lay there crying, without making a sound.

248

Candace stood up.

"Paris," she said; "Oh, Paris, I want to die!"

"Hush, Candy," Paris said. "Get a grip on yourself. Do something useful. Go see if you can find a hack with a coloured driver. We'll take these folks to Barry's place, or to mine."

"Yours," Candace said. "It's closer to Junction, and Dion doesn't live there. And then?"

"Then I go hunting," Paris said. "For Dion."

"Paris, no!" Candace said. "Paris, you can't! You don't actually know——"

"Don't I? Your school, Hector's mansion—Bruce's house. Not even smart enough to change his tactics. Only this wasn't gunpowder. That new stuff. Invented by a Swede. Nobel, I think his name is. Dynamite. More powerful."

It was shock, Candace realized, that made him talk like that. Almost pedantic. Too calm. Too perilously calm.

Bruce turned to him.

"No—killing, Paris," he said; "promise me. It won't bring —Lucy back. Nor heal my wife's broken heart. Vengeance is—God's. Only one thing you can do for me——"

"What's that?" Paris said.

"Come hear my speech," Bruce Randolph said.

The church was packed. Paris, Barry, Laurel and Candace were the only white people there.

They had brought the little coffin and put it at the foot of the pulpit. There were a crowd of white men outside the church, waiting. Dion Cadwallader was among them.

Bruce stood up. His voice was very low.

" 'Now is the winter of our discontent,' " he began; then his voice gathered strength. "I have no comfort to offer you, my people, being myself comfortless! Before me lies a murdered child. I do not say my child, for she is yours, too! The child of a race—the emblem of a sore-stricken people. Our child—and more. It is the flower of our hopes that lies here so still. Our hopes, our dreams, our faith, will be buried with Lucy Randolph. They're dead now, too:

249

for we made the tragic error of believing ourselves free!"

There was a stir in the tight-packed crowd, a shuffle of feet, a murmuring.

"Tragic and hopeless, for we shall never be free!"

"Never, Bruce?" a bass voice boomed.

"Never! Not ever so long as one man like those who did this thing remains alive to rear up in his incredible, baseless, senseless arrogance, in that indefatigable, indomitable, unconquerable, and yet—it is I who say it! I who sired this martyred baby—somehow, strangely admirable will, which, linked forever to resistance to all change, coupled with a blind negation of all logic, a denial of simple decency—can and does and always will base pride itself upon a biological accident—his whiteness! Upon that. Upon the fact that Nature endowed him poorly—was, in his case, parsimonious of pigmentation; cheated him of the warm and glowing colouring she granted so generously to her more favoured children——"

"Paris," Laurel whispered: "do you reckon they understand him?"

"Doesn't matter. He's not talking to them. He's talking to those rats outside. And they'll get enough of it—I hope. . . ."

"Based pride upon that!" Bruce thundered, "holding it enough, so that this flowering land must remain eternally poor and backward; and he, himself, will produce nothing, contribute nothing to civilization worthy of a second glance!"

The growls outside the windows were audible now.

"For, holding his paleness to be the be-all, end-all of existence, he feels no need to bend his energies to aught but the maintenance of his wasteful, unproductive membership in the mystic brotherhood of white men. And maintain it, he will! Make no mistake about that, my people! The Yankee has gone home at last, wearied of the struggle with this stubborn people. For the Yankee had his doubts; at bottom, he was logical. But the Southerner has neither doubts, nor logic, nor, sadly, even those rudimentary vestiges of the concept of fair play the Northerner still retains. Lacking logic, he not only doesn't see the essential idiocy of basing pride, honour, virtue and all else upon the accidental, incidental colour of his hide; but fails to remark the inviolable connection between means and end, using, therefore, the foulest methods that ever disgraced humanity to win what was not worth a candle in the first place!

"We know that now. We have seen our shacks, and our poor, pitiful, hopeful schools burned; ourselves, at best, whipped; at worst, lynched with a sick, sadistic barbarity calculated to turn the stomach of a Tartar!"

"Oh, Paris, honey!" Laurel whispered. "He's going too far!"

"Let him!" Candace snapped. "He's got every right!"

"And now," Bruce's voice sank, "they extend their pitiless warfare upon the heads of women and babies. Nothing will they leave us in their furor to preserve the only poor, shoddy, piteous thing they have, this megalomaniacal conception of racial superiority, instead of trying to *do* something, be something worthy of respect. Nothing. Not even our few brave beginnings: the first systems of public education, the first—and only—enlightened public legislation the South has ever had——"

Dion Cadwallader thrust his head through an open window.

"That's damned well enough, nigger!" he said.

Bruce ignored him, as if he were not there.

"They will not leave us that. The Yankee has retired defeated and left them victorious upon the field, left them —and this, my friends, is perhaps most terrible of all—to even write the books. To vilify us before posterity. For no history will ever be so thoroughly revised, rewritten and so completely falsified as the chronicle of our days. . . ."

He lifted his head, and said it, softly:

"For it appears that these honoured dead have died in vain—and that government of the people, for the people and by the people—and right and justice and decency and human liberty and the dignity of man—over one-half our land—have truly vanished from the earth!"

Then he turned. Sat down.

The silence was absolute. Through it, Paris could hear only the choked whisper of Candace's crying.

He got up. Walked up to where Bruce and Eulalia sat.

"Come on, Bruce," he said; "we've the burying to attend to. Barry and I will be pall-bearers. Right after that, you Eulalia, and the boy are coming home with me."

Numbly, Bruce nodded. They came out of the church, carrying the tiny casket. They were not molested then. There were, maybe, some things even beyond Dion Cadwallader.

Some things. A funeral was. He had all his Gaelic forebears' superstitious respect for the dead. But that was all. Besides that final thing, Dion respected nothing.

After the funeral, Barry caught Paris's arm.

"They're coming after him, boy!" he whispered. "Di told me as I passed."

"We'll take them to the steamboat landing on my place," Paris said. "Light a bonfire. If we rush, we'll be in time for the eleven-o'clock boat. I've got five hundred dollars in my safe. Bruce can take that. I hate like hell to use the same methods as with Samson; some of them might remember how we got Samson out, and rush us at the landing. But the train's too dangerous. They could send a wire ahead to Jackson or Meridian and have him taken off on a trumped-up charge. No, it has to be the boat. Get off in Cincinnati, take a train to Boston, from there. . . ."

"Paris," Bruce said, "I won't have you taking the risk——"

"Oh, to hell with that!" Paris said.

"Paris," Candace said; "may I come, too? That is, if you don't mind, Laurel?"

Laurel stared at her. When she spoke, her voice was bleak.

"No, Candace, I don't mind," she said.

They made it. Leaving Barry with a repeating carbine in his hands to guard the house, Paris rode down to the landing with Bruce, Eulalia and the child, talked to the Captain when the stern-wheeler nudged up to the dock. The Captain accepted them without too much argument. The state had been quiet for some months, now.

Then Paris rode back to Griffin's Way and waited, gun in hand. But it was nearly morning before they came.

"Barry," he said, "you get on home. With Ingra in the family way and——"

"And Dion leading that mob. That's what you started to say, isn't it, boy? That's why I'm staying. To keep you from having to do it. I'm going to—aim for him—first."

"Oh, Barry, no!" Candace said.

"Look, boy," Paris said; "You do as I say. Take Laurie and Candy over to Walfen while there's time——"

"And leave you here?" Laurel said. "No, Paris, honey. Give me a gun. I know how to shoot and——"

"Goddammit, Laurie!" he began. But the noise of the first shot shattering the window, drowned his voice.

He and Barry dropped to their knees by the windows, the carbines in their hands.

"Lie down on the floor, girls," Barry said; "that way you won't get hit—maybe. . . ."

A volley ripped out from the trees. All the front windows crashed in at once.

"Paris!" Dion's voice called out. "We want that nigger! Give him up peaceable, and we'll let you go!"

Paris lifted his gun, sighted toward that sound. Held his finger on the trigger. Did not fire.

But Barry did.

Another volley.

Then, before they realized what she was doing, Laurel stood up. Raced to the door. Tore it open. Reached the porch.

"Di!" she screamed. "He's not here! He's gone! Paris put him on a boa——"

They heard that shot. It sounded different. Long drawn out. Deliberate. Aimed.

And through it, Laurel's voice, diminishing out of sound into a sigh, soft, slow, terrible.

253

"Dear Lord! Dear Lor——"

The choking gurgle that died out into something more than silence: into the absence, the negation of sound.

Then all three of them were there.

Paris bent, picked her up.

"Bring a light, boy," he said.

Barry brought the lamp. By its glow, sighting down his rifle barrel, Dion Cadwallader saw what Paris held.

"Dion!" Barry cried out, his voice breaking. "You fired that shot! Wasn't a baby enough for you, you bastard? Did you have to kill her, too?"

Paris started back into the house; but Dion's animal howl stopped him.

"Paris, wait! I call a truce! Hell, I call the whole thing off! You heard me, boys; the war's over! Don't nobody shoot! Paris, for God's sake, I've got to see. . . ."

Paris stood there, waiting, holding her. Barry stood beside him with the lamp held high. Candace clung to one of the columns that supported the room. She was crying.

Dion and the others came out from the darkness under the trees. Stopped at the foot of the stairs. He stood there, staring at—that bonelessness, that rag-doll dangle, that lolling, that trailing, that stillness, that unbreathing, that no longer spreading stain. He didn't need to ask. But he had to.

"Is she—is she?" he said.

"Yes," Paris said. There were tears on his face. They glistened in the light of the lamp.

"Oh God!" Dion said. "Oh God Oh Lord Oh Jesus—Laurie!"

Then he whirled, fled back down those stairs. Much more slowly, Barry followed him.

Paris turned. Tried to open the door. He couldn't, burdened as he was with all that was left of Laurel. So Candace opened it for him. But she didn't follow him into the house. She stood there, looking at the Cadwallader brothers, facing each other at the foot of the stairs.

"Dion——" Barry said. His voice was quiet.

"Oh, Barry, please!" Candace said.

"I didn't know it was her!" Dion said. "'Fore God, Barry, I didn't know!"

Barry's eyes were pitiless. He turned his back to his brother. Stood there, with his arms folded across his chest, waiting.

Candace came running down those stairs. Halfway, the sound of the shot halted her. Made statuary of her. Arrested her into a caricature of motion.

"Oh, Barry!" she wailed. "Barry——"

"Don't look," Barry said; "you get on in that house, Candy, d'you hear?"

She turned, went up those stairs step by step by step for all those twenty million steps for all that eternity of climbing.

Barry didn't follow her at once. He stood there a long, long time, looking downwards. It was too dark for him to see his brother's face. There was a special quality to the darkness. It seemed to have gathered at that spot. Pooled.

"I tried to stop him!" Reeves Jurgen muttered. "But Di always was mighty quick with a gun—Reckon that was the fastest draw he ever made. . . ."

Barry climbed the stairs then, opened the door. Went in. Knelt down beside Paris and Candace before that slight, small figure on the bed. Said a prayer. For her. For all those dead in sorrow. Lifted his gaze at last towards the shattered windows.

And saw the light of the new day come stealing in——

For these, the living, who had held fast. Endured the night. Waited for the morning.

For Ingra. For himself. For their child. Maybe even for Candace and for Paris.

He didn't know. It was still too soon to tell.